# THE SKIN TRADERS

By Nick France

1.

The water was getting deeper. Up to her waist in the cool dark sea, Madihah lifted her sultry brown eyes to heaven and offered a silent prayer. There was no moon. Faint reflections from the dim shore lights, danced upon the waters ahead.

"It is not far, it is not far."

Taking slow deep breaths, she quietly repeated her mantra, trying to free her mind from the fear that haunted her every step. There was a man in front. He was tall, dark skinned, with good hair. She could faintly hear the breathing of the man behind. There were others. Shadowy figures in three meandering lines. Slowly and obediently, wading out to sea.

Most carried the few belongings they could manage. Small packages held above their heads contained parcels of food, photographs and tiny memories of home. Madihah had nothing, just the ragged clothes that covered her tiny frame.

"Wade out up to your knees. Then head towards the light, and the boat will be waiting." That was all they had been told. It was a lie. The water had passed above her knees shortly after leaving the shore, yet there was no sign of any kind of vessel.

Looking out into the inky blackness, she blinked and rubbed her tired eyes to see if she had missed something. A sudden pain forced her eyelids to shut as the sharp saltwater tingle made her eyes sting. Tears rolled down her cheeks as she lifted the still-dry neckline of her blouse to wipe her face.

Cold, wet and starting to lose the feeling in her fingers and toes, the water was above her waist and getting deeper. There was no turning back, she would either reach a boat or drown trying. Feeling sick and afraid, her body ached, her head dizzy with fatigue, she was so tired. It had been many days since she had last slept. Soon there would be time to rest while they made the crossing. Two hours they had promised for the journey, but that could be just another lie.

With only soft sandals to protect her tiny feet, Madihah stepped awkwardly on a loose rock, sending her falling slowly backwards. As her head slid under the surface, she breathed a mouthful of the vile salty water. Panicking, arms flailing, she fought to return to the surface. Her soaking headscarf wrapped itself around her face. Blinded for a second, she struggled to regain her footing. 'Was she going to drown? Now? Because of one little slip? After everything she had been through to get this far?' Rough hands gripped her shoulders, and her head was once again above the water. Pulling the scarf from around her face, she took a desperate gulp of air, exposing the smooth, youthful features of her pretty, dark brown face. Upright and coughing up brine from her lungs, she took another deep breath and looked up to the night sky. Her eyes shone with wonder as she gazed at clouds that she may never have seen again.

The man behind released his grip, and without a word continued forward, ever forward. The water was deep, much deeper than they told her it would be. 'Up to your knees' they had said. Those words constantly ringing in her ears, and soon, very soon, it would be up to her neck. Madihah could not swim, there were no swimming pools back home; at least, none that her family could afford to use; and it would have been far too dangerous to attempt to learn in the sea.

If only she had been able to afford a lifejacket. They had looked cheap and shabby; but having one might at least have helped keep her head above the water. She had no money, nothing left to bargain with, except for her body, and luckily, she had managed to get thus far relatively untouched.

Madihah knew that not all the people that waded alongside her were going to make it. That was certain. It was still very possible that none of them would. So many had died trying to get this far, some had been beaten, others raped and tortured. There were those that starved when they could no longer afford to buy food and water from their "guides". There were others unable keep up, the old, the weak and the sick. Many of them just died where they fell. The desert had claimed so many victims. The "guides" and their greed had claimed the rest.

She heard a shout and looked ahead. It was a little hazy, but in the far distance, amidst the blackness, there was a small dim glow. It was a boat. It had to be a boat. Her heart leapt with joy.

A small wave splashed against her face. Some of the water went up her nose, and as she choked, forced her head skywards to catch another breath. The uneven surface beneath her feet was becoming more difficult to reach. On tiptoes and at full stretch, to keep her head above water, she was going to have to try to swim for the boat.

The light seemed to be getting closer, but the water was terrifyingly deep. In desperation, she stretched her body as far as she could, to keep her nose and mouth just above the water. Her stomach ached with the effort. She tried to doggy paddle; some of the others were managing. Madihah started to panic.

"It is not far, it is not far." Her tiny hands flapped at the water as it slopped over her face, filling her eyes and mouth. She coughed, fighting for breath. Tears mixed with the salty water that threatened to take her. So Close. Just a few moments more was all she needed.

"I do not want to die," she sobbed amidst the coughing, with the last of her strength ebbing away.

The current was getting stronger. Another slip and the pain of the last few months would have been for nothing.

The boat was near; almost touching distance; but the water was now so deep she had to try to push herself off the seabed to stay above the water to breathe. As Madihah sank beneath the waves, she held her breath and kicked upwards, taking a full lung-full of air as she broke surface, before sinking once again. She feared she would surely drown, and, in her panic, grabbed hold of the man in front. Looking up she realised that they were right beside the boat. He, and another man, hoisted her high into the air. A pair of hands from above grabbed her arms and threw her into the craft. She landed painfully, but at least she was out of the water, and still alive.

The boat was quite small, little more than a dinghy. She rubbed her bruised back and shoulder and huddled into a small space between two other women. Other migrants were being crammed into the small vessel. Madihah was certain it would sink, 'with so many people on board. How could such a boat ever make it across the sea to Europe?'

Just when it seemed that there was no more room to breathe, another small boat pulled up nearby, and the cold wet masses, still waiting in the sea, began to move towards the empty craft.

A small outboard motor kicked into life and Madihah breathed a sigh of relief, at least they were moving.

The boat slowly rocked against the waves. The distant lights of dry land twinkled and gradually disappeared before her eyes.

It seemed like an age before they pulled up alongside an old wooden trawler. The fishermen had probably sold their boat to the smugglers, as trafficking people proved far more profitable than catching fish.

One by one, the bedraggled human cargo gathered on the deck of the fishing boat. Madihah was ushered below, into what she assumed was the hold. She sat on a plank that had been roughly set up as a makeshift bench. The foul stench of rotting fish filled her nostrils, and, she would have been instantly sick, had she eaten anything in the last few days. The walls were caked in blood, which she prayed was merely fish blood, and the floor ran sloppy with fish guts, bones and entrails.

A white woman and her family sat down next to her, she had a kind face. The woman had some biscuits, that had somehow managed to stay dry and she gave a few to Madihah. They began to talk, as best they could. From the woman's accent it sounded like she came from Eastern Europe, but it was hard to understand; especially with the noise of so many people now being crowded into such a confined space. The tired old engine began to grind into life and the fishing boat started to move.

As the craft began to turn, it pitched and rolled against the waves. Some were obviously not accustomed to sea travel and were instantly sick, and the levels of stench, heat and overcrowding became just too much for others. There were screams of revulsion and terror. The engine clattered for a while, then settled into a dull rhythm. The next part of the journey had begun.

They had travelled for half an hour when the boat stopped. The hold door opened and yet more people pushed into the hold.

One of the white woman's family started to panic; so the woman called to a member of the crew to see if they could go on deck. She offered money to one of the crew and he agreed; but Madihah had to remain, she had the wrong colour skin to go on deck.

As the hold door finally slammed shut, they heard a sound. Metal on metal. A large bolt slid into place effectively locking them into the hold. Some of the women began to scream, and the children cried in the darkness. There was no way out. If the boat sank, she thought, it would be their tomb.

The fishing boat, fully laden, limped out to sea. Madihah was sure that this was the last she would ever see of the outside world. If the boat, by some miracle, did not sink, she would surely suffocate.

For several hours, the boat rocked. The rough sea and the stench of sweat, sickness, excrement and fish guts, along with the loud whirring and rattling of the old engine, made Madihah feel very unwell.

'A few more hours', she kept telling herself, 'just a few more hours and we will be in Europe.'

Others were praying. Madihah was not even sure whether even God could hear them. He was supposed to be everywhere, but she could not imagine even he could exist in such a place. 'A few more hours ...'

A loud crunching noise emanated from the engine and fell silent. It was then she felt her feet were wet. Madihah's clothes had begun to dry out since being on the fishing boat, but she could feel liquid swish around her feet. It might have just been urine, but no, she knew there was far too much liquid for that. It was water, seawater, and it was starting to rise. The boat was sinking.

She should have felt frightened. Fear had been the norm for so many months, and although her life hung by a thread, the thought of death no longer scared her. She pushed her face as close as she could to the roof, to try to gasp as many breaths as she could, before the end. It would take a miracle to save her, to save them all. Panic ran through the entire hold as the water rose. The men closest to the exit shouted and beat on the door, trying in vain to break it down. However, the door was strong and the bolt outside held firm.

Madihah, face to a small crack in the roof, breathed in long and hard. Closing her eyes, she had one last thought, 'So this was how it was going to be'.

The events of her short life had taught her that life was cheap, and an early death was common and almost expected; people you loved would die long before their time, from either starvation, dehydration or sickness.

In her whole journey, in just getting this far, she had seen beatings, rapes and killings. She had witnessed many unspeakable acts against innocent people. Death would be a blessing, a final source of peace. She was going to drown, and nothing was going to save her.

She was fourteen years old.

Egypt, six months earlier.

2.

The "Amunet Palace Hotel", surrounded by tall palm trees and fragrant herb gardens, stood proudly on the southern-most edge of Cairo's tourist zone. Recent investments, from a far eastern business partnership, had taken the once crumbling façade, and turned it into a picture of opulence. Gone were the tired, cracked walls and broken paving stones. In their place, the bright new terracotta rendering positively gleamed.

Traffic hurried beyond its' imposing walls. Horses, mopeds, trucks and bicycles each jostled for position amidst the hundreds of horn-blowing cars. Even the pavements held no peace for the weary. Beggars and traders aggressively vied for the attention of the pale sun-starved tourists, as the daily life of the city, commerce and traditions came to life once more.

In the dining hall of the "Amunet Palace" the breakfast shift was drawing to a close. Dirty dishes were stacked onto trolleys. Tables and serving areas were being cleared, cleaned and reset for lunch. Inside the kitchen, the chefs and pot washers were discussing menus and their work for the day ahead.

Waitress Anja Peterovic cleared the last of the tables. She was looking forward to a few hours well-earned rest in her shared quarters. Waitressing to overindulged, and mainly overweight, tourists was not her dream job. She had come from a poor Hungarian family and dreamt of making a good life for herself, somewhere else. In fact, given the events of her early life, anywhere else would have done. During the previous two years, she had worked her way south across Europe, employed in various temporary jobs, as a cleaner, waitress, bar staff, receptionist, anything she could do to get by.

Anja felt it was probably time to be moving on again. She was twenty-five, tall, slim, attractive and very bright, with wavy dark brown hair that rested softly on the top of her shoulders. She kept in good shape and rarely touched alcohol and kept herself, pretty much, to herself. This, to most, made her seem quite moody and aloof, which was very far from the truth.

She was extremely positive in nature but had soon learned that giving too much of herself, could be costly, practically, physically and emotionally.

Whilst working at the "Amunet Palace", she had made one very good friend. Liesel hailed from a small village near Copenhagen and was the main reason that Anja had stayed so long in such an awful job. They only spoke English to each other as neither spoke each other's language.

Anja slowly drifted towards the small room she shared with about half a dozen of the other female waiting staff. As she turned a corner, she spotted Liesel walking slowly a little way ahead of her.

"Liesel, wait for me."

Anja's soft Hungarian accent rang down the hallway. Liesel turned, and Anja could clearly see there were tears in her eyes. Liesel pulled a tissue from her apron pocket and blew her nose. Dabbing her eyes, she tried to pretend that nothing was wrong.

It did not work. Unable to hold back her tears, Liesel began sobbing.

"Anja, it is so terrible."

Distraught, Liesel took a deep breath to steady herself. Replacing the tissue, she ran the fingers of both hands through her long black hair. As she did so, a small strawberry shaped birthmark became visible just below her hairline, and for a moment, the fair skin of her long slender neck, was exposed.

"They say I been doing things I did not do."

Liesel struggled with the words as sadness overwhelmed her. Around the corner a small stern-faced woman appeared, it was Liesel's supervisor. Liesel did not trust her, and it was obvious from the way she glanced at them, she suspected that Liesel was up to something. Anja, gripping her friend by the elbow, whispered softly in her ear.

"We should not talk here."

Anja guided Liesel along the corridor and out through a side door. Arm in arm, their eyes blinked as they stepped into the warm morning sunshine. It was going to be another hot day.

They passed the staff car park and, as they did so, Anja glanced across at her old moped, parked in a corner next to a small hedge. Anja's mind wandered for a moment and wondered to herself why she had ever bought it in the first place. Yes, it had been cheap, but she hardly ever used it.

All it ever seemed to do was sit there, paintwork fading, in the hot Egyptian sun. Maybe she would sell it. The extra money would come in useful for when she finally got away.

As they rounded the building, Liesel reached into her apron pocket and pulled out a packet of 'Gitanes' and a lighter. Without offering one to Anja. She tapped the pack and pulled out a cigarette.

"So, what are they saying you've done?"

Liesel, hands shaking, raised the cigarette to her lips and clicked her lighter into life, sucking in the air as the flame licked the end of the cigarette. Liesel inhaled and then blew out a puff of smoke. She coughed, and for a moment, was silent with her thoughts. Tears welled in her swollen red eyes once more, and Anja put her arm around Liesel's shoulders. Liesel was an honest, sensitive soul and Anja hated to see her so sad.

Liesel was unsure just how to put her feelings into words, 'English words', but she just said them anyway, as best she could.

"They say I steal things and look at places where they don't want."

"What things, what places?"

Liesel was finding it very difficult to find the words to explain the accusations 'they' had made against her. As a poorly educated cleaner her command of English was not important, just "hello" and "good morning" would have probably been enough to get her the job.

"I make cleaning in office, like I always, every day I make clean office, I good cleaning, I no steal."

A tear ran free and trickled down her cheek.

"What made them think you did?"

"I make clean office," Liesel repeated, taking another draw from her cigarette, "then manager come, see I looking at pictures on desk. He very angry."

"What pictures were they, and why would they be important?"

"I not know," Liesel looked to the floor, "but they photograph of some of holiday peoples".

"You mean guests?"

"Yah, guests."

"Are you sure they weren't just photocopies of guest passports?"

"No, they like holiday photographs, people on they holidays."

"On their holiday?" Anja corrected.

"Yah." Liesel was still tearful. "Is right, on they holidays."

"Were they the managers' photographs? Maybe they were his family on holiday?"

The smoke rose from the cigarette and began to make Anja's eyes water. Anja was not and had never been a smoker, although both her father and uncle had been. The smell of the smoke took her, for a second, back to a dark place in her young life. Her uncle. She cast the thought from her mind as quickly as it had arrived, as Liesel continued.

"No, some looked like they guest and some looked like they workers, the cleaners, the cooking persons."

Anja thought to herself, 'why would the hotel have holiday photographs of the guests, or members of staff?' Then came a realisation.

"We have a photographer, here at the hotel, he takes pictures of guests, and perhaps he sometimes takes some of the staff too. The hotel makes some money out of them by selling them to the guests, that's probably all it is."

Anja tried to reassure her friend with a gentle hug.

"But why he so angry?"

As Liesel was worked herself back into a state, she drew heavily on the cigarette, hoping the nicotine would help numb her fears.

"He say I steal, he say he get rid of me and he see I don't find other job in all Egypt. I no afford to leave, I no money for plane ticket, I no money to get home. I no doing steal, I not make stealing."

Liesel burst into tears and all Anja could do was to hug her friend until her crying subsided into gentle sobs.

"I'm sure everything will be okay," Anja reasoned. "You know what hot heads these Egyptian men are, he will have forgotten it by now. It's probably living their entire lives in such a hot country that makes them so angry."

Anja walked Liesel back to the room she shared with some of the other cleaners. They both needed to try and get some rest before their next shifts began.

Leaving Liesel at the door, Anja kissed her lightly on the forehead and touched her hand, before heading back towards her own block.

As Anja pushed open her door, a couple of waitresses were watching the news on the small portable television. Anja slumped down into an old armchair. Putting her head back, against the soft cushions, she closed her eyes and relaxed. In the background, she could half hear the babble of the other waitresses chatting, punctuated by the latest headlines from the TV set. The Egyptian Finance Minister had resigned. An English boy had gone missing while on holiday. More trouble in Israel. Anja's mind was elsewhere, she was worried about her friend.

Anja drifted off into a deep and mildly troubled sleep, awakening with a start, several hours later, as one of her roommates shook her arm.

"It's time."

Anja opened her eyes as a tousled haired, brown eyed, dark skinned face looking down at her. She had slept through most of the morning. She stretched, yawned and pulled herself to her feet. It was all too tiring; there must be a better life out there.

Anja made her way back to the dining hall, and the whole process of laying out the buffet, fetching and carrying plates, supplying drinks to the guests and cleaning up spillages, began once more. The nicer guests gave her small tips with a few US dollars here and a few Egyptian pounds there. She began scraping the contents of the half-eaten plates of food into some plastic containers, from tourists whose 'eyes were far bigger than their bellies', and in a lot of cases their bellies were very big indeed.

The hours dragged by slowly, with another tiring shift finally over, Anja made her way back towards her 'servants' quarters, but decided to stop in on Liesel and see how she was feeling. A few of the cleaners were still on duty but she knew that Liesel's next shift did not start until later that evening, after the dinner session had ended.

As she approached Liesel's shared room, Anja noticed the door slightly ajar. She knocked lightly. There was no reply. She guessed that the quietness beyond meant that anyone inside may be sleeping. Trying to remain as quiet as she could, Anja eased the door open and peered inside.

There were six beds in total. Three beds were neatly made with each cleaner's personal items stacked tidily. There were two that looked as though they had recently been slept in; where the occupants had rushed out to their shift; before having had time to make them.

The sixth, which Anja knew to be Liesel's, was completely stripped. Liesel's clothes, which had been hanging on a rail next to the bed, just a few hours earlier, were gone.

Anja felt someone behind her and moved aside as one of Liesel's roommates pushed past.

"Where is Liesel?"

The roommate just shook her head, maybe she did not understand the question; maybe she did not even understand English.

Anja, felt a small shiver run down her spine, and repeated the words more slowly.

"Where, is, Liesel?"

"I don't know," came the reply.

"She was here this morning, but when I came in for my apron about an hour ago, all of her things were gone."

The roommate paused for a moment; she seemed to be looking for something.

With a wry smile, she lifted up a pillow, picked up a mobile phone from beneath adding:

"Maybe she found a better job somewhere else? That wouldn't be difficult."

Anja knew that something was wrong. Liesel had been so upset earlier and would never have left without saying goodbye.

Besides, she could not leave. She did not have any money.

3.

Anja returned to her room, feeling completely deflated and confused she sank down in her usual spot. Her mind raced, trying to make sense of the day's events. Liesel would have said something. Somehow, she would have found Anja and told her that she was planning to leave. Maybe the management had just escorted Liesel from the hotel without even giving her a chance to say goodbye. Especially if they had proved somehow that, she had been stealing. But where would she have gone?' Liesel had very little money. Cleaners were paid even less than waitresses, which was one of the main reasons they all shared rooms with about half a dozen others. It was highly likely that poor Liesel would end up on the streets, homeless.

What could Anja do? There was no one at the hotel she could trust; and to ask one of the managers would have aroused too much suspicion.

Then another thought occurred to Anja. 'What if the police had been called and Liesel had been arrested? Surely someone would have noticed'. Anja slid thoughtfully back into her favourite armchair. 'What if it was to do with the photographs? But, how could looking at a few holiday photographs have led to accusations and the dismissal of a cleaner?'

Anja decided that the only way she would know for sure, would be to see the photographs for herself. There was a good few hours before the breakfast shift began; and although it had been a long day, and Anja felt very tired, she had to try to find out what had happened.

Liesel had mentioned 'the office'; there was only one main office. It had a small number of desks, computers and filing cabinets.

Without further consideration, Anja headed towards the main office. At that time of day, it was unlikely that anyone would be in there working, but it was always possible that one of the duty managers may be around, so she would have to be careful.

As Anja approached the office door, she noticed, through the smoked glass window, that the room was in darkness.

She tried turning the old brass handle and knew straight away that the door was locked; without a key, there was no chance of getting into the room. Anja wracked her brains for a solution.

The duty managers would each have a key, but none of them would just hand it over to a confused waitress.

An idea occurred to her. Nonchalantly, she slowly retraced her steps along the corridor. With a quick glance over her shoulder, to check that no one was looking, she opened and crept through a side door.

Anja found herself at the bottom of a very plain looking staircase. The guests normally used the main staircases, but the staff often used the back stairs, as a short cut, especially if their destination happened to be a long way from the central staircase. There was no one around. Poking her head over the black metal handrail, Anja looked upwards towards the top of the stairwell. Standing completely still, she held her breath, listening intently for any sign of life. After about twenty seconds she exhaled, all seemed perfectly quiet.

Anja crept up the next flight of stairs and peered around the door. The upper floor contained mainly guest rooms. She paused, listening for sounds, voices, footsteps, or anything that might cause her alarm. There was nothing, just silence. Anja slipped through the door and calmly strolled along the upper corridor, to the cleaning storeroom, which, she knew just happened to be almost directly above the main office. Anja tried the door. That too was locked. Anja knew that the recent hotel makeover had not extended to the locks of the cleaning storeroom. She turned the door handle to the open position.

Anja forced her shoulder against the door. No reaction, just a dull thud, having just earned herself a bruised shoulder. Again, she tried. The lock creaked. There was hope. At the third attempt, the lock splintered away from the doorframe and she fell inside the storeroom.

Anja pulled herself up from the floor and, on her knees, peered down the corridor. Silence. At least there were no witnesses to her breaking and entering. She pushed the door closed and found a small table to prop it shut.

The storeroom was about the same size as one of the guest suites, but instead of the opulent décor, soft bed and Jacuzzi, there were trolleys stacked with clean bedding, mops and buckets, vacuum cleaners and all manner of cleaning chemicals, black plastic bags, dusters and cloths, water bottles, coffee and sugar sachets and a couple of spare kettles.

At the rear of the room was a small metal framed window, complete with frosted glass that, by the look of the rust, had not been opened for years. Anja knew she needed to open the window if her plan was going to work. As there was not much in the way of tools to pick from, she took one of the mops and slipped its' metal shaft behind the handle of the window and pulled. The metal rasped as the rust began to give way, with Anja straining against the frame. Finally, the grip of the rust around the window surrendered, and with a loud creak, Anja finally managed to prise it open, with a gap wide enough for her to climb through.

Anja poked her head out of the window and looked down. There was a four-floor drop to the ground. To her left she saw what she was looking for, the fire escape ladder that hung suspended above the first-floor balcony. The ladder hung in this way to stop anyone from the ground gaining access to the upper floor bedrooms and office; but would simply rattle down into place if the building were ever on fire. It was a few feet away and just out of reach. Anja thought she might be able to jump across, provided she could get enough lift when leaping from the small ledge below the window.

Anja eased herself out of the window, with the mop tucked firmly into her armpit. 'This may be a useful, if somewhat unorthodox, weapon if confronted' she smiled at the thought. With her left hand holding onto the edge of the window frame, she threw the mop onto the fire escape platform of the room next door. It made a light clattering noise and rolled towards the edge of the fire escape landing. For a second, Anja thought it would fall, but it safely came to rest against one of the metal struts that surrounded the platform.

Next, it was her turn.

She bent her legs as best she could on the narrow ledge. Launching herself, Anja twisted in the air, her hands flailed out to reach the rail of the next-door landing. She missed with her right, but the fingers of her left hand wrapped around the rail.

Anja felt pain surge through her as the left side of her back and shoulder took the full weight of her body.

She swung in the air for a second, then with her remaining strength, managed to grab the rail with her right hand. Two handed, with a very sore shoulder, Anja was able to pull herself up and over the rail. She slumped down on the small landing next to the mop and massaged her aching body. She smiled to herself looking at the mop that had had a much easier time in getting across.

Anja took a moment to gather herself and breathed deeply. Picking up the mop, she pulled herself to her feet, and winced as the pain shot through her left side. She had pulled a muscle in her back, at the very least. Having committed herself thus far, she knew there was no time to lose. Slowly Anja crept down the metal stairs, trying not to make a sound. Her shoes made a light clanking sound against the metal, so she took them off, tied the laces together and strung them around her neck. With just a pair of stockings about her feet, she felt the hard, cold metal square grids of the fire escape steps digging into the soles of her feet. It was an uncomfortable, but thankfully silent descent.

One level down and she was at the double fire doors of the main office. There was a small open window just to the side of the door. It was too small to climb through, but just big enough to slide an arm in.

Anja knew the inside of the office reasonably well. She knew the position of the desks, the filing cabinets and, best of all she knew that the fire escape doors had a 'push bar' across the middle. If she could just get the mop through the window, and get enough angle, and enough strength, she could push the bar to force open the doors from the inside.

She slid the mop carefully through the open window; it was a bit of a stretch as the window was just above Anja's shoulder height. She managed to lever herself up by standing on the lower handrail of the fire escape landing, steadying herself as best she could.

So, there she was, a hotel waitress, half way up the back-fire escape of the opulent "Amunet Palace," breaking into an office with a mop. Anja half grinned to herself as she thought through the ridiculousness of her current situation.

Each time she tried to push, the mop slid down behind the bar. Running out of strength, Anja sighed. 'Maybe this was all just a waste of time. What was this going to prove anyway? Even if the photographs were still there, how could she connect this to Liesel's disappearance?'

She was just about to give up when the mop connected; the bar dropped and, as if by magic, the doors swung silently open.

4.

The office was dark. With sunlight fading, Anja was going to have to turn on a light if she hoped to see anything. She pulled the fire escape doors to, but did not lock them, as that might have made a noise.

There was a desk towards the back of the office with a small lamp clamped to its' edge. Anja felt around underneath and quickly undid the wing nut that held it in place. It unfastened quite easily, and she lowered the lamp to the floor and slid underneath the desk. She clicked the switch and the lamp lit up her hiding place. Taking her shoes from around her neck, she placed them on the floor beneath the desk, and stared over at the grey metal filing cabinets.

Anja knew that the filing cabinets would be locked, but she also knew that their keys were stored in the top drawer of the desk. The desk was old, and the lock was weak, so it did not take Anja long to break the wooden drawer front using a letter opener, that had been carelessly left on top of the desk.

With the keys safely in her hand, she crept over to the filing cabinets. The dull glow, of the lamp beneath the desk, gave off enough light to seek the material she was looking for.

Sliding each cabinet drawer open, Anja felt around for the files inside. Each time she thought she might have found something relevant, Anja returned to her hiding place to leaf through the contents in more detail. Each time, she found the usual files one might expect relating to the hotel business, general invoices, promotional photographs, rosters and timesheets.

On the sixth check, her heart leapt. In the bottom drawer of the third cabinet, she found a thick file containing photographs and papers. Anja carefully lifted the file out of the drawer. It was quite full. As she returned to her hiding place, some of the files slipped out onto the floor. She cursed to herself and bent down to gather them up. She was close enough to the dim light to realise that these were some of the photographs that Liesel had seen that led to her disappearance.

Anja gathered them up in her arms. Cuddling them to her chest, she made her way back to the rear desk. Carefully lowering herself to her knees, she began to examine the contents of her haul. There were documents that appeared to have names on the top. The rest of the words were in Arabic, which Anja could not read. There were photographs and passports. Not copies of passports, but actual passports. There were holiday photographs, just as Liesel had said. Looking closer at the people in them and the backgrounds of the locations, she was sure that most of the photographs had not been taken in Egypt. The other thing that struck Anja was that many of the photographs were pinned to forms. Again, the forms in Arabic, with some of the standard wording printed on the forms in what looked like a Cyrillic style of lettering.

Anja sat wondering to herself. 'What did all of this mean?' She began leafing through the passports, some faces looked familiar, but they could have really been anyone. Guests and staff came and went so regularly, it was hard to get to know or even remember anyone. Then she opened one passport, and immediately recognised the face looking straight back at her. It was Liesel's passport. She could not have gone, not without her passport. She slipped Liesel's passport into her pocket. Anja would return it to Liesel when she finally found her.

Anja was on high alert. A noise, did she hear a noise? She sat as still as she could beneath the desk. Holding her breath, she peeped above the desk towards the main office door. Maybe it was just the fire doors rattling, as they were only just 'pulled to'.

She continued to work through the files, flicking them open, looking at the photographs. She opened what must have been the twentieth folder, and she froze. The photographs were of her. Anja Peterovic herself. A shiver ran through her whole body. There were pictures taken at the hotel. Not ones she had posed for, but photos of her working, talking to guests, talking to Liesel and worse still, pictures of her sleeping. Someone had crept into their private quarters and taken pictures of her while she slept!

She took the file that contained her photographs and stuffed them inside her blouse. With Liesel's passport safely in her pocket, Anja decided she must tell someone. Someone official. The police. Yes, she had to show the police what she had found and get them to search for Liesel.

Anja gathered the contents of the file and carefully returned them to the filing cabinet. As she pushed the drawer back into the cabinet, she heard a noise. It was a key turning in the door lock. The old brass handle was turning. In a moment she would be caught, and probably endure the same fate as Liesel.

Anja's chest tightened as she quickly made towards the fire doors, trying not to trip over anything in the semi-darkness. Then she remembered she had left the lamp, still lit, beneath the desk, along with her shoes. It was too late to do anything about them.

There was no time to open the fire doors, so she ducked down behind the furthest filing cabinet, which happened to be closest to the fire exit. The light switch clicked on, and the fluorescent strip lights, that ran the full length of the office, flickered into life.

Anja took a deep breath. At her feet was a small fire extinguisher. Quietly she picked it up and listened. She heard the shuffle of feet and a chair being dragged across the floor. Silence. An object clunked on the desk. Her mind was racing now, 'It must be the lamp. Whoever that is has found the lamp and my shoes'. Anja tensed. She was about to be caught red handed, with no excuse but the truth; and the truth would certainly condemn her to a terrible fate. There was nothing else for it. Anja held her breath and waited.

5.

Anja could hear them breathing. She could sense their presence. She could smell their sickly-sweet sweat. Near, so very near and treading carefully, Faint footsteps on the wooden floor. Closer. Closer. Anja's hands were sweating. Tightly, she gripped the fire extinguisher. Another second, her adversary would be upon her. So close. Nicotine and stale perfumed aftershave. The smell was familiar, but no time to think why. A bead of sweat ran down Anja's forehead and dripped off the end of her nose. A voice inside Anja's head screamed, 'Strike first, strike fast, strike now.'

A hand moved towards her. Anja struck out with all her might. The base of the fire extinguisher made contact. Straight into the face of her 'would be' assailant. Falling backwards, the stunned body hit the floor. It was a woman. Anja's 'would be' assailant was a woman. Anja recognised her straight away as Marina, her supervisor. Not a person she would lose any sleep over. Bitch. She may not be involved in whatever was going on. There was no time to find out.

Anja looked up from the body as two men entered the office. A shocking sight met their eyes as Anja stood over the unconscious, bleeding Marina. The improvised weapon still in her hands dripping with blood. Anja hurled the fire extinguisher towards the two men, pushed the rear doors open and ran out onto the fire escape.

It was almost dark outside. The bright lights of Cairo glistened in the distance. Anja felt the warm night air brush her face as she quickly made her way down the steps, missing every alternate step as she went. There was just one thing on her mind. She had to get to her moped, before they did.

There were voices above her. Shouts, in Arabic. Soon others would join in the chase. If she were cornered, it would soon be over. Anja had to escape. She had to tell the police. 'But what if she herself was arrested for attacking Marina? What if no one believed her?' She had Liesel's passport, but she could have stolen that herself.

She still had the file with her photographs in it. Anja had no idea what the words in the file meant, so it might be proof of nothing. She, Anja, was in possession of her friend's passport and pictures of herself. If the words on the form were not incriminating, she could be facing serious jail time in an Egyptian prison for assault or maybe even murder.

These thoughts and more flooded through her mind, as she ran for her life. The main priority was to get away. Whatever she was now involved in, she was in trouble, big trouble.

Anja got to the first-floor fire escape landing and released the catch. The ladder rattled down to the ground. They were gaining on her. The clatter of her pursuer's shoes on the metal stairs were closing in as she started down the ladder. Sliding the last few feet, she stumbled and landed awkwardly on the ground. Scrambling to her feet, she could see them approaching the top of the ladder. Her feet hurt, her shoes were still under the table in the office, for now, she would have to endure the pain.

The car park was not far from the fire escape. A few hundred yards lay between her and her moped. Anja was tired, but she had to run on. She was fast. She had always been athletic and had won medals at school. If she could just out-run them and, provided the moped would start, she could soon be free. She ducked behind some bins and followed a little gap behind some packing crates that were stacked behind the kitchens. The men must have lost her in the darkness and had now split up. Some shouts were close, but others were much further away. Her plans did not extend any further than the hotel gates. Chest pounding, she slipped from behind the crates and rounded the building half running, half crouched; and there in front, just a hundred feet away, stood her moped.

Anja reached it in seconds, jumped astride and fumbled around her pockets for her keys. She always carried her keys and purse, never trusting the hotel safe, or her locker for that matter. Feeling the warm leather fob, she pulled it out; the keys rattled in her hands. Only half a dozen keys, but it seemed to take an age to find the correct one. On they came. Anja could hear them getting nearer. They were close. Very close. She thrust the key into the ignition and turned. There was just a gentle click.

'Don't tell me the battery is dead,' she whispered to herself.

A stocky man had rounded the building and ran across the car park.

Immediately seeing Anja he shouted to the others that he had found her. Another turn of the key and a sluggish grind of metal on metal emanated from beneath her. One more failed try and she would have to give up on the moped and run, but what chance could she have. A third turn of the key and the engine reluctantly fired into life. The closest runner was almost on top of her. Letting off the brakes and revving the engine, she lurched forward, just as a burly fist whistled past her head. A second later and she would have been on the floor.

Anja rode as fast as she could, wobbling a little, but without toppling over, raced for the entrance gate.

A delivery truck was checking in at the gatehouse. A security guard had inspected the load and had raised the barrier. The truck rolled through and the gateman began to lower the bar, and slowly descending as Anja approached. She forced her head as low as she could, skimming the top of her hair on the underside of the steel pole as it descended. She was still alive and had made it outside of the hotel with her own file and Liesel's passport safely tucked inside her clothing.

6.

Anja emerged from the hotel grounds still astride her moped. Unlike the nicely paved hotel entrance, the track that led from the gatehouse to the main road was rough and rutted. She bumped along desperately trying to avoid the rocks and boulders in her path. Progress was slower than she had hoped, and she could already hear shouts and curses, as the barrier raised behind her.

Her front tyre glanced against a well-camouflaged rock. Losing control for a moment, she narrowly missed a couple of local men who were offering some tourists a moonlit photo opportunity with their camels. She came to a brief halt and took a breath. Regaining her composure, Anja shouted "Ana Asifa, Sorry" to the dismayed gathering.

Revving her engine back into life, she picked up speed, and quickly reached the junction where the track met the road.

Anja had planned to turn left, but the main road was far too busy to cross, so instead she had to take a right turn and joined the busy throng heading back towards the city centre. She slipped into the stream of traffic and managed to overtake a couple on a bicycle and a small melon truck. The needle of her fuel gauge was just above the red; but she felt reasonably confident there was enough gas, to at least make it to the city, abandon the moped and slip into the back alleys on foot. Anja was fit and was sure she could easily outrun any of the hotel security guards in a sprint.

Anja raced on, as fast as her old moped would allow. Darting past several bicycles and a packed bus, she knew they would be close behind her. Quickly peering over her shoulder, there were two black cars she recognised, vying for position behind the bus. They were managing to keep up with her.

Anja continued to weave in and out amongst the heavy traffic. A truck, piled high with straw bales, lay dead ahead, and seemed to be braking hard, despite the fact his brake lights were not working. Anja was going too fast to stop.

She swerved to the left and, as she did so, found herself staring right into the radiator grill of an oncoming lorry.

The lorry driver braked hard and blasted his horn. Pure instinct kicked in and Anja managed to overtake the straw laden truck to her right, and tuck in, just in front of it, before the lorry was upon her. Anja felt a whoosh of warm diesel tainted air in her face as the lorry thundered past. Her heart thumped wildly in her chest. The manoeuvre had been dangerous but might have just given her the extra distance advantage she needed.

The road was getting busier. The closer Anja got to the city centre, the more built up it became. Dozens of pedestrians were trying to cross the road, mingling in amongst the mass of vehicles. It was hard to travel at any kind of speed. She overtook another moped with two men, without helmets. The passenger sat behind, arms crossed, with a defiant, 'I don't hug men' expression on his face.

The traffic began to thin, and Anja managed to nip in between a gaily coloured coach and a tall box van. There was a crossroads ahead, a busy intersection controlled by traffic lights. Anja knew she needed to get across these lights before they changed to red, to stand any chance of escape.

She edged out in front of the box van and glanced over her shoulder. The black cars were no longer in sight, but she did notice a motorbike working its' way through the tightly packed vehicles towards her. She recognised the helmetless rider immediately as one of the hotel supervisors. He was coming for her and closing in very quickly.

The traffic lights were close, but, at the speed he was travelling, the motorbike might just catch up with her before she made it to the intersection. Shaking with fear and adrenaline, Anja took off at full throttle. Never had she felt more alive, terrified and excited all in equal measure.

A bus pulled across her path and she had to dodge to avoid a collision. The moped wobbled for a second, but she kept her balance. The lights ahead were still green. At any moment, they could change. Inside she could feel the seconds ticking away before they switched to red.

"Stay green, stay green!" Anja shouted as she approached.

The lights turned red just as she arrived at the white line. A split-second decision. She was going to chance it. She had to.

If she could get across the intersection, before the opposing traffic started to move, she would surely escape.

With all the speed she could muster, Anja shot across the white line. The chasing motorbike had the same idea. Just as he caught up with her, Anja deftly twisted her moped away from him. An opposing car had jumped the lights early. The female driver had not expected either rider to be in her path and managed to manoeuvre to avoid hitting Anja. The car struck the motorbike head on, sending the helmetless rider hurtling through the air. Terror filled his eyes as his face met the pavement. It would be the last thing he ever saw.

Still at full speed, the moped's tyres screeched on the uneven road surface. As Anja turned sharply, she found herself looking straight into the eyes of a small Egyptian boy, standing in the road. He was directly in her path, seemingly frozen to the spot with fear. She knew straight away, at this speed if she hit him she would kill him.

Instinctively Anja swerved missing the boy by a whisker. The moped, slipped onto its' side, wheels spinning, with Anja's left leg trapped beneath. It bounced violently against the kerb. Anja screamed in agony as the left side of her body scraped across the road, as she and her precious moped skidded into the path of the oncoming traffic.

7.

Anja's world began to move in slow motion. The oncoming vehicles crawled towards her. The deafening blast of their horns seemed, to her ears, long and drawn out. It was like a dream. The motorcyclist floated gracefully through the air. Looking into the eyes of the boy, she could almost see into his very soul, and then like a bolt from the blue she was back in the moment.

A small car clipped the back wheel of the moped and spun her round. Anja screamed and passed out. Miraculously, the remaining traffic came to a halt and she and her moped slid across the road and came to rest at the kerbside.

An old man, begging at the side of the road, rose from his blanket and beloved trinkets, and rushed to Anja's aid. Two young women wearing hijabs stopped to help. Several others scrambled out of their cars and ran over to offer their assistance. A large crowd had gathered and the sound of emergency sirens filled the air.

Anja's eyes flickered open, confused and barely realising what had just happened. As her eyes began to focus, she noticed the motorcyclist lying motionless in a pool of blood at the roadside. Her memories began to return. Raising herself onto an elbow, she scanned the crowd for her pursuers. All that met her gaze was a sea of concerned faces.

She tried to move but the moped had her firmly pinned to the ground. The pain in her left hip was unbearable. A paramedic knelt by her side, as several of the passers-by lifted the moped from her leg. A pool of blood seeped from a wound just below her knee. Anja wept as the medic pulled on his latex gloves and began to apply first aid.

From a safe distance, the hotel security men climbed out of their vehicles and surveyed the accident. With so many helpers, motorists and onlookers milling around, they knew it would have been impossible to intervene. Any attempt to grab Anja would have raised too much suspicion.

They loitered long enough to witness the ambulances and police cars arrive. Seemingly unnoticed, they returned to their vehicles.

After applying a splint to her damaged leg, Anja was carefully lifted onto a stretcher and into the back of the waiting ambulance. A second ambulance arrived, presumably to transport her adversary to the morgue. When the doors to Anja's ambulance closed she began to feel a little more at ease. Somehow, she had managed to evade capture, for a while at least.

A siren rang out as the ambulance fought its' way through the traffic. The medic readied a pain killing injection, but Anja pulled away. "Laa, No" she said shaking her head. The medic shook his head and lowered the needle. Although she was in a great deal of pain, the last thing Anja wanted was to be sedated.

They arrived at the hospital within minutes with Anja taken straight through to the emergency triage room. Her left leg was extremely painful, and the left side of her body sore and badly bruised. A nurse brought her a small plastic cup of water and helped prop her head while she took a sip. It tasted good; she was extremely thirsty, so she greedily gulped the remaining water, laid back on the trolley and awaited her turn.

After an initial check from an emergency nurse, an orderly wheeled Anja to the X-ray department. The doctor informed her that she had fractured her leg quite badly in two places, and it would have to be set and plastered. They advised her that she needed to stay in hospital for a few days for observation, but may be allowed home for family' care in a few days. 'That might be a little tricky,' she thought to herself as another orderly wheeled her into a treatment room.

Still refusing painkillers, Anja screamed as they pulled and twisted her leg back into place. Once her leg was set into the correct position, a technician applied the plaster. Her leg was throbbing with pain, and after about ten minutes, she finally agreed to take some pain-killing tablets. After the plaster had been applied, Anja was moved to a side monitoring room for about an hour, and then onto a ward.

She winced as two orderlies lifted her from the trolley to a bed. The ward seemed relatively clean and modern, the paintwork looked fresh and the air-conditioning appeared to be doing its' job.

A man with a clipboard stood by her bed, it sounded as if he was talking about payment, but his voice became ever more distant as the effects of the painkillers kicked in. Anja drifted off into a deep and disturbed sleep.

Anja slept through the whole night awaking from her slumber somewhat groggy and confused. As her mind began to clear, she began to take stock of her surroundings. She was sharing a room with five other women. Three were quite old, and two were younger than herself. The older women were sitting up reading. One young woman was sleeping and the other, who wore headphones, was either listening to music or watching TV; Anja could not quite tell which. A male orderly was busily sweeping the floor. He looked up from his broom and smiled at her, he had a nice friendly smile, so she smiled back.

A nurse appeared at her bedside and offered Anja a cup of tea and some breakfast. Although Anja was not very hungry, probably a side effect of the painkillers, she ate a little bread and sipped some tea. The nurse placed a plate of biscuits and a jug of water on the cupboard at the side of the bed "for later". Anja knew she would need all the strength she could muster and made a mental note to consume all the fuel she could, before she made her next move.

"Where are my belongings?" Anja asked, worried about the files and passports she had been carrying.

"I'll go and check for you," replied the nurse.

Anja lay back in her bed and surveyed the cast on her leg. She was still alive, but she may not be safe for long.

The nurse returned and said that her personal effects were perfectly safe.

"Your brother called by last night, paid for your treatment and collected your belongings, and he said he would be back later to see how you are and possibly take you home."

"My brother?"

Hiding the shock in her voice, she thought quietly to herself, 'but I don't have a brother'.

As the nurse disappeared, Anja knew that her mysterious 'brother' must have been someone from the hotel. Who else would have known she was there? Worse still, she no longer had any actual evidence against them. All she had was her testimony, which her employers would simply deny; also, her fingerprints would be on the fire extinguisher covered in Marina's blood.

Cast or no cast, broken leg or not, she had to escape from the hospital.

The male orderly came near to her bed as he swept.

"Do you speak English?" Anja enquired. She thought that her native Hungarian would have been a lot less likely.

"I do," he replied, he had a strong English accent, somewhere from the north of England she guessed.

"I'm from Liverpool like, well Bootle, to be exact," he said, guessing she may be curious.

"They call me Scouse Mick, I'm just over 'ere on me gap year, earning some extra dosh before heading off to Uni like."

He seemed friendly and maybe someone she could trust, even though he seemed quite hard to understand.

"So how do you pronounce your name?" He said examining her chart.

"A-N-J-A is that Ann-Jar?"

"Ann-Yah," she corrected him

"Ann-Yah," he mimicked and smiled

"I need a favour, but it needs to be our secret."

"Anything for a boss lookin' bird like you," he winked and smiled a rather leering smile.

"I need to get out of this hospital, right now."

"Shouldn't you be restin'?"

Anja had to think of a legitimate reason to want to go outside.

"I'd really like a smoke."

"I'll get yer a ciggy, and take yer out for a smoke, no sweat, you stay right there darlin' and I'll go and fetch yer a wheelchair."

Anja waited anxiously, sat on the edge of the bed, and looked all around. It was a nervous wait, very aware that her 'brother' might appear at any moment.

'Scouse Mick' arrived back about twenty minutes later with a wheelchair.

"Sorry darlin', took me ages to find one that didn't have a squeaky wheel," he remarked jovially.

As she eased herself into the wheelchair, she felt his hands touch her breasts.

"What are you doing?" Anja said sternly.

Mick tried to laugh it off.

"You can't blame a fella for trying to cop a feel, can you? Must get it all the time in your job."

He was cocky, extremely confident and obviously fancied himself as a 'ladies' man.

She was going off him rapidly, but as he was her only means of escape, she might just have to hold her tongue and play along until she was free. Then another thought occurred to her, how would he know what she did for a living?

"Just get me out of here," Anja snapped.

"Keep your hair on," he laughed, as if it were nothing.

A nurse spotted him pushing Anja across the ward and shouted across.

"Where are you going with that patient?"

"We're just goin' out fer a ciggy like," Mick replied with a smile and a wink.

Anja was caught in a new dilemma, even if this orderly was completely trustworthy, what was she going to do once she got outside the hospital, in a wheelchair, in a gown with no money and her leg in plaster? Maybe she could get a taxi somehow, to somewhere. Somewhere safe. But where? And more to the point, if he was not trustworthy, what was she going to do then?

As they left the main building, Mick paused for a second and bent down as if to tie his shoelace. As he stood, Anja felt a sharp scratch at the top of her left arm. Almost immediately, the world around her began to swirl. Almost at the same time she realised she could not move a muscle. Not even to speak. Anja was paralysed. All she could move was her eyes and eyelids.

A couple of male orderlies stood outside the hospital entrance smoking. Anja tried to shout to them for help, but it was no use. She was panicking inside. Where was he taking her? Mick wheeled her quickly towards a private ambulance parked close to the hospital entrance. As they approached, the rear doors opened and a man, she immediately recognised, stepped down.

Scouse Mick had tricked her.

"Is this 'er?" Mick asked the man that had come to meet them.

"Yes, you have done well."

The man was tall, greying slightly and smartly dressed in a white doctor's coat. Although Anja did not know his name, she recognised him as one of the hotel managers.

He must have been the 'brother' that the nurse had spoken about.

The hotel manager gently took control of the handles of the wheelchair and rolled it onto the lowered platform at the back of the ambulance and pushed a button. The mechanism whirred as the wheelchair began to rise and eventually rolled it and Anja into the back of the vehicle.

As the manager moved to close the ambulance doors, Mick put a hand on his arm.

"So, where's me ackers then mate?"

"Your ackers?" The manager appeared confused.

"Me Dosh."

The manager clearly did not understand.

"Dosh?"

"Me M-O-N-E-Y, me fuckin' money!"

Scouse Mick grabbed hold of the manager's arm in a vice like grip, his anger rising. The manager pushed him away. Mick clenched his fists, but as he tried to lash out, he had failed to notice the two approaching orderlies. One immediately grabbed Mick in a chokehold. The manager neatly pulled a pistol from inside his jacket. They marched Mick towards the back of the open ambulance. Anja could see the shocked expression on his face as he stared at her, his eyes pleaded with her to help him. She was completely powerless. In one swift movement, the manager had attached a silencer and pressed the muzzle against the back of Mick's head. As he fired, Mick's face exploded. Blood and splinters of brain and bone sprayed the interior of the ambulance.

Anja saw the red spray of dust hurtling towards her, with a bullet leading the charge. Mick's face had become a gaping hole. To Anja it was as if the jaws of hell were opening, about to suck her into its' evil depths. Her mind was a swirl of terror, shock and revulsion, fuelled by hallucinogenics. The bullet missed her own head by inches. Its' dull thud echoed as it landed behind her. A soft thump lost against the loud screams raging inside her head. They hurled Mick's lifeless corpse into the back of the vehicle. An oversized rag doll without a face. Mick's blood oozed across the ambulance floor in an ever-growing pool.

Anja saw the last crack of daylight slowly disappear as the ambulance doors slammed shut. Trapped in the darkness of the worst horror scene she could ever have imagined.

Again, she tried to scream but no words would come. There was no hope. They had her, and for poor brave Anja, this could be the end.

8.

It was 8am as Jade Turner woke from her slumber. It had been a nice dream, somewhere sunny, on holiday maybe, or was it in the park? A few moments after waking, it became harder to remember the exact details. Mum and Dad were with her, they were having fun. A very nice dream. She had not set the alarm; after all, it was Saturday. Jade's 'lie in and then pop to town to do some shopping day'. She rolled over onto her side, 'just a few more minutes', she thought to herself. Jade dozed. Outside the rain teemed down. The splashes of the raindrops danced on the window ledge outside.

Her thoughts turned back to Mum. It had been two years since her lovely mother had passed. Jade opened her eyes and yawned. Glancing over to her bedside table, there sat the photograph that she held so dear, taken on Mum's last holiday. Mum was well then, or so they thought. Her Mum and Dad laughing as the sun beat down on their little caravan in Wales. Her mother had bought her a little toy camel, wearing a sombrero of all things, from a little antique shop not far from the caravan site. A small cheap gift that she treasured. It always reminded her of that holiday. It stood proudly on the bedside table next to the photograph. They had been such happy days.

Jade rubbed her eyes, sat up on the edge of the bed and stretched. Today, she decided, was going to be a good day. She got up, slipped off her nightdress, and looked at herself in the full-length mirror of her wardrobe. Jade had shoulder length 'out of a bottle' blonde hair, with a delicate hint of black roots.

She stretched up to try and make herself a little taller than her usual medium height, 'with a bit of work, I could be a model' she thought to herself. Jade had always been one for showing off, and like her mother, was a vibrant soul.

Jade did a twirl and her hair flicked up, the snake tattoo in full view on her left shoulder. Jade so regretted that tattoo now. She had been in a dark place when that happened, and now she was stuck with it, a reminder of those days.

To have it removed would have been expensive and painful, and Jade really did not like pain.

Jade picked up her mobile phone from the bedside table and switched it on, the array of multi-coloured icons popped into view. She checked her emails, updated her Facebook and Twitter pages and then clicked the camera icon. Jade took a couple of "selfie", photographs of her face, in various contorted shapes and then clicked the 'share' to Instagram button. Her work for the day was done. She needed to get dressed, have breakfast and head for town. It was going to be a big day, meet Emma at the hairdressers, clothes shopping, lunch, then hit the travel agents.

As Jade descended the stairs she could hear the crackle of bacon frying, the smell drifted around the entire house. Her father, Harry, was cooking his speciality, bacon and egg sandwiches. He had been to the local shop earlier and bought a nice fresh white giraffe loaf. Harry was far from the best cook in the world, but he tried his best. Vicky had always been the cook. She could cook anything. Harry thought about Vicky, every day. He missed the little things about her. She would touch his arm, his back, put her hand on his knee, she used to squeeze past him in the kitchen. He had loved it when she touched him. The memories were happy ones, but they left him with a feeling of sadness. He looked up from the frying pan, and as Jade entered the kitchen, he could visualise a young Vicky standing there. Beautiful, bright, eyes shining and full of life that was Jade. Vicky would have been so proud of her daughter.

Harry wiped a tear from his cheek.

"It's just the steam," said Harry. "It makes my eyes run."

"Smoke more like," Jade smiled at him.

Jade opened the refrigerator door and lifted the tomato ketchup from the shelf.

"Maybe we should get a cook?"

"Maybe we should get a housekeeper?" replied Harry. "A nice young Swedish one for your old Dad."

"In your dreams," Jade retorted with a grin and switched on the television.

The news came on, the newsreader droned on about asylum seekers trying to cross the channel, trouble in Gaza, small boy still missing on holiday in Tunisia, economic turmoil in Greece.

"They haven't found that boy then?" Jade commented.

"Not by the sound of that," replied Harry.

Harry started serving up the sandwiches, a layer of bacon, then a fried egg on top, he broke the yolk of each and spread it across the bacon. Tomato ketchup smeared and spread across the top slices of bread, and then put in place to complete the sandwiches.

"Perfect, a feast fit for a King." Harry was proud of his creations.

"Or a Queen," Jade interjected, taking a bite.

The runny yolk ran down the side of the sandwich and onto her chin. Jade grabbed a piece of kitchen roll and wiped her face, before the yolk and sauce mixture landed on her blouse.

"So, what are you up to today?" Harry's soft voice barely audible above the television.

"Meeting Emma in town. Bit of shopping, maybe lunch, oh hairdressers, of course..."

"Of course." Harry interjected.

"... then maybe we'll get some holiday brochures."

Harry's friendly blue-grey eyes stared at Jade, 'so like your Mother' he thought, 'so much life'.

Harry's wife, Jade's mother, Vicky had died two years before; it had been a massive strain for them both. The cancer had not been diagnosed straight away; Vicky had always been the life and soul of the party. She was the one who Jade took after the most, Harry the careful one, Vicky the wild one. Vicky was beautiful, caring, supportive and loving. She always knew Harry was the shy sensitive type, and she had helped to bring him out of his shell over the years they were together. Their life, although not free from life's problems, was a happy and contented one.

Then Vicky got tired, just a little at first, she could not do as much as she used to. She often found herself a little short of breath after climbing the stairs.

She became too tired to play sports, too tired for shopping, and worst of all for Harry, she became too tired for making love. The headaches started soon after, 'migraines' she called them. She had been overdoing it that was what she told herself. The first blackout had been a real shock. Vicky was in the middle of washing up, when she collapsed at the sink and slumped to the floor. She woke within a minute. She had been alone in the house, and had not wanted to alarm Harry and Jade, so had not mentioned it, but she had a nagging feeling that this was more than just tiredness.

The second blackout came while she was in Birmingham, shopping with Jade. They were in a clothes shop and Jade had been trying on some new dresses ready for a friend's birthday party. Vicky watched as Jade modelled a pretty yellow dress she had found, witnessing the worry in her daughter's eyes, just moments before passing out.

Vicky awoke, surrounded by a crowd of shoppers, Jade was crying, and holding her mother's hand, walking alongside as the paramedics carried her on a stretcher to the waiting ambulance.

The tumour in her brain was getting bigger, and had started to impact on Vicky's speech, her memory and her ability to walk and move. It was in a place that was too awkward to operate on, so all the doctors could do was to offer painkillers and chemotherapy. Vicky became ever weaker and the family knew that it would not be long.

Within two months of being diagnosed Vicky transferred to a hospice and a few days later she was gone. The cancer had eaten her away, bit by bit, with a stroke finally claiming her. Harry was devastated, his world totally shattered. He withdrew into himself and drank heavily to ease the pain. Jade too was in a terrible state. Her schoolwork suffered, she started playing truant, smoking and hanging out with a gang of kids from the local council estate. She got a tattoo of a snake across her left shoulder. Harry did not like it, but being in such a dark place himself, he could do nothing.

Along with his depression, Harry started to suffer blackouts. The doctor told Harry he must quit drinking if he was to see his daughter grow up and marry. Still he drank. One day he woke up to find Jade standing over him, he was lying on the kitchen floor, in a pool of blood and a pain in his abdomen. He had been making a cup of tea, laced with whisky and had passed out, fallen, and landed on the open dishwasher. A knife had been sticking, blade upwards, out of the cutlery box and as he fell, stabbed himself. Jade came home and screamed at the sight. She thought he was dead. Amazingly, for Harry, the knife had not penetrated too deep, having missed all his vital organs and arteries. Her scream woke him. It was at that point he knew that he was in serious trouble. He finally sought help from his doctor, joined Alcoholics Anonymous and slowly, but surely, freed himself from his drink problem and mentally moved into a better place.

Two years passed, the wounds began to heal. Harry found a new job. Jade encouraged him to start dating, but he could not bring himself to commit to anyone as he missed Vicky so much. She had been his soul mate, his lover and best friend. He was lonely, but he knew he could never replace Vicky, and no one would ever be able to live up to her.

It was a wet and miserable Saturday morning in Lichfield, one of England's smallest cities. Harry drove Jade into the centre and dropped her off in a car park.

"Will you be home for tea?" Harry asked.

"What are we having?" Jade replied, already knowing the answer.

"Chippie Tea," they both chimed in unison. Jade took off her seatbelt, opened the car door and stepped out into the rainy Lichfield air.

"See you later," Jade whispered to Harry, leaned over and kissed him on the cheek. She noticed the small flecks of grey in amongst his mop of brown curly hair. The grey had started to appear soon after her Mother had died. He was still only in his mid-forties, but she knew the stresses and strains of the last few years had made him look so much older. She loved her Father with all her heart. She was his protector, just as her Mother had been, and she would always be there for him, no matter what.

"Missing you already," Jade shouted and waved as Harry drove away.

Jade looked about her. It was raining quite hard, so she pulled the hood of her raincoat over her head and walked down a small covered alleyway towards the shops. The dark grey clouds loomed over the town, and people started taking shelter under the canopies of market stalls and covered walkways. Inside the cafes and shops, trade was booming, as the shoppers escaped the downpour.

Jade made straight for the hairdressers. She had an appointment and was going to enjoy the next few hours. A small bell jangled as she opened the shop door, relieved, she pulled down her hood. A few water droplets fell from her coat and landed on the mat. Jade wiped her feet and walked over to the reception desk.

Emma was already there, sitting proudly in her chair. Her hair had already been washed and was now being styled by Alphonse (his real name was Brian, but Alphonse made him sound more Mediterranean).

A small cup of espresso steamed beside Emma. This was the life, nothing else to do on a Saturday but 'be pampered' by a handsome gay man in a high-end hairdressing shop. Alphonse was not gay, maybe he was slightly effeminate, but acting overly camp was good for business; and he could get even closer to the girls and women that frequented his shop.

"Hello Jade, what's going on with the raincoat girlfriend?" His manner friendly as he wiggled his finger in front of his face, as if to scold her fashion sense.

Alphonse flitted around her, Jade was his type, but to cross the boundary between business and relationship was not on his mind today, and it would ruin his reputation.

"Oh, I couldn't find mine, it's me Dad's," Jade shrugged, and slipped Harry's raincoat from her shoulders.

Jill, the young Saturday girl, who had been sweeping hair, put down her long-handled brush, took Jade's coat and hung it on a coat peg at the back of the shop. Alphonse turned to Jade, scissors in hand, standing behind Emma.

"I won't be a tick love," said Alphonse, "Jill, luvvie, could you just make Jade a coffee, white no sugar wasn't it?"

Jade nodded gratefully, a nice coffee, a morning of pampering, a nice lunch, then add to that some shopping and choosing holidays, what could be better?

The morning had gone smoothly. Jade and Emma left the little hairdressing shop together, arm in arm they strolled towards the shops. That was Jade's way. Jade was a friendly young woman at the tender age of eighteen. Everybody loved Jade. Certainly, she had had her moments after her Mother had passed away, but she was feeling healthy again. Emma had been a dear friend from her early school days and came back into Jade's life at just the right time, to help to stop her completely going off the rails.

They had been best friends ever since their very first day at Chadsmead Infant's school; the teacher had sat them together for their very first lesson. Jade had been the first to speak and had asked to borrow some of Emma's crayons.

Their friendship never looked back. The years went by and slowly they drifted apart, each studying different subjects and hanging out with different friends. Emma was more interested in science, technical drawing and history.

Emma was not keen on sports, but despite her lack of interest, she was quite a fast runner and had won a few trophies at the school sports days. Jade preferred sports, music and art. Jade also had a string of boyfriends that seemed to take up most of her time outside school.

Emma was a sensible shy girl, she loved horses, reading, romantic films and was very studious. Jade, on the other hand, was more outgoing, lively, did not read much and preferred clubbing and watching 'reality' television. Jade was also a big fan of One Direction and ogling nice looking men, mainly in magazines. They were both so very different, which is probably why they got on so well together.

Huddled together beneath Jade's latest purchase, a brightly coloured umbrella covered in pictures of boy band One Direction, they took a stroll past the grand entrance to Lichfield's magnificent medieval cathedral, a beautiful, three-spired stone building. The cathedral always inspired Emma as she loved architecture. When she was older, she was going to be an architect. They had recently finished their AS Level exams and at least four years of study lay in wait for Emma. Jade was not the least bit interested in academia, she was going to get a job in a shop or something. Maybe a clothes shop, so she could try on all the new things that came in and get staff discount.

Jade was always the chatty, outgoing one, Emma was quiet, but Emma found a real trust with Jade. The world was a scary place for Emma, but when she was with Jade, she felt safe. Jade and Emma, it was always Jade and Emma, they went everywhere together. So close, they could have been sisters. Emma being the shy one, always looked up to Jade, went along with her flights of fancy and always laughed at her jokes, even when they weren't funny.

Jade had big ideas, when she was seven she had decided that she was going to be famous. Jade would have been a singer if she could have actually held a tune. That did not stop her; she was always singing, always positive, bright and breezy. Emma would never have dared to be as outgoing as Jade, but she went along for the ride. Emma often wondered what life would have been like had she never met Jade, would she have had such a good time in her childhood? She had voiced this concern to Jade, but Jade had just called her a 'daft sod', gave Emma a big hug and said that they were always meant to be best friends, no matter what.

Jade made people laugh, possessing a very disarming quality. Everyone loved Jade. She did not have the slimmest of figures, but in her way, she was beautiful, the sparkle in her eyes, the vivacious laugh and flowing blond hair. She loved her family, she loved her food, and she loved boys, well, 'older boys' to be more precise.

They spent the next few hours wandering around the small market in the square, trying on clothes and gathering a sizeable collection of brochures from the travel agents. After about an hour and a half, Jade decided that it was time for coffee and some lunch, so they headed towards some of the older looking shops and the place where their favourite teashop resided.

'The Spark' was Jade and Emma's favourite. A handful of colour swatches sat in small picture frames, dotted across charming retro wallpaper; with a mixture of non-matching wooden chairs and tables all helped give the room a real bohemian vibe. In the corner sat a 1970's Schreiber living room cabinet with an old dis-connected dial phone placed on top. An elderly couple were just getting up from two soft easy chairs set in the window and Jade loitered close by making sure no one else could grab the only non-wooden chairs in the place. These were her favourite 'watching the world go by' chairs.

Emma glanced up at the blackboard that listed 'Today's Specials' as Jade made herself comfortable in a leather easy chair.

'Carrot, Coriander with Parsnip', that sounds nice remarked Emma.

Jade nodded in agreement. They giggled as they ordered "two soups" (they always laughed when the ordered "two soups", as they remembered the fabulously funny Julie Walters sketch of the same name); two flavoured cafe lattes, one hazelnut and one caramel. Emma also ordered a BLT (Bacon, Lettuce and Tomato) sandwich on crusty white bread and Jade had a big slab of date and walnut cake.

As they ate, they leafed through the first of the brochures and chatted about holidays.

"Where shall we go, on holiday?" said Emma quietly.

"Somewhere exotic, somewhere where there's camels," replied Jade, with a playful gleam in her eyes.

'Why does she have this fixation with camels?' Emma thought to herself.

She had seen them at the zoo when she was younger and thought they were rather smelly, spitty animals, they chewed in a funny way, and had sloppy tongues.

Jade was only teasing, but Emma still did not always catch onto that fact, even after all these years.

Jade continued to speculate "Greece, Turkey, Spain, Majorca, Ibiza, clubbing? How about a clubbing holiday? Sun, sea and sangria?"

They began to leaf through the brochures, discounting quite a few as they went, too expensive, too far, too dull.

Emma was not really one for clubbing, or sangria for that matter, her perfect holiday would have been somewhere warm and quiet, curled up with a good book

"How about Italy? Just think of all those, hunky Italian men, all that olive flesh.'" Jade was 'on a roll'.

Emma shrugged, and Jade could tell that none of her ideas had impressed so far.

"This has to be the holiday of a lifetime, so where do 'you' think we should go?" Jade was putting Emma on the spot.

"Maybe we should see what's on offer at some of the online travel agents?" Emma started to say, "Maybe France or Portugal…" thinking these places weren't so far, and the flight wouldn't be too long, and they were somewhere where her parents might approve of. Emma was also feeling very nervous about flying. Jade was already way ahead of her.

"I'd like to see the desert, the sand, the tribesmen, the camels," ('there she goes with the camels again' thought Emma). "How about somewhere like Africa?"

"Isn't that a bit dangerous? What about the insects, and haven't they been in the news recently, isn't there trouble going on over there now?" Emma was feeling rather fearful inside, her hands trembled ever so slightly.

"You worry too much," said Jade, "it's all going to be fine. Africa is a big place and there can't be trouble everywhere, surely".

Jade was never one for keeping up with current affairs, the recent Arab spring risings had barely even registered on her radar.

They finished their lunch and walked into the city, the rain was slowing to a light drizzle and the clouds, which had earlier seemed so dark and grey, were slowly changing to a much lighter grey.

Jade folded her umbrella as they made their way across the square, towards the bus station.

Sitting down at their bus stop, they continued to flick through the brochures, suggesting and discounting destinations as they did.

As they boarded the bus, Emma handed over her change to the bus driver to pay for both of their tickets, Jade did not even look up from her brochure, something had grabbed her attention. She sat on the first available seat and Emma slid in beside her.

"This looks good, it has everything."

"Where are you looking?" Emma expectantly replied, with a small feeling of dread.

"Morocco," Jade was getting excited, "it's got everything, sunshine, food, shopping; and only three hours flight…"

"Morocco?" Emma was not so sure.

"…and it has camels," Jade smiled, her bright blue eyes twinkled as the sun began to peep through the clouds.

Emma felt she was losing the battle and very soon, they would be flying to Morocco.

9.

The bus dropped them at the end of Jade's street and they ran to her house. The rain had increased during the journey and was pouring down so heavily, that Jade asked Emma to stay for 'tea' and maybe a 'sleepover'.

Emma gratefully accepted, as she really did not fancy walking home on her own in the storm. Harry would have gladly driven her home, had she wanted to go, but the thought of a 'sleepover' sounded like a nice idea.

Harry went out and bought some fish, battered chips and mushy peas from the local fish and chip shop, while Jade and Emma prepared the table. Out came the tomato ketchup, the salt and vinegar, and the spicy barbeque jerk sauce that Harry like so much. Jade boiled the kettle, while Emma spread some thick slices of white bread with butter. Harry returned home just in time to see Jade pouring the mugs of tea.

This to Harry was his paradise; he did not crave anything else. He had a new job as a carpenter for a local company, which he quite enjoyed. He had his nice little house, it was not massive, but it was affordable. He had a lovely little garden, with a shed, greenhouse and his small workshop in the back of the garage. Most of all he had his lovely daughter, who looked after him so well. He was a rich man indeed.

They sat eating their cod and chips, while Jade and Emma excitedly talked about their trip. They discussed a multitude of countries, listed the pros and cons of each, and still they could not decide where to go, for the budget they had available. Emma again suggested looking at the internet to try to find a better deal than those listed in the brochure. Jade opened Harry's laptop computer and started scrolling through the hundreds of websites offering cheap deals.

"Look here, Morocco. Let's see what we can find."

Jade giggled as she trawled through the webpages, the pictures of the Sahara, the hotels, the pools, all-inclusive deals, shops and restaurants.

Jade typed the words "cheap holidays morocco all inclusive" into the search engine and clicked the search button. Twenty-three million, three hundred thousand results. This was going to take a while. For the next few hours, Jade searched through the websites, looking at pictures, prices and descriptions. Jade was about to give up for the evening when she spied a website she liked the name of.

"Peachy Beach Holidays" was a price comparison website that seemed to be offering some great deals with some big names of the travel world amongst the choices. This had to be worth a look. It did not take long before she had downloaded the "app" and found an offer that even Emma had to agree was a good deal. It was an all-inclusive hotel just outside Marrakech. They could visit the famous Souk and there were lots of interesting trips that Emma would like, and a nice pool and bars that appealed to Jade. The all-inclusive meant that everything, apart from a few trips, was included in the price.

Harry checked the details and agreed it was a great deal. The dates, the deal related to, were within a matter of days, which was why the price was so good.

"They'd rather fill the plane with a few passengers paying a lot less, than fly with so many empty seats," Harry remarked.

Jade looked at her Father lovingly, a little too lovingly, and Harry knew very well what that look meant.

"Da-a-ad, would you like me to fetch you a beer?" Jade put on the little voice that she knew Harry could not resist.

"…and shall I get your credit card, while I'm doing it?"

Harry was going to pay. He was always going to pay. He loved his daughter so much, he would do anything for her, and at least she had looked for the best deal she could find.

Emma made a phone call home to tell her parents, and to get her passport number for the booking. Within half an hour, the trip was booked and paid for. They were going to Marrakech.

Just a few days later, they had packed and were heading down the motorway towards London. Harry had offered to drive them to Gatwick airport, and Keith, Emma's father, would pick them up two weeks later.

It was a three-and-a-half-hour drive from Lichfield to Gatwick, but for Jade and Emma, the time went by very quickly.

They both kissed Harry as they said farewell.

"Ring me when you get there," Harry shouted and waved at they crossed through into passport control.

Harry could not fight the tears in his eyes; he had tried so hard not to show his feelings on the long drive. He was going to miss Jade terribly. She was his little girl, and she was growing up fast. It would not be long before she found a husband. She was going to be a brilliant wife, and mother, just as Vicky had been. One day soon, he would be a grandfather, but he would be living alone. This was the first time he had been truly on his own, and the reality of his future was starting to dawn on him. It was going to be a long and sad drive home.

Harry needed a drink, his body suddenly craved alcohol, a little voice inside his head whispered to him 'just one drink, it can't hurt, just one little drink'. His mind took control, 'one little drink would lead to another little drink, then another, then another'. He fought the temptation, his demons were still there, always there, gnawing, nagging away at him. No alcohol, not now, not ever. He dried his tears and headed for the coffee shop. He ordered a strong double shot café latte and an apricot pastry. Harry picked up a newspaper someone had left on the table and only half read the headlines. Migrants, asylum seekers, small boy still missing in Tunisia, the boy's father had been arrested, more trouble in the Middle East, and a proposed interest rate hike from the Bank of England.

Harry stared into space. Two weeks. What was he going to do at home on his own for the next two weeks?

10.

Jade and Emma emerged from coolness of the Boeing 737 into the blazing sun of Marrakech. They were directed, along with the rest of the tourists, to the arrivals hall, and stood in the long queue, passports in hand waiting to be checked. The queue moved reasonably quickly, and soon they found themselves standing behind a painted yellow line in front of a row of boxes, wherein sat the sour faced customs officials. Jade was ushered to one of the boxes and handed over her passport and the arrivals form she had completed on the plane. The official looked at her suspiciously, and Jade felt very uncomfortable, expecting to be whisked away at any moment, for some embarrassing bodily search.

Without a word, or change of expression, the official handed back her passport and pointed to the next queue that ran behind the boxes. A second official seemed to just want to check that the passport had been stamped and Jade moved quickly through into the baggage collection hall.

Emma took ages, like Jade, a stern looking man eyed her suspiciously, then looked at something on his computer, before stamping her passport and pointing her towards the second queue.

Reunited, Jade and Emma breathed a sigh of relief, hugged each other and walked arm in arm, towards the baggage reclaim. It took nearly twenty minutes for their bags to arrive, and Jade managed to sweet talk a young man from Manchester to lift the bags off the carousel for them.

Now they had their bags, they just had to get to the hotel, and their holiday could properly begin.

They entered the exit hall and approached a sign for their tour operator, a small Moroccan man in a neat uniform, who spoke excellent English, asked their names.

"Jade Turner and Emma Watson for the Hotel Ishq Palace."

"Ishq Palace, coach number 19," replied the representative, and pointed outside towards the waiting coaches.

Jade and Emma, dragging their suitcases, ambled outside into the hot sunshine towards the coaches, an amazing experience for two young women who had, aside from a short trip to the Isle of Wight, never left England's shores. In their first brief sight of Morocco, the outside of the terminal looked like a different world compared to the one they had left back home.

They found their coach with ease; the driver slid their suitcases into the large luggage compartment and they climbed aboard.

Driving through Marrakech, they passed its' terra cotta coloured walls, that were strangely full of holes, Emma worried that the holes might be bullet holes, as she had seen on television in the 'war ravaged' areas of the Middle East. There were people calmly walking across the road, intermingled with the traffic weaving around them. Jade remarked that there must be loads of accidents. Young men rode on mopeds without the protection of helmets; while others wore helmets that were un- fastened. There were carts, beggars, donkeys, food stalls, all the bright colours she could have ever imagined, and probably every kind of smell, shielded as they were by the air conditioning and smell of diesel fumes.

The ride from airport to hotel was short and uneventful. The humorous holiday representative kept them entertained with his tales of Morocco and a few jokes to put them in the holiday mood.

They were feeling very tired when they arrived at the vast hotel complex. Stepping down from the coach, they were immediately shepherded into a large and rather plush reception area. As they queued for the reception desk, smartly dressed waiters appeared with trays of ornate stemmed glasses filled with brightly coloured ice-cold cordial, and two drinking straws each. They quietly admired the surroundings as they sipped their drinks.

At last, it was their turn to check in. The man who greeted them was young and friendly, he smiled as he took their details, and Jade could not resist winking at him as he wrapped the 'all-inclusive' band around her wrist. Armed with room keys, a leaflet with a map of the hotel on one side, and restaurant times on the other, they tied luggage tags to their suitcases, for the porters to take care of while they went to the restaurant.

The restaurant was buffet style with a massive choice of dishes.

It seemed like, wherever in the world you were from, and no matter how fussy an eater you were, there was something there for everyone.

Jade, a far from a fussy eater, filled her plate in minutes and carried it back to a free table. As she sat down, a passing waiter asked her what she would like to drink.

"White wine", she replied. "No, make that two white wines please, one for my friend."

"Would you like some water too?" The waiter asked politely.

"Oh yeah that would be great mate," Jade responded.

Emma arrived at the table a few minutes later; she had been wandering around the restaurant, looking at the copious array of dishes on offer before making her decisions. Her plate was nowhere near as full as Jade's, but even she had a fair selection of different foods to try.

"Wine's on the way," beamed Jade as she tucked into an unusual looking meat dish.

They sat and ate quietly. The waiter brought the drinks and received a cheeky wink from Jade in place of a tip.

Once dinner was over, they decided to explore the hotel. They found the bar, then another bar, and a sign that seemed to point to even more bars. They wandered down to a pool area, which was vast and had two bars.

"Let's have a drink," Jade said as she walked towards the bar nearest to the pool.

The bar area was full of people, but they managed to push their way through the crowd and ordered a cocktail each plus some vodka jelly shots. Jade surveyed the potential available men, while Emma looked up at the stars.

As she scanned the crowd, Jade caught the eye of a good looking, dark skinned young man dressed casually in tee shirt and frayed denim shorts. She winked. He smiled and nodded back at her. He began walking over, along with his friend.

"Look out," Jade whispered to Emma, "I think we've pulled."

Emma trembled at the thought; she really was not prepared for an encounter like this so soon into their holiday. The two men were probably in their mid-twenties and both looked like they might be local.

"Hello pretty ladies, my name is Roman, and this is my good friend Tariq."

Roman, with a mass of black curls, lowered his head and held out his right hand. He took Jade's hand and kissed it gently. He looked up and as their eyes met, gave her a broad friendly smile. Tariq offered his hand to Emma, but she did not offer hers'. Snubbed, Tariq withdrew his hand and rubbed the top of his shiny bald head and sighed.

"Hello Roman," Jade giggled, blushed and turned to Emma saying, "Are you okay?"

"I'm fine," said Emma sipping her cocktail. She was obviously nervous of these strange men, but they did seem friendly enough.

"And, what do you do, Roman?" Jade asked Roman with a giggle.

"We are private tour guides, we can show you the best places to visit in Marrakech," replied Roman.

"...And get you the best deals in the Souk," remarked Tariq.

Emma could see where this conversation might lead and pulled Jade by the arm.

"Maybe we should go and find our rooms," Emma whispered nervously.

Roman sensed that the girls might be a little afraid, so he backed away.

"We may see you by the pool tomorrow, have a good evening."

Roman and Tariq both nodded and headed back towards the main hotel. Emma sighed with relief, and they went in search of their room.

Following the signs, it did not take long to find their accommodation,

"Room 412," announced Jade.

"Sorry. You weren't upset that I wanted to go, were you?" Emma said apologetically.

"Don't worry," said Jade, "I thought they were a bit oily anyway, and besides, there's plenty more fish..."

Jade laughed as she unlocked the door to their room.

Emma flicked on the light. Their room was impressive. Twin beds, with swan shaped towel sculptures and delicate rose petals scattered over each. A Jacuzzi, by the window overlooked the pool.

As they gazed out of the window, they watched the pool lights twinkle against the moonlit night, casting spots of colour across the water as it lapped gently.

"This really is a beautiful place," said Emma.

"Definitely a holiday to remember," replied Jade.

11.




Jade and Emma awoke to the sun peeping around the edges of the curtains. They felt well rested and content.

"Jacuzzi before breakfast?" Jade asked cheekily.

"Why not?" agreed Emma.

They relaxed for almost an hour, as the bubbles caressed their bodies. Jade turned up the level and the power of the jets steadily increased.

"That's a lot of bubbles," said Jade, and jokingly added "and not all of them from the Jacuzzi."

They both laughed loudly, and a fit of 'the giggles' overtook them as the bubbles frothed and foamed.

After a while, they dried, dressed and set off for breakfast. Having stayed in late, they had not checked the time and only just managed to catch the restaurant before it closed. A friendly waiter gently ushered them through to a table nearest the buffet, so they at least managed to grab some bread, eggs and coffee before it closed.

As they finished the last dregs of coffee, they noticed some people they recognised from their flight heading towards reception. Realising that this must be the "Welcome" meeting from their holiday representative, they hurriedly left their table and followed the crowd. They passed reception and through another door, which led into a small theatre. There was a large map of Marrakech projected onto a screen above the stage. As they entered the room, each holidaymaker was handed a small envelope, and a glass cup filled to the brim with mint tea.

There were two reps on the stage, who took it in turn to speak, Angelique, who was French and Safiyah was Moroccan. The speech included details about the hotel facilities, the animations team activities plus the meal and pool times. They talked a little about the history of the area and then onto the trips they recommended and would eventually sell.

Jade was not keen on the mint tea, and Emma ended up drinking both cups as she found it very 'refreshing'.

They both looked enthusiastically at the trips. Emma was short of money, but Harry had given Jade plenty of spending money, so she agreed to pay for them both.

The trip they picked was a day out in Marrakech, including a trip around the Souk. Emma had seemed very nervous about venturing into the Souk on their own; but with the protection of a local guide, it did not seem anywhere near as daunting. As soon as the meeting was over, they hurried over to join the queue for booking their trip. The next trip to leave was early the following day.

They returned to their room and gathered their things for the pool. Jade had brought a beach bag in which she put their sun-cream, her celebrity magazine and Emma's E-reader. Emma loved her E-reader; she loved that she could take thousands of books on holiday in something that weighed less than a single book. With floppy hats, sunglasses and dressed in their beachwear, with beach towels under their arms, they made their way down to the pool.

The sun was shining and, even in the shade, it was very warm. The pool was busy, and it took about ten minutes to find a couple of sunbeds with an adjacent sun umbrella. The hotel 'animation team' were going about their business, trying to get the holidaymakers moving. Jade agreed to go for the "Watergym" session, while Emma preferred to sit in the shade of the umbrella reading.

Emma watched the "Watergym" session with delight, seeing Jade throw herself about, falling into the water constantly laughing. Jade looked over at Emma and signalled her to join in, but Emma was having enough fun just watching.

After the session, Jade strolled up and wrapped a towel around her.

"That was fun," she said, rubbing herself dry with the towel. "You should try it."

"Maybe I will tomorrow," replied Emma.

"Doubt it," Jade shook her head. "Tomorrow we'll be in Marrakech."

They spent the next few hours relaxing in the sun and taking the occasional dip in the pool to cool off.

They went to the pool bar for a light lunch and bumped into Roman sitting on his own.

"Hello pretty ladies, how are you today?" Roman was dressed in only his shorts and sandals, and Emma could tell that Jade liked the look of his toned body and arms.

"We're fine," said Jade casually. "Just catching the rays, you know."

"Rays?" Roman seemed confused.

"The sun's rays, you daft sod," chided Jade.

"Oh yes, rays of the sun, sorry I thought you mean fishing or something."

Roman's manner was cool and relaxed. He moved his sunglasses on top of his head, amidst his curly mop of hair, closed his eyes and turned his head skywards.

"This is indeed a beautiful day, as is every day here in Morocco," his voice had a friendly warmth about it, and both young women began to feel at ease in his presence.

"Where is your friend?" Jade asked.

"Oh Tariq? He is making a delivery, he'll be back soon."

"Is he a delivery driver then? I thought he was a tour guide," queried Emma.

"Yes, he is, ehrm, we are." Roman corrected himself then laughed. "He is delivering some tourist books to a hotel in Casablanca."

"Ooh Casablanca, that sounds romantic," cooed Jade.

"Sadly it's not as romantic as the film makes out; it's more of an industrial town. There is a 'Rick's Bar' but not like Humphrey Bogart."

"Humphrey who?"

Jade obviously had not heard of him, so Emma cut in.

"It's a black and white film, so you won't have seen it, I bet your Dad knows all about it."

"Oh, a Grandad film." Jade started to show a small sign of realisation

They talked for about half an hour, finding out a little more about Roman, as he found out more about their lives back in England. As Roman said farewell they returned to their sunbeds.

"He seems nice," said Emma eventually, "I think I must have just mistrusted him when we first met."

"Yes he does," agreed Jade "And I'm sure his friend is nice too, who knows we may get to see them again before the holiday is over."

12.

Next morning Jade and Emma breakfasted early. The holiday rep had warned that there would be lots of walking, so they made sure they applied plenty of sunscreen and wore their trainers. The coach arrived to pick them up at the agreed time and taking their seats the Marrakech adventure began.

The morning schedule was a tour of the old town, visiting places of worship, museums and many old buildings. Jade had started to lose interest with all of this 'old stuff' and her feet were starting to ache. She wanted to get to the shops. That was where the real holiday lay for her. Emma happily followed the guide, while Jade sat and rested her feet. A young mousey shorthaired woman sat next to her, she was a similar age and as they began talking, Jade recognised a French accent.

Her name was Sabine and she had arrived on a flight from Paris a week earlier and was staying at the same hotel. They chatted away like old friends. When the museum tour was over Jade introduced Sabine to Emma. All three decided to team up for the last few days of Sabine's holiday. It would be fun. Sabine had come on holiday on her own. 'A brave thing to do' thought Emma.

The tour included lunch at a traditional Moroccan restaurant in the Souk. The waiter brought out a large tagine and they hungrily tucked into the rice and lamb dish. Even though it was a hot day, the warm meal was most welcome, as they had worked up quite an appetite from the miles of walking they had done that morning.

With lunch over, the tourists were given a guided tour around the various areas of the Souk. The colours of the fabrics, the smells of the food, the heat of the furnaces all made for an unforgettable experience. It was exciting, hot and busy. The tiny streets interwove as an intricate maze, full of shoppers, traders and tourists. Mopeds weaved their way through crowds of pedestrians. To Emma, it all seemed too dangerous and chaotic.

Once the Souk tour was over, the holidaymakers were given an hour of 'personal leisure time', to explore the main square.

They had heard from the holiday rep that the various monkey men, snake charmers and henna ladies controlled the centre of the square, and to be aware 'at all times' and not to take any photographs of people without asking their permission, as they would probably demand a fee.

The three young women wandered around the square. There were dozens of stalls overflowing with oranges and selling fresh orange juice. They remembered a warning they had heard at the hotel, 'don't have ice in your juice, it's not made from bottled water'. A man with a monkey on his shoulders walked towards them. Sabine looked at him, she gave him a simple "No" and he backed away, looking for another tourist on whose shoulders he could place his monkey.

Suddenly, Jade felt someone grab her right hand. She turned to find an old woman, dressed in a black shawl, scribbling a design onto the back of her hand. She completed the intricate flower design in seconds. The old woman stood proudly holding out her hand, obviously awaiting payment.

"English?"

"Yes," replied Jade.

"One hundred dihrams."

Jade was a little shocked, she had not asked for this drawing on her hand, and worried that it might not wash off. Although it was rather pretty.

"Non, cinquante, pas plus," said Sabine.

"Cinquante, d'accord," replied the woman.

"Just pay her fifty dihrams," said Sabine, obediently Jade paid.

Emma pushed her hands deep into the pockets of her shorts, she wasn't planning to get caught like that.

"It is only henna," Sabine explained, "and it will wear off in a few days, it sounds a lot, but it's only cost you about five euros at the most."

"Sabine seems quite confident, she must have been to be holidaying in her own," remarked Emma once they were safely back in the comfort of their hotel room.

"Yes, a handy person to have around."

Jade was getting ready for her shower, bath towel wrapped around her, evening clothes laid out on the bed. They were both looking forward to a good evening.

A few hours later, they were in the reception bar, joined by Sabine, and a few others from the earlier trip. They laughed about the monkey men and snake charmers that had managed to obtain money from some of the party, and Jade proudly showed off her henna tattoo. It was a fun evening, filled with merriment and laughter. Slowly, as the night wore on, the party broke up as one by one they sloped off to bed.

Next morning, Jade and Emma came down to breakfast at a more reasonable time than they did on the first morning. They ate at a leisurely pace and drank several cups of coffee. They remembered to bring their mobile phones with them and attempted to call their parents, which they should have done on the first night. The telephone signal was terrible. They each stood in different parts of the restaurant and reception trying to get a phone signal.

Emma briefly connected to her mother and said they were both fine, but they may not be able to get back in touch, until they were back at the airport, because of the signal problems. Jade failed miserably so Emma asked her mother to contact Uncle Harry to let him know they were safe.

They returned to their room and prepared for a day at the pool. They wandered around looking for three sunbeds, as they thought it would be nice to spend the day with Sabine. Luckily, they managed to find three unoccupied with a sun umbrella. They sat a while and waited. Jade took part in "Watergym" and Emma sat and read her book. When Jade returned she sat thoughtfully on the edge of the sunbed and said:

"I wonder what's happened to Sabine. She said last night that we'd see her around the pool today. I'm sure she still has a couple of days left before she flies home."

"Do you know her room number?" asked Emma.

"I'm sure she said it was 642."

"Let's go and see if she's there, maybe she's ill or something?"

Jade and Emma left their beach bag and towels, still claiming the three sunbeds, and went in search of room 642. On arrival, they knocked the door. Silence. They knocked again. Still no reply.

"Sabine, are you in there?" Jade shouted. Still silence.

"Maybe we could check at reception?" Emma suggested.

"Good idea."

They made their way to reception, and the attractive man who had originally checked them in, looked up from his papers and asked if he could help.

"Yes, we're looking for our friend Sabine from room 642," Jade enquired.

"642, 642," he repeated the room number several times as he flicked through his computer screen.

"Oh yes, room 642, Miss Sabine Desrosiers. She checked out early this morning."

"Checked out?" Both Jade and Emma said in unison.

"Yes, it seems there was some family emergency and she had to leave in a hurry."

"Oh, that's a real shame," said Emma.

"Do you have any contact details for her?" Jade asked.

"I'm afraid that would be against regulations to give you that kind of information," replied the receptionist.

"It's only a phone number; we just want to make sure she's okay." Jade gave him her baby doll look, the look that always worked on her father.

"It is impossible," he snapped. Suddenly his tone became very stern and made them both feel quite uneasy.

"...And if that is all?" Not waiting for a reply, he returned to his papers.

There was nothing more they could do; Sabine had returned home and that was that.

They returned to their sunbeds and tried to relax, but it all seemed so surreal. A few hours later Roman appeared again. They called him over and asked for his advice.

"These things happen," he said as he sat on Sabine's sunbed. "But I don't mind asking around and see if I can get her contact details for you."

He was friendly and seemed genuinely concerned and willing to help. They chatted for a while until Roman received call on his mobile phone and he had to leave.

"It's Mother, she needs me to collect something for her," he said as he arose.

He kissed them both on the hand and left them to carry on soaking up the sun.

Jade and Emma were soon immersed into the full holiday routine. Wake up, Jacuzzi, breakfast, "Watergym" for Jade, relaxing, reading, lunch, more relaxing, reading, Jacuzzi, dinner, partying in the bar, then back to the room for a good sleep. This daily routine continued, and the days quickly rolled by. Roman would pop and see them from time to time, sometimes with Tariq, who also seemed to be a nice man, just a bit quieter than Roman.

It was Thursday, two days before they were to fly home, when Roman asked them if they would join him and Tariq for a night trip to Marrakech.

"It's so beautiful at night," Roman said. "Once the evening comes, the monkey men and snake charmers go home, and the real nightlife begins. There are food stalls, acrobats, storytellers, it's a very different atmosphere than you will see in the daytime. More relaxed, more of the local people enjoying themselves, you will love it."

"We could not afford to pay you for a trip like that," said Emma, now more relaxed in their company.

"There would be no charge, you are our friends, and we would not dream of such a thing," said Tariq.

"In fact, to save money, we could even go to Mothers' for some supper," said Roman.

"That sounds nice," replied Jade.

"That's settled then, we'll pick you up this evening at seven, we'll meet you in reception." Roman's eyes flashed in the sun.

As Roman and Tariq left them, Emma seemed a little nervous.

"I'm really not sure about this."

"What's not to like?" Jade replied. "We only have a couple of days left, and we'll never get the chance to see Marrakech at night again, it sounds so exciting."

"Okay." Emma seemed resigned to her friend's adventurous side taking over.

Roman and Tariq were as good as their word, and that evening at exactly seven o'clock they were smartly dressed and waiting just outside the hotel foyer, next to a very expensive looking black Mercedes. Jade and Emma, wearing the best clothes they had packed, entered the reception area, and spotted them outside. Roman went in to meet them while Tariq slid into the drivers' seat of the vehicle.

"I really don't think we should be leaving the hotel complex with these men, we hardly know them," Emma whispered nervously.

"It will be fine," said Jade. "They seem like really nice guys to me."

"But what if they want to, you know, do things with us?"

"They won't, they seem like perfect gentlemen, and we're going to meet Roman's mom, it's going to be the night of our lives, just you wait and see."

"I'm still not sure."

"Look if you really don't want to go then stay here, I'll go on my own. It'll be fine."

Emma looked Jade up and down, standing there in all her finery. She was a beautiful young woman. Emma knew that she had more common sense than Jade, and whatever happened, Emma would have to go along and look after her friend, to make sure she did not end up in any kind of trouble.

"Okay you win," sighed Emma.

"Goody, goody, let's get going then."

As Roman approached, they walked out to meet him. Roman held the rear car doors open while Jade and Emma eased into the back seats. Roman joined Tariq in the front. Tariq switched on the engine and slowly dropped into first gear.

"This will be a good night." Roman said to Tariq as they drove towards the walled city.

The centre of Marrakech was indeed a very different place at night, and everything Roman had promised. Tariq bought them a few drinks of orange juice from one of the local stands, as they stood and watched the acrobats perform. It was a breath-taking evening, lights, sounds, colours, the assault on their senses was awe-inspiring. Never had a place felt so amazingly alive. Emma began to feel a little light headed and felt her head spinning.

"Emma are you okay?" Jade was concerned. The words began to jumble in Emma's head.

"I feel really dizzy, I think I'm going to pass out," said Emma weakly.

"That will be the excitement of the evening," said Tariq. "It's a lot to take in all at once."

"And maybe a touch of sunstroke or dehydration," said Roman, "I think it might be best if we take you to Mother's now."

"I agree," said Jade and despite the even tan she had been developing, Emma's face began to look very pale.

"Let me carry you." Tariq swept Emma off her feet.

Moments later, the four, Tariq carrying Emma and Jade arm in arm with Roman, strode purposefully towards the Souk.

13.

The Souk was alive, its' noise and energy overwhelmed Jade's senses. The aromatic smells of exotic food; the bright vibrant colours of rugs and fabrics; and a thousand different spices spread out as far as the eye could see. Orange flames licked from small furnaces as metalworkers created the most intricate filigree jewellery. To any other tourist it would have been a palace of wonder. A real-life Aladdin's cave. Jade could not even register these delights. Her stomach felt sick. Roman led them through the maze of clothing and trinket stalls that littered the outer reaches of the market. A thousand eyes appeared to bore into her, friendly smiles and welcoming waves offering hospitality at every turn. Jade's head whirled as if in some nightmare. As she hurried along beside Tariq, she reached down and stroked her friend's hair. Emma's head lolled around Tariq's left arm as he carried her, twisting and turning to avoid the passers-by. Emma's eyes lay half-open and she let out a weak groan. Jade could see that Emma was fading fast.

"Could it be food poisoning?" Jade asked Roman, her voice shaking with worry.

"It could be." Roman held Jade's arm to try to reassure her as they hurried through the tiny streets.

"Maybe we need to take her to a doctor?" Jade's plea ignored as Tariq and Roman strode purposefully on.

At last, they arrived at a tall brown panelled door, with an ornate brass handle and a small barred peephole. Roman produced a key from his pocket and bent to unlock it. Opening the door, Tariq slipped quickly inside, with the stricken Emma still collapsed in his arms.

"Mother will be upstairs. She will know what to do."

Roman's voice was calm and confident, but it did little to assure Jade. Tariq carried Emma through to a small courtyard, and an open doorway beyond. Jade followed them closely, while Roman momentarily held back. He paused until the others were out of sight. Carefully and quietly, Roman locked the front door.

The riad was small, a lot smaller than the places Jade and Emma had visited with the tour guide on their second day. The courtyard was quite dark, the only visible lights emanated from the windows of the upper floor.

Jade followed Tariq through the open doorway and up the dimly lit stairs beyond. Roman caught up as they reached a landing that ran around the upper floor and unlocked a roughly painted door. Roman led them inside.

The room was large but dimly lit, filled with assorted ramshackled furniture. Tariq laid Emma down on a threadbare two-seater sofa as Roman called out:

"Mother?"

A small, pale, stocky, grey haired woman, of what Jade considered East European origin, entered the room from a side door.

"You have them I see." Mother's tone was ice cold.

"Yes," replied Tariq.

"My friend is sick; shouldn't we call a doctor?" Jade was panicking.

"No need for doctor," said Mother. "She fine enough."

Mothers' hard sounding voice confirmed Jade's suspicions, the accent was distinctly eastern European, possibly even Russian.

Mother knelt beside Emma, felt her pulse, pulled back her eyelids and then opened her mouth. It looked to Jade as if Mother was checking Emma's teeth.

"Look at me child," Mother slapped Emma's face. "Look at me."

Jade moved to intervene but Roman held her back.

"How many fingers?" Mother held up three fingers of her right hand.

"Three." Emma slurred the word, but it was clear enough to know she had understood.

"She be fine when she sleep it off." Mother's broken English and brusque manner alarmed Jade; she shrugged off Roman as he attempted to put and arm around her shoulders.

"Slept what off?" Jade was shaking with panic.

The room fell silent for a second, a silence that was only broken by the sound of a small whimpering voice, coming from the next room.

Jade glanced through the open doorway and saw a young woman, with short mousey hair, sitting in the corner rocking gently.

Backwards and forwards she swayed, with her hands up over her face, crying. A half-empty bottle of vodka lay on the table beside her.

Immediately alarmed, Jade moved closer to the doorway to get a better look. As the woman wiped the tears from her eyes, Jade recognised her immediately.

"Sabine?" Jade's voice was simultaneously anxious and curious.

The young woman looked up, a vague recollection showed in her eyes, but she seemed far too bewildered to fully comprehend the situation. Jade rushed into the room to get a closer look.

"Sabine, I thought you had gone home."

Sabine sat on an old hard wooden chair, dressed only in an old and rather scruffy dressing gown.

"Roman, what is going on? Why is Sabine here; and what is wrong with her?"

"This is start of your new life," said Mother. "You work for me now."

"What, I, I don't understand, what is this place? Roman, she's not even your mother."

"I never said she was MY mother, she could be somebody's I guess, but I doubt it." Roman laughed and Tariq smiled.

"This is all wrong; we're getting out of here."

Jade looked at Sabine.

"Come on Sabine, help me with Emma, we're going back to the hotel."

Jade rushed over, grabbed Sabine by the arm, and tried to drag her out of her chair.

Sabine did not seem to want to go. As Jade pulled her arm, Sabine sank to the floor. Then Jade came the sudden realisation that Sabine must be drugged or drunk or both.

Jade ran to Emma's side and tried to lift her up. Although Emma was of slight build, she was as good as dead weight. Jade struggled in vain to lift her best friend's limp form and Emma flopped back onto the sofa.

There was nothing else for Jade to do but to try to save herself and bring back help for her friends.

Quick as a flash she kicked Roman in the left knee as hard as she could. Roman yelped with pain, buckled and fell to the floor.

He swiped at empty air as he fell, but Jade was too quick for him. Jade dodged his flailing arm and ran for the door. Tariq turned towards her, but she beat him to the doorway and ran along the landing towards the stairs.

Roman staggered to his feet as Tariq raced along the landing in close pursuit. Jade had just reached the top of the stairs when Tariq caught up with her. Roman limped onto the landing in time to see Tariq grab Jade around the neck, gripping her tightly in a chokehold. With all the strength she could muster, Jade stamped hard on Tariq's instep. He cursed, and as he began to release his grip on her throat, she sank her teeth hard into his forearm. Tariq screamed and lashed out, catching Jade on the side of the head with his fist. This rough blow sent Jade careering, head first, down the stairs. Jade landed in a heap at the bottom. Her neck lay bent awkwardly sideways. Roman staggered past the bleeding Tariq and down the stairs, but he was too late. Her neck was broken. Jade was dead.

14.

The cry to worship from a distant minaret echoed across the town and woke Emma from her deep sleep. It was morning. Her head was aching, and she felt sick. Slowly opening her eyes, she discovered she was not waking up in their plush hotel room after all. The room was windowless, the only light provided by a low wattage bulb dangling from the high ceiling. As her eyes began to focus, she saw only peeling white walls and the thin off-white dirty sheet that covered her body. It was then she realised that under the sheet, she was completely naked. There was something cold and hard around her wrist. She looked down to see her wrist handcuffed to the metal bed frame.

'Was this a dream?' She shook her head, trying to clear the fuzziness from her brain. It did not feel like a dream.

Vague recollections of the night before came flooding back into her mind. They had been in the square watching the acrobats. Tariq had brought them orange juice. She had felt sick, and there was a distant memory of being carried by someone. She recalled nothing else until she woke the few moments earlier.

There was a light tap on the door. Not waiting for Emma to reply, the door slowly opened. Emma held her breath, her heart pounding in her chest. She wondered if this was her captor coming to do something terrible to her. Emma was terrified.

"Salut, 'ello?" A timid quaking voice came from behind the opening door.

"Hello?" Emma replied.

A mouse haired head popped around the edge.

"Sabine?" Emma was startled, joyful and confused at the sight. As Sabine shuffled over to the bed, in her scruffy dressing gown, a million thoughts raced through Emma's mind.

"What's going on? Where am I, and where's Jade?"

"She's dead," Sabine replied slowly. "Jade is dead, they killed her last night trying to escape." Sabine's soft French accent belied the horror of the message it had conveyed.

"Oh my God." Emma paused as she struggled to catch a breath.

"Jade dead, she can't be." Emma began to cry.

"She is, I'm very much afraid, and we have to be careful not to join her."

Sabine stopped talking and listened carefully for a moment. There was a noise outside the room. She moved towards the door and whispered:

"Tell them you are a virgin, and with that, Sabine was gone."

Through the wall, Emma heard words being exchanged between Sabine and another woman but could not understand them. All went quiet. A few moments later, a short stocky woman entered the room with Tariq following closely behind. He grinned at Emma. It was the woman who spoke first.

"I am Mother." Her words showed no sense of kindness, paternal or otherwise, "and now you work for me."

"Work, what do you mean, why am I here and where is Jade?" Emma managed to speak through the tears. She was very frightened and began pulling at the chain, shaking uncontrollably.

"Your friend cannot help you now," said Tariq, "but I can be your friend."

"Mahlchyat, Silence." Mother was about to have her moment. She always enjoyed this part, the changing of their mood. She could actually see the changing thought processes in their eyes. The initial confusion. The sudden realisation of the situation they were in, and finally the fear and submission. The power it gave her. It was like a drug and Tariq was not going to interrupt.

"You will answer when I ask, otherwise you will be quiet, I am your Mother now and you will do as you are told. You will be fed and drink when I say, and there is your 'en-suite' so you stay clean for your guests."

Mother pointed across the room to an old enamel sink, that had seen better days, and a tin bucket with an old dirty tea towel draped across the top.

Emma was at first stunned and then burst into floods of tears, as her situation began to sink in.

"Now child, stop crying. I need to know, how many boyfriends have you had, and how well do you satisfy them?" Mother seemed to be taking this in a very 'matter of fact' manner.

Cold questioning as if she were conducting a job interview for a maid.

"I, I, I don't have a boyfriend," Emma stammered.

"I can be your boyfriend." Tariq interrupted "I can be your boyfriend right now."

He looked at Mother.

"It's my turn."

Emma suddenly remembering what Sabine had said, blurted out:

"I'm a virgin."

She screamed the words through the sobs.

Mother's eyes lit up, and Tariq squirmed, moved over to the bed and began to stroke Emma's hair.

"You said it was my turn, I could have the next one."

Emma could smell Tariq, stale sweat and urine, as he sat on the edge of the bed. He pulled down the sheet to expose her pale young body and reached down to touch her breasts.

"Enough, you killed the last one, and this little virgin will fetch a good price."

Mother was talking business, nothing personal, just cold hard business.

Emma was shaking with fear, tears rolling down her cheeks, as Mother signalled for Tariq to leave the room with her. As he got up from the bed, Emma quickly pulled the thin blanket up to her chin to cover her nakedness. The door slammed shut behind them and Emma was alone, crying her poor little heart out. She never dreamed that anything like this could ever happen to her, and what of poor Jade, her best friend? Could she really be dead? Looking down at the chain, she knew if this was real, if this was not a dream, she had just three options: to try to escape and perhaps suffer the same fate as Jade; go along with whatever they had planned for her; or kill herself.

Another thought occurred to Emma, whatever they did have planned for her, if she were to kill herself, then the truth would never come out. They would just become another missing person statistic.

Whatever was in store for her, she would have to deal with it, stay alive and maybe there would be an opportunity to escape somewhere along the way. Hopefully, whatever it was, wouldn't involve Tariq raping her.

Then there was Sabine, she had also been tricked.

72

Perhaps between the two of them they could come up with a plan to escape.

15.

It was several hours later when Sabine once again poked her head around the door. This time she brought bread and tea. They both sat on the edge of the bed, Emma wrapped in the sheet while Sabine still wore her old dressing gown.

"The night we had drinks in the bar, after our trip, Roman drugged me", she said quietly. "They brought me here and Roman had sex with me."

Emma was silent. Sabine had tears in her eyes. Emma put an arm around her waist.

"It was horrible, he was horrible, I didn't want to do those things, but I could not move. I was so frightened."

They both fell silent as they sipped their tea and ate the dry bread.

"We have to get out of here," said Emma breaking the silence.

"But how?" Sabine replied. "The doors are locked, we have no clothes, no shoes, nothing, and you are still chained to that bed".

"I have an idea of how to get out of this handcuff, when I was a little girl I broke my wrist and damaged my hand when I fell off my bike. Ever since then I could do this..."

With just a few grunts, Emma managed to dislocate her thumb, slide her hand through the handcuff and relocate her joint.

"Does that hurt?" Sabine's tears stopped for a moment as she watched in awe.

"It's a bit uncomfortable but it doesn't hurt much."

They heard a noise coming from the other room, so Emma reversed the process and slipped her hand back inside the handcuff.

Mother entered the room. She seemed in a surprisingly good mood. Emma guessed that money was on her mind.

"Today we have some special guests arriving, finish your breakfasts, we will be welcoming them in an hour."

Mother backed out of the room, closing the door behind her.

Emma and Sabine looked at each other, they had one hour to get away.

"We will never escape before they come." Sabine's sweet voice sounded completely demoralised.

Emma sighed, she knew Sabine was right, somehow, she would have to deal with their guests and make it through alive.

"I have already had to entertain several of the guests," Sabine continued, "I was scared, but had to play along, all I thought of was treating it like I was at the dentist. It is not love making; it is a way to endure."

It was good advice, Emma felt that whatever happened over the next few hours and days, it was not her fault. All she had to do was survive. Another thought occurred to Emma, if they could just make it through the next few days, her family would come looking for her. They would leave 'no stone unturned' in trying to find her. She told Sabine and it seemed to give her fresh hope.

An hour went by, and Mother sent Sabine to her room to wash and prepare herself. Emma sat alone, still wrapped in her sheet. There would be no way to overpower the "guests" or Mother for that matter; but she was quick and maybe there would be an opportunity to make a run for it. She had no clothes, just the blanket to wrap herself in, but she also had the element of surprise with her dislocating wrist trick. All she could do now was wait and see how the next few minutes played out.

There were voices, men's voices; they were clearly right outside Emma's door. Mother entered the room with two men. They were both tall, broad, very dark skinned and had a rough African look about them. Mother left the room and closed the door. The two men stared at Emma and exchanged glances. They made no sound as they approached the bed. Emma pulled the sheet up around her neck and started shaking. One man took the other end of the sheet and pulled, casting it across the room and onto the floor. Emma, completely naked, curled up into a ball, trying to cover as much of herself as she could despite her shackled arm. Their eyes bore down on her small slightly tanned frame. Emma was completely at their mercy and she began to cry.

Through the tears, she glanced up and could see them nodding to each other. One man reached down and lifted her head; he pulled her eyes open, then pulled her lips apart, and seemed to be examining her teeth.

For a second, the irony of the earlier dentist analogy crossed her mind. 'Was this what these types of men do before they 'did it''? They both stepped away from the bed and whispered something to each other that Emma could not understand, then they left the room.

Emma lay on the bed chained and uncovered. She waited. About five minutes later Sabine returned with an armful of shoes and clothing.

"Mother said we have to get dressed." Sabine produced a key to unlock Emma's handcuff.

"What is going on?" Emma enquired, rubbing her sore wrist.

"I'm not sure, but I think is has something to do with those men."

They dressed in the clothes that they had arrived in; it was so nice to put their own clothes back on. 'Maybe now', thought Emma, 'there would be a chance to escape'.

Once dressed, they crept out of the room and there stood Mother, the two dark skinned men, plus Roman and Tariq. The latter two taking hold of a girl each, by the arms, while the African men rolled up a sleeve on each girl's arm, picked up two prepared syringes, and injected them simultaneously.

The drug took effect very quickly, Sabine collapsed, and Emma could feel the world around her swirl once again.

Emma and Sabine were still semi-conscious as Roman and Tariq carried them down the stairs and into the Souk. Turning down a side alley and eventually onto a road, a car was waiting. The two African men got into the front of the car. Roman and Tariq bundled the sleeping girls into the back. As the car disappeared into the distance, Roman and Tariq watched as the sun glinted off its' darkened windows.

"It was my turn."

"Shut up and count your money."

Roman had no time for Tariq's whining. They had work to do, there were still more girls to find and the day was still young.

16.

The black Mercedes nosed out into the crowded Marrakech streets, and travelled south towards Tazenakht. On the back seat, Emma and Sabine slept soundly, the drug had worked very quickly. After a few miles, they turned off the road and slowed to a halt on a patch of rough waste ground. The vehicle pulled up alongside a container lorry, the doors of which were wide open. The Africans got out of the car. Doused in sweat, two swarthy Middle Eastern men shaded their eyes as they climbed out of the container.

Shaking hands, the Africans led them back to their car. Taking a side each, the Middle Eastern men opened the car doors and slid in next to Emma and Sabine. It was an easy task for the associates to open their lips and check their teeth. They pulled their eyelids open and one man pulled a small torch from his pocket and shone it into their eyes. There were nods and smiles of approval. The tall Africans lifted each young woman from their respective car seat and carried them over to the container. As they stepped inside, the heat was overpowering. It was a metal box, with a roughly sawn wooden bench on either side, bolted to the floor. Small holes in the container roof, provided tiny shafts of light. The light barely permeated the darkness, the holes allowing just enough air for the sad sweltering occupants to breathe.

The existing occupants, and there were many, were in a poor state. Tearful, weary and sweating profusely, they were mainly young women, girls and some boys. The few clothes they wore were no more than rags. In the obvious oven heat of the container, the fewer clothes they wore the better. Each occupant, shackled to a metal rail welded just above the benches, was easy prey for anyone who had a care to take advantage. A handful of near-empty plastic water bottles were dotted about the floor, not an easy reach for anyone handcuffed to a bench. The best they could hope for was for the bottles to roll near each of them as the vehicle moved.

As she started to regain consciousness, Emma felt her wrist being attached to one of the shackles near to the container door.

Her head lolled about as she tried to focus, and regain use of her muscles, and desperately tried to work out where she was.

One of the African men looked sympathetically at a pretty young Asian girl, probably little more than fifteen years old, and shook his head. She looked up at him with pleading eyes, as if he might be her last hope, her saviour. There was no hope; this was business, nothing more, nothing less. As they stepped out of the container, back into the relative cool of the blazing sun, the Africans received a thick brown envelope. They shook hands, returned to their car and departed down the dusty track towards the main road.

Sabine began to stir. The effects of the drugs began to wear off, and they soon realised they were not the only people to board this lorry; but they appeared to be the last. At least forty others were crammed into the container, and it was hot. Emma and Sabine knew that their time with Mother had only been a prelude to the real dangers that lay ahead.

It occurred to them that they may no longer be in Marrakech. Following their long-enforced sleep, they had no idea how much time had passed, or where in the world they were.

The full realisation dawned on Emma. If they were no longer in Marrakech, or even Morocco, their families would never be able to find them. Their only hope was to find a way to escape.

The back of the container slammed shut. The lorry's engine fired into life and started moving. They pressed their faces against a few small holes, drilled into sides of the container for extra circulation, as they tried to breathe. 'If any of us made it alive out of this sweatbox, it would be a miracle,' thought Emma.

The lorry rode across many miles of rough terrain while the women bounced around uncomfortably inside the container. All had sore wrists from the shackles that restrained them. The screams of pain and the stench of sweat and fear filled the air in an all-consuming hell. After about three hours the truck stopped. The rear doors opened, and a flood of fresh air filled the container. They were in the middle of nowhere. Emma considered her dislocating wrist trick and making a run for it, but where to? They were in the desert, and even if she could outrun her captors, she would surely die of thirst.

Sabine held Emma tightly. Sabine was no longer the confident companion of a few days earlier; she was a broken terrified spirit.

The driver threw some more bottles of water into the back of the container, before he slammed the doors shut once more.

The cramped conditions and lack of oxygen made the journey unbearable. The lack of toilet facilities added to the smell, and amongst this, Emma was sure there was a new smell, the smell of death. At the next stop, the driver opened the doors and found there were in fact two dead women hanging from their shackles. Their bodies thrown by the roadside. One of the men put an upright finger to his lips, made a shushing noise, before running his finger across his throat. They understood well enough what he meant.

'Be quiet, or we cut your throats.'

Night was falling and, from the noises they could hear outside, it seemed that they were approaching a border crossing. They did not know whether it would be better for them to make plenty of noise, to alert the border guards, and risk being murdered by the drivers, or stay silent and face whatever fate had planned for them. It was a tough choice, but out of fear, they chose silence.

After many miles, the lorry stopped once more. The container doors opened, and at last, the occupants were unshackled and led into a large white building.

A hotel in the middle of the desert.

17.

Tired and weary, the captives disembarked into a large air-conditioned reception area. A dusty chandelier, suspended from a peeling plaster ceiling, cast a thin shadow over a large ornate fireplace. Cracked leather easy chairs, wooden tables and ragged curtains betrayed its' years of decay. Some prisoners struggled to walk, whilst most appeared to be in shock. Forced to kneel on the floor, like naughty schoolchildren, their hands placed behind their backs with heads bowed.

Emma pretended to close her eyes. Peeping through her eyelashes, she could see that a dozen or so, thickset, armed men surrounded them. One very tall man stood in front of the group and began reading a list of names from a notebook. With each name called, a woman was 'selected'.

"Prema." A man grabbed Sabine's arm and dragged her to her feet. She squealed as she disappeared down an adjacent corridor. Emma's heart sank.

"Hadya." Obediently, Emma rose to her feet as a hand reached for her arm. The best she could do was play along, whatever awaited her, Emma knew she must endure and survive. She was led to a small room that contained a bed. There were no bedclothes or pillow just a badly stained mattress. The only light glimmered from a single bulb that hung high from a dirty ceiling. A bucket lay on the floor beside the bed.

"You. Hadya." Her captor declared, pointing at her face. "You name is now Hadya. Now you learn."

He moved towards the door, as if to leave, but instead he closed it leaving them both inside the room.

"You sit." He pointed towards the bed. "You virgin, yah?"

Emma, caught completely off guard by the statement, felt a shudder of fear run down her spine.

"I pay good. I very good, big man"

The man's English was basic but completely terrified Emma. He stood in front of her, as she sat on the bed, shivering with fear.

"Now, your clothes off."

He took out his mobile phone and began filming her as she started to remove her clothes. There was no point in arguing, he was enjoying every moment, and he was obviously planning to enjoy her undressing over and over again.

With tears in her eyes, Emma was down to her underwear. It was as far as she wanted to go.

"No everything, my brother back in Ukraine he like to watch."

His accent strong and guttural. He smiled, his thick neck, short-cropped hair and scarred face stank of cheap cologne mixed with several days of sweat.

Emma turned her back to him as she removed the last of her clothing until she was completely naked, and very afraid.

"Now you kneel."

She turned towards him trying to cover herself with her arms as best she could. Obediently she knelt. Her knees felt the roughness of the hard wooden floor.

"Now, you undress me."

Emma did as she was told. She did everything she was told. She removed his clothes for him. His body completely covered in thick black hair. Naked, he looked almost like a gorilla, the matting punctuated here and there with tattoos. As she lay back on the putrid mattress, she tried to think of home and her family. She tried to remember the words to her favourite songs; anything to take her mind away from this place, this horrible moment. What was happening was an animal act, a criminal act. They would all pay for what was happening to her. She would win. She would survive. It was not her fault. Emma tried to blank it out and entered a state of pretending. She was in hospital, 'this was a procedure, one that would soon be over'. At least he had the forethought or sense to use a condom.

He got up, dressed and left. Without so much as a word or a look back at her, he closed the door behind him. To him she was just a commodity; he had paid and got what he paid for. Emma lay on the bed and wept.

Emma lay naked in the loneliness of the room for about an hour, quietly sobbing to herself. She felt cold as she rubbed her eyes, sat on the bed, and slowly began to dress. She was in complete distress.

Raped by a man older than her own father, she was sore and bruised and felt violated. However, inside her, deep, deep inside her, she felt a fire. At first, she thought it was rage, and she was never an angry sort, but this was something else, it was her survival instinct, whatever they did to her, she would survive. Even if they raped her every day, multiple times a day, she would survive so that the world would know what had happened to her, Jade and Sabine. Sabine. Emma knew she had to find Sabine.

Emma crept over to the door and carefully turned the knob. There were voices in the direction of the reception area. Curiosity got the better of her. Emma slowly walked down the corridor towards the voices. The women were sitting on the floor, crying, wailing and rocking. Women from the container were there and at least another thirty others. The men that had been doing the 'teaching' were distributing bread and water. Some of the girls fought, kicked out and punched, but every attempt met with laughter and a hard slap. The whole process designed to degrade. The changing of their names, It was to remove their own identity.

Emma spotted Sabine in a corner, weeping quietly to herself. Sabine was gently sucking on a piece of bread she had dunked into her cup of water. Emma walked over, avoiding as many of the men as she could. She knelt beside Sabine and leaned in to hug her. Sabine pulled away, an instinctive movement given everything that she had just been through. Sabine looked up and realising that it was Emma, held onto her tightly.

Minutes later, the young women were dragged into a circle, surrounded by the men, and the grim role call began again. Each girl cried as she was chosen; but not Emma. She went in silence. A silent recognition and for her own protection. She would not resist. She would try not get hurt. It was a different man, younger, slimmer, and in different circumstances, Emma may have actually found him attractive. Her second experience was similar to the first, only less words exchanged. Again, he used a condom; maybe it was for the protection of both, maybe they were being 'saved' for something else. Again, the young man left her lying weeping on the bed.

The process repeated over the next few days, two a day, then three, then four. Emma found a place in her mind she could retreat to while "it" happened.

She felt nothing, only determination, she was certain that the first week was all about breaking their spirits. Ready for the next thing, whatever that was. The men, they were always the same group of men, were taking it in turns, and what was once horrific became routine. Some of the women began to smoke crack, which was in ready supply. Emma had never taken any kind of recreational drug. She tried to convince Sabine not to indulge, but Sabine needed the relief and escape to oblivion that the crack gave her. Sabine wanted to lose herself.

After being imprisoned for a little over a week, the mood began to change. The women became not just sex slaves, but housekeepers too, scrubbing floors and cleaning out the bedrooms and toilets. Emma suggested to Sabine that perhaps they were expecting some VIP's or maybe some rich drug dealers.

Awoken early the following morning and forced to shower, Emma suspected that something was awry. It was especially unusual, as the cleanliness of the men was always poor, and as such, the cleanliness of the young women and girls had not seemed to matter. This day was different. The place was as clean as a seedy looking hotel-come-brothel could ever be. It was a warm day, but the building seemed much warmer than usual.

At around the middle of the day, Emma heard vehicles approaching. Voices were audible in the reception room. Several of the men began rounding up their captives and gathered them into the reception. A fire crackled in the large marble hearth. As they faced the reception desk, a large group of smartly dressed men stood before them. Forced into a line, each woman had to undress, and stand tall. The smartly dressed men walked slowly along the line of young women, some women whimpered in fear, as they were pawed to check their 'firmness' and forced to open their mouths so they could inspect their teeth.

One by one, the women paraded up and down the reception, in a degrading catwalk show as the men made notes. It was nothing more than a human cattle market.

When it was Sabine's turn, led up and down the room, she tried to cover her nakedness with her arms, but one of the men slapped her until she 'revealed all'. Just as her turn was nearly over, one of the 'customers' stood in front of her, stopping Sabine in her tracks. He eyed her up and down and moved closer, invading her personal space once more, he grinned.

"Dance for me."

He whispered the words close into Sabine's ear, his stale garlic breath made her wretch. With a laugh, he stepped back from Sabine.

"Dance for me bitch ...."

He drew a large knife with a curved blade from beneath his suit jacket and ran the blade down between Sabine's breasts.

"... or die."

Sabine shivered with fear.

"Dance for me," he repeated quietly in her ear, as he brushed his body against hers.

As she began to sway, he grabbed her wrist.

"Stop, but how can you dance, there is no music." Addressing the others, he began to clap his hands slowly.

"Clap, I want you to provide the music."

He gestured to them all to join him, and slowly, they all began to clap.

"Faster, you clap faster."

He grinned as they did what they were told. He liked being in control.

"Now we have music, you dance now."

He pushed Sabine into the middle of the floor. Sabine stumbled for a moment, in a trancelike state she nervously began to sway in time with the clapping. As she danced, the women looked down at their feet. Emma was horrified; she clapped along with the others. She had to. There was no choice.

A few minutes, which seemed like an age, passed. He obviously grew bored with his game and called for them to stop. Mind made up, he pointed to Sabine and two of the other girls, both Europeans. He nodded to the 'hotel manager' who made some notes as the man pulled a wad of notes from his hip pocket. The transaction was complete. The three 'purchases' were firmly led across the room towards the blazing fire,

"Now you are mine."

He pulled an iron from the fire and branded one of the women on the back of her left shoulder. She screamed in agony and fell to the floor as the smell of burning flesh filled the room. Sabine was next; two men grabbed her and held her tightly as she too felt the intense heat burning her flesh. Sabine passed out. The third woman suffered the same fate and lay on the floor whimpering.

The line of women could only watch in horror, this was probably going to be their fate too; it was just a matter of who their master might be, and how soon they were going to be chosen. As she started regaining consciousness, they hoisted Sabine to her feet. The three women were crying, as three cloaks wrapped around them. The pain, as the rough material rubbed against their wounds, was excruciating. As the three were about to be led outside, Emma knew that unless she did something drastic, this could be the last time she ever saw Sabine, and she knew that Sabine would never be able to survive without her. This was her only chance to be with her friend and boldly she stepped forward.

"I can dance too."

He looked straight at Emma, she returned his gaze.

"I can dance, take me too." She started moving, slowly, seductively, looking straight into the eyes of Sabine's new master.

"Take me." Emma whispered running her tongue gently across her upper lip.

For a few seconds a hush descended on the room. Sabine's master smiled.

"Very well, I like to watch you dance."

He reeled off some more notes as Emma walked towards the fire. She went there willingly and suffered the pain. She screamed out as the white-hot brand ate into her skin, melting and scarring as it did. Emma barely believed what had just happened. It had been instinctive and utterly the bravest thing she had ever done. She was probably being taken to a worse place than the 'hotel', but at least she would be with Sabine.

Emma pulled on the robe, mentally saying goodbye to her old self, and her old identity. The four slaves staggered from the building and towards a waiting people carrier.

Hoods pulled over their heads, they were bundled into back of the vehicle. It was a hot day, but at least the car had air conditioning giving them some small relief from the intense heat. Their shoulders throbbed with pain as the vehicle finally pulled away. For the next hour and a half, they sat in silence, not daring to speak for fear of suffering more pain.

Eventually the vehicle stopped. Although they could not see, the sounds and smells of a town were clear to them. It could have been anywhere, they had travelled so far, and didn't even know which country they were in.

The best they could guess was that they were still somewhere in Africa.

They were pushed, blindly, down an alley and then through a steel door. As the door closed behind them, it was obvious to Emma that they had entered a hard-surfaced hallway, due to the echoes she could hear and the cold on the soles of her bare feet. Less than a minute later, they were in a large bright room. As their hoods were removed and their eyes adjusted to the light, they could see the curtained walls of what appeared to be a reception area for 'clients'.

The four of them gazed all around. There were about half a dozen men sat in easy chairs obviously waiting. One looked up at Emma and smiled, this was not a nice smile but a leering 'I want you' kind of smile. They had been there barely five minutes and already it was Emma's turn. It was over quite quickly, the man seemed put off by the blood seeping from her shoulder wound, so probably regretted his choice of 'fresh meat'.

Emma lay on the bed as he left, feeling tired, drained and used. It was a feeling she had begun to become accustomed to, even after so short a time. She thought of how quickly humankind can become savages. After just a week, some of the girls had quite happily eaten their meals with their dirty fingers. The men who used them were little more than savages anyway, driven by greed and lust. Her shoulder throbbed as she thought to herself, 'this is not the end, I will survive, they will pay for what they've done to us'.

After a while, she put on her robe and stepped out of the room and into a corridor. There were people moving in different directions, men leaving on their own, and couples entering rooms. She could hear all manner of noises coming from behind the thin doorways, and the walls seemed equally thin. It was a busy place, and maybe, being in a town, with many people coming and going, there would be an opportunity to escape.

Emma wandered around the building and found herself in a kitchen. On a table in the corner sat a microwave, a kettle and some plastic plates and cups. An old fridge sat below the table. It looked dirty and probably did not work. There was a table and six plastic chairs running around the outside of the room with a further six stacked the opposite corner. They lacked the quality of the padded reception chairs, but they would suffice. Emma was about to sit on one when she saw a needle that had been carelessly left there. Looking closer, she found further evidence of drug use in the room.

Emma decided to explore some more, on the basis that if she was exploring, she would not be working. There was a toilet just off from the kitchen, it needed a good clean and the rancid smell almost made Emma choke. Further down the corridor was a bathroom, which consisted of a bath, and a chair, presumably to hang a towel on while you bathed. A man walked into the bathroom behind her.

"Are you lost?"

He was a slim young man, dressed in combat trousers, boots and a white Nike tee shirt probably in his early twenties He was dark skinned with several days' stubble on his chin.

"My name is Malek, I work here."

He had a kind face, but as Emma already knew that did not mean anything in this dark world. He reached out a hand, as did she, and in a strange moment, they shook hands. Malek did not try and touch her in any other way.

"My uncle Nassim owns this place. It was he who brought you here. He is a hard man, but if you work hard he will be fair to you."

Emma listened, it was strange that he only wanted to talk, to someone who to everyone else was just a "thing" his uncle owned. His English was excellent; and it turned out that he had been educated, for a while, in London, paid for by his uncle after his father had died. He was working as a kind of odd job man to help pay him back for his education. Emma could tell he was not happy there, and like her, found himself trapped in a life that was not of his making.

"I guess they'll be wondering where we are."

Malek smiled as he motioned towards the door.

Emma had told him nothing about herself, she had barely even uttered a word, and did not altogether trust him, but at least he seemed kinder than the rest.

They walked back to the reception area passing a young woman with pretty face and shoulder length brown hair leading a client into a room and could not help noticing that the woman had a large scar down her left leg, and quite a pronounced limp. Malek and Emma entered reception and, as Emma had guessed, there was another customer waiting. It was her turn to go through the whole performance again.

A few days passed, and the routine began in earnest. Emma barely saw Sabine. They worked different shifts.

When they were not working, they were sleeping and trying to gather strength to get through the following shift. Day followed night, followed day. On one particular evening, it seemed quieter than normal. The stars glistened through the barred windows as the women gathered in the 'kitchen'. This was their living room. As Emma entered, she noticed some women around the table sharing a crack pipe. Amongst them was Sabine. Emma pulled her friend to one side.

"You have to stop this."

Emma shook her, and Sabine winced. Sabine's shoulder had become infected, and the pain had obviously started to affect her mind.

"I can't," Sabine cried, "I need this, it's all I have."

18.

After nearly a week, a week of dreadful food and endless clients, Sabine and Emma had barely exchanged a word. Sabine seemed to have settled in with her 'druggie' friends, and Emma spent most of her time sitting alone. Emma was in her own world, constantly trying to think of a way they could escape their hell. It was a Friday. Emma called it Friday. She had started counting days and this day felt like it might be a Friday. Uninvited, Sabine sat beside Emma and put her good arm around her shoulders.

"Oh Emma, I am so sorry, I have been so horrible to you, and after all you have done for me."

Emma could see the tears in Sabine's eyes, and could tell they were genuine and came from deep inside Sabine's heart.

"Please forgive me."

"Of course I forgive you Sabine; you are my best and only friend."

"We will get out of here, won't we?"

"We will, we will be home soon, our families will find us and we will be saved, you'll see." Emma tried to be as convincing as she could.

Another week went by, and as usual, Emma saw little of Sabine. Too many clients, not enough time off, they began working double shifts, late into the evenings and even some mornings. Emma was exhausted and her will to go on was beginning to fade.

It was a Tuesday morning, when Emma saw Sabine again. Emma was tired, but Sabine was strangely upbeat.

"How are you Sabine?" Emma's voice trailed through her tiredness.

"I'm good," replied Sabine, in her soft French accent, "I think I've found a way out of here."

Emma looked Sabine straight in the eyes,

"A way out, how?"

Malek appeared in the doorway and Sabine immediately stiffened.

"Ssh" whispered Sabine "Not here, will see later if I think the plan is going to work."

An hour or so later it was Emma's turn for a bath. As she soaked in the lukewarm water, she allowed herself a glimmer of hope. Sabine had a plan. Somehow, she had discovered a way out. Unable to contain herself, Emma made a fist with her right hand and ever so slightly punched the air.

An hour later, Emma, was impatiently waiting for Sabine to appear and decided to look for her. She wandered through the building checking the toilet, the rooms and the reception. There was no sign of her friend. 'Could she have taken her chance and escaped already?'

Emma wandered back down the corridor. There were a couple of women carrying towels, banging on the bathroom door. Emma could not understand the words they were saying but it was clear they wanted to get into the bathroom. Malek heard the commotion and came to investigate. He tried the handle, it turned, but the door would not budge.

"I think it must be stuck," he said, straining to push it open.

There was no lock on the door, so something else was holding it shut. In desperation, Malek took a run at the door and struck it with his shoulder. The door cracked open forcing the chair that was wedged underneath the handle on the other side, to split and break.

The bathroom was dark inside, illuminated only by the single light bulb from out in the corridor. The bath stood alone. The single piece of furniture visible in the darkened room. A tap softly dripped. The only break in the silence was the peaceful sound of water raining over its' sides splashing gently onto the floor. Limpid crimson water rolled out in an ever-growing pool across the tiles.

Amidst the rose-coloured water of the bath lay Sabine. Pale, eyes closed, head beneath the water. The open wounds on her wrists dripping the last of her blood.

"No." Emma screamed and covered her eyes. Collapsing on the wet floor, she broke down into floods of tears.

As Malek stood over the bath, he looked down on poor Sabine. Naked and submerged in the sea of pink. A shard of a stained plastic plate lay on the tiles beside the bath. This was how she had cut her wrists. Her eyes and mouth closed, Sabine looked as if she were asleep.

Malek leaned over and touched her forehead. She was cold. The warm blood had left her body and immersed her pale form. Her expression was one of contentment and serenity. Sabine had escaped and finally, sadly at peace. This had been her plan all along, and now at last Sabine was free.

The bullish figure of Nassim stormed into the bathroom, and barked at Malek, in words that Emma could not understand. Malek ran out of the bathroom, Emma could clearly see he had tears in his eyes. Nassim, face red with rage, began shouting at Emma and the other women.

"Clean this mess up."

Nassim punched the wall, leaving a deep crater in the partition from his giant fist.

"Bitches!"

Emma stood in shock, her only friend, had surrendered. Sabine had left her, and now she was all alone. She felt a gentle arm around her shoulders.

"Come on, we must do as he says."

Emma looked up at the woman who had whispered so gently to her, and then dropped her gaze, noticing the long scar that snaked down her left leg.

"She, she was my friend, I don't know what I'm going to do now."

Emma could barely see the woman's face through the tears in her eyes. Emma needed a friend. More than anything else in the world, she really needed a friend. As the woman took Emma's face in her hands, Emma gently tilted her head, so their eyes met.

"What is your name?" The woman's voice was soft and calm.

"M-my n-name is Emma, Emma Watson."

The woman smiled gently, a friendly warm smile. As the tears rolled down Emma's cheeks, the woman took Emma in her arms and held her close, just as her mother would have done.

"I'm very pleased to meet you Emma Watson."

The woman had kind eyes. Emma held her and sobbed into her chest.

"…my name is Anja, Anja Peterovic."

19.

Keith arrived at the airport ahead of time. He was worried. Emma had not been in touch since that single phone call on their first night at the hotel, which was most unlike her.

He followed the signs for the short stay car park and stopped at the barrier to collect his ticket. Driving up a couple of levels, he rolled his car into a nearby parking bay, dowsed his headlights and turned off the engine.

Outside it had started raining. Grabbing his raincoat from the back seat, he slipped it on over his shirt.

"Bloody English weather," he muttered as he locked the car door.

With hood up and head down against the rain, he ran across to the terminal building. The big sliding doors silently opened, and Keith felt a warm blast of air muss his hair as he entered. The arrivals board stood right in front of him. Keith blinked a couple of times to bring the words into focus and could see that the plane from Marrakech was on time. This meant he had at least an hour to kill before Emma and Jade appeared.

It was a luxury to have a spare hour. Life was as frantic as ever, he had a busy job, and there were always chores to do at home. On Saturdays, they had relatives to visit, DIY and a lawn to mow. Emma always needed to be dropped off and collected, even though she was 'all grown up'. He did not mind, he had always wanted a family, and for him family life had come rather late. His friend Harry had his daughter early in life, but being an older father was not so bad.

Keith stopped at a coffee shop ordered a double shot skinny latte with a lemon muffin. The young woman who served him smiled. It was a friendly smile and Keith could not help but smile back.

She had a twinkle in her eye. He may have been fast approaching middle age but 'oh yes. I've still got it' he thought to himself.

He collected his purchases from the counter and spotted some newspapers on a rack close by. Taking one of the red top newspapers, he put his raincoat over the back of a seat and sat down. Keith slowly brought the mug to his lips and loudly slurped his coffee. 'Hopefully the pretty young thing behind the counter didn't hear me', he thought.

Keith started to read. He knew it would not take long. The paper was filled with sensational celebrity stories, who was dating who, who was cheating on who, and who with. The usual array of scantily clad women filled pages three to six. He quickly skipped past these just in case the woman at the counter was watching him. She was not. She was serving someone else, also with a smile and a twinkle.

Skimming to page seven, there was the continuing story about the missing boy who had been on holiday with his family in Tunisia. The details were sketchy at best; his name was Justin. He had been abducted while the family were on a shopping trip. They had apparently let go of his hand for a moment and he was gone. The red top seemed to think the father had something to do with it. 'There they go again' thought Keith, quick to judge as usual.

He flicked to the back of the newspaper, Chelsea football news, Liverpool football news, expensive signings, 'transfer-windows'. Keith yawned; it was just the same old news, different day, different people involved, but the same old news.

He reached over and put the paper back in the rack. For the next twenty minutes, Keith sat and stared into space, supped his coffee and finished his muffin. He made the odd sly glance at the pretty woman serving drinks; she did not look back. 'Oh well, she had her chance' he joked to himself.

Keith decided to take a walk around the shops, not much to see, the usual overpriced fare. He wandered into one of the news outlets and bought a large bar of fruit and nut chocolate for them all to share on the way home before heading off in the direction of the arrivals gate.

There were crowds of people waiting at the gate; including about a dozen taxi drivers with pieces of card each with a name written in black Sharpie or "big pen" as Emma called them. There were lovers awaiting their partners and other parents, like Keith, awaiting their children.

The board said that the Marrakech flight had landed about five minutes earlier, so Keith guessed it would be at least half an hour before the girls emerged. He opened the wrapper and broke off a piece of chocolate, the delicate creamy sweetness tasted nice as it melted in his mouth. Time went on. He was getting impatient; they seemed to be taking forever. Twenty minutes later a flood of people emerged from the gate, smiles greeted loved ones; tanned faces met paler ones. One by one, the waiting people drifted away. Then Keith saw Jade, but no, as he got closer, it was not her after all. She looked very similar, dressed in similar clothes. But no, this woman was slightly taller, and looked like she used botox. Jade never went in for that sort of thing. A swarthy looking man stepped forward to greet her. They seemed to know each other as they kissed and went off together his arm around her shoulders.

Another half an hour, and most of the passengers seemed to have passed through the gate, just Keith and a young woman remained waiting. At last, an elderly woman in a wheelchair appeared, being pushed through by one of the flight attendants. The woman in the wheelchair reunited with the remaining young woman, probably her daughter.

Keith was left standing alone at the gate. Other people began to gather, obviously for the arrival of another flight. Keith was getting very anxious. He decided not to call home as he did not want to worry his wife Andrea unduly, so decided to call Emma's mobile phone, but that just went straight to voicemail.

There was an enquiries desk across the concourse and Keith marched towards it. The clerk on the desk seemed efficient and friendly, and offered to check the manifest to see if the Emma and Jade had actually been on the flight. He could confirm that yes, they were on the flight, and had cleared customs about half an hour before. As there were no bags from that flight left unaccounted for, he could only surmise that Keith had missed them as they had come out in the initial rush.

Keith thanked the man and headed back towards the arrivals gate. He looked around the shops; then wandered outside to see if they were standing in the road; waiting for him to pick them up. No sign. He started to panic. He found a young female police officer and explained the situation. Side by side they approached the enquiries desk.

The clerk reiterated his story, that they must have been on the plane, had cleared customs, collected their bags and must have left the terminal.

The police officer asked the man to put out a call on the tannoy system, which he readily agreed to do. The message went out across the whole airport and Keith and the police officer waited. After half an hour, the police officer told Keith there was nothing else she could do and said that they had probably taken a taxi back home. Keith explained that taxi back to the Midlands, from London, would have cost them a fortune, and was not something anyone would do when they were going to get a lift anyway.

The police officer suggested he phone home to see if they had been in touch. This he did, and, no, there had not been any phone calls from either of their daughters. Keith's wife Andrea was very worried. The only other thing they could do would be to check the airport CCTV. The police officer said that Keith would have to wait until the following day for that to happen; and only when they were sure that their daughters were actually missing.

Keith thanked the police officer for her time and walked slowly back to his car. What else could he do? He got back to his car and called Jade's father Harry, explaining the situation. Harry told him to return home, and hopefully Jade and Emma would soon be in touch.

The following day there was still no news. Harry and Keith met to plan their next move. The authorities insisted the girls must have arrived home, and after much insistence from the two fathers, they trawled hours of CCTV footage since the time the flight touched down. As the images flickered across the computer screen they spotted a few passengers that looked a little like them. However, there were none that exactly matched their exact description.

Both families feared the worst. They knew their daughters could not have been on the flight, even though all of the administrative evidence suggested they were. They must still be in Morocco, and in some kind of trouble.

There was just one choice remaining, they would have to be on the next flight to Marrakech and try to find them themselves.

20.

Fourteen hours later, the Boeing 767 touched down at Marrakech airport. It had been a long flight. Few words had passed between the two friends. Harry had been tempted by the offer of a shot of whisky, from the attractive blonde airhostess, 'the one with the nice legs'. Thankfully, he had resisted. Harry instead, opted for coffee, instant and tasteless, but very hot. As Harry almost burned his lip with the first sip, Keith smiled with relief. He knew of the demons that Harry fought on a daily basis and was extremely proud of his friend. Harry had seriously considered the shot; longing for the relief that smoky oak taste would bring. Deep down he knew this was not the time to be sinking back into old habits. There was plenty of time for that once their adventure was finally over.

Clutching their bags, they descended from the plane, stepping onto Moroccan soil for the first time. Walking across the tarmac, they realised that, in their haste, they had forgotten to pack, or even purchase, any sunscreen; and in the baking heat of the midday sun, they could feel their skin begin to burn.

The line of disembarked passengers all moved towards the waiting bus, which whisked them away from the runway. They arrived at passport control in minutes and joined a long snaking queue. Hordes of tired pale faces stood about them waiting impatiently. The lengthy flight had comprised mainly British holidaymakers, escaping the cold and rain of home. Two young children seemed to be playing a game of 'who could scream the loudest', and a number of disgruntled grown-ups appeared to be complaining to each other about them. One small bald headed man was talking on his mobile phone close by.

"I'm sorry I can't quite hear you," he said, cupping his opposite ear with his hand.

"It's these bloody screaming kids."

"Oy!" The mother shouted, pointing to the man on the phone.

She was young, massively overweight and wearing tight fitting clothes, that were at least two sizes too small.

"Are yaw torkin' 'bout mar kids?"

Her accent was broad; and it was immediately obvious to Harry and Keith that she was from the West Midlands. The mother continued indignantly.

"Ee corr 'elp it if ee's too 'ot."

Other travellers chimed in to show their displeasure, as the volume of voices began to rise, the arguments, and the temperature, became more heated. The two fathers just stared ahead, watching the queue in front of them slowly subside.

After what seemed to be an eternity of waiting, they finally made their way out of the terminal building and into the warm sunshine. For a moment, they stood in silence, breathing in the dusty air and taking in the very scene that had greeted their daughters just a few weeks earlier.

With only a small amount of hand luggage to carry, they took a taxi straight to their daughters' hotel. The car's air conditioner sputtered and clearly did not work, so Keith rolled down his window to try to give them some air to breathe. A warm breeze filled the vehicle. Their shirts stuck to their backs and sweat streamed down their faces. The old toothless driver pointed at various buildings as they passed, speaking in a combination of French and broken English. He laughed at his own jokes, jokes that only he could understand. Neither passenger spoke throughout the journey, they were preparing their thoughts for whatever awaited at their destination.

After about half an hour, they arrived outside the hotel. Harry paid the driver and gave him a healthy tip. They stood and watched as the toothless taxi driver drove away laughing and waving. Harry shook his head. As a gesture of solidarity, they looked at each other, took a deep breath, in unison, and purposefully made their way through the tall sliding doors into the hotel reception.

The downward blast from the overhead air conditioner blew refreshingly cool air as they entered. It was a welcome respite from the oppressive heat outside; and it was more than tempting to stand there a while and cool off. The inside of the hotel was impressive, but admiring its' expensive decor was the furthest thing from their minds.

A smartly dressed middle-aged Moroccan man greeted them at the door and ushered them towards the reception desk. His hair was grey, thinning and greased back, as were his eyebrows.

As the man held out a hand, he gave off a combination of deodorant and strong aftershave. Sweet and overpowering in equal measure. Harry shook the outstretched hand, as did Keith; coughing lightly as he breathed in cool air, transfused with the man's mixed aromas.

"Welcome my friends; would you like a nice cold drink before you check in? Your suitcases are outside, No?"

He expected them to say 'yes', and assumingly claim some kind of tip. He glanced outside at the empty space, then, with a slight look of disappointment, he withdrew his hand and turned his gaze back to the friends.

They carried a small rucksack each, it was all they had time to pack, and they had not wanted to waste any time at the airport baggage reclaim with large suitcases. Between them, they had some duty-free bags containing the few toiletries they had bought at the airport.

"We aren't staying," said Keith quickly "Our daughters are missing, and we are trying to find them."

"You hope to find them here?" The man seemed confused.

"They were staying here, and then they disappeared." Harry exclaimed.

The man seemed very calm, confident and relaxed.

"We will see what we can find out. What were their names?" He stepped behind the reception desk and began typing into the computer.

"Jade Turner and Emma Watson," Keith was hopeful but agitated.

"Jade Turner, Jade Turner, ah here we are, Miss Jade Turner and her friend Miss Emma Watson. Room 236," he paused. "A very nice room overlooks the gardens."

It looked like he was waiting for his next computer screen to come up, or maybe he was just stalling.

"And they checked out on," he paused again, as if to build suspense. "Saturday. Saturday evening. For their onwards travel back to the United Kingdom."

The last sentence sounded like he was reading it from a well-rehearsed script.

"That's just it," replied Keith, "they didn't return to the UK."

"Well they are not here; they checked out," the man replied with a smile.

"Can we see their room?" Harry asked.

"I'm afraid that just isn't possible, room 236 is now occupied again." His reply was emphatic, and final.

"Well, where could they have gone?" Harry's voice betrayed his rising anger.

"Maybe they met some boyfriends at the airport and went home with them, back in the United Kingdom, or somewhere else."

"But they don't have boyfriends," shouted Harry in frustration.

"Parents never really know what their children get up to when they are not looking. Especially on holiday."

"What are you implying?" Keith's frustration had turned to anger.

"Your young people are a disgrace, morally and emotionally corrupt. They lack discipline and respect. The mess we have to clean up, the abuse we are subjected to. You would not believe what we must endure."

The man had done all the implying he was prepared to do. Turning off his computer, he looked up and motioned behind them. Two large security guards approached from the reception bar opposite. It was clear that the two Englishmen were intent on creating a scene and some of the guests were starting to take an interest. That would never do.

The guards politely asked them to leave, with an undercurrent of menace. Keith and Harry were escorted through the sliding doors and out to the gate beyond. At the gate, and no longer on the hotel premises, the guards stood their ground waiting for them to leave. The friends needed a plan.

They considered hanging around outside the hotel grounds and showing photos of the girls to tourists coming in and out; but the chances of the transient guests remembering two English girls, out of the thousands of people that pass by every day, was quite remote. Nearby a young boy stood alongside a couple of camels, trying to convince a young Spanish couple to don some Moroccan robes and have their photographs taken with them. Offering the boy a few dirhams, Keith and Harry showed him the photographs. He thought they looked a little familiar. 'But then' he said 'that most English people looked the same to him.' Realising there was nothing further to be gained at the hotel, they considered approaching the local police, but what would they do?

As far as the world seemed to be concerned, Jade and Emma had left their hotel at the allotted time, flown home on the correct flight, arrived safely in England and just chose not to go home.

As frustration and desperation began to take hold, Keith had an idea.

"I'm pretty sure the girls would have gone on a trip to Marrakech at some point. Why don't we at least head down there, show their photographs to some of the tourists and traders, and see if anyone remembers seeing them?"

Harry was dubious, but as it was as good an idea as anything else he could think of, agreed to give it a try.

A taxi driver was sitting in the shade of a palm tree just outside the hotel complex. He quickly agreed to drive the pair into the city. The taxi seemed much newer than the last, and its' driver, Hadir, was a great deal younger and had many more teeth than their previous chauffeur. The air conditioner purred as they turned onto the main highway.

As they drove, they explained their plight to Hadir. Hadir's English was excellent. He listened carefully to their story, of how badly the hotel had treated them and to Keith's idea.

"I see your problem. The hotel will not want to take blame or want any investigation. It is bad for business. The police will not help you either, too much corruption. You can try the stallholders in the main market place, Djemaa El Fna, but also I could take you to the British Embassy on Avenue Mohammed V, maybe they can help."

On the drive into the city, the friends decided to split up, so they could cover more ground. Hadir dropped Keith in the 'Place de la Liberte' square, in the more modern area known as Gueliz, just outside the ancient walls of the Medina.

"If you find your way back to this road, Avenue Mohammed V, you cannot get lost," Hadir said as Keith slid out of the back seat.

"I'll call you when we've been to the Embassy," said Harry.

They shook hands and wished each other luck.

"Whatever happens we'll meet back in this square later on," was Keith's parting sentence, before Hadir swung the taxi west towards the consulate.

The Avenue Mohammed V ran diagonally north-west to the southeast, bisecting Marrakech like a seam joining the old and new towns.

Harry stared out of the windscreen admiring the tree-lined vista as they drove away from the Medina. On any other day, in any other circumstance, this would have been a most pleasurable experience. The hot sun reflected off the bright pink facades, the tall palm trees, the upmarket cafes, shops and restaurants. It was busy, yet peaceful. Ordinary people just going about their day. Harry noted the red and white kerbs stones, highlighting the edge of the pavement. 'Like an endless barber's pole laid along the road' he noted.

After about fifteen minutes, they arrived at the address only to find that the consulate had already closed for the day.

What do we do now? Harry had tears in his eyes, as he tried to fight the tiredness and desperation he was feeling. Hadir thought for a moment.

"The main British consulate is in Rabat, it's a good few miles from here. It would probably take us the rest of the day, but I could take you if you wish."

Harry reached into his pocket, pulled out his mobile phone and called Keith. Keith had just arrived outside Djemaa El Fna, and had begun to ask a few of the locals if they recognised the photos of Jade and Emma. Harry explained that he probably would not be back until the evening and Keith replied that it was definitely the best idea. As Harry was saying goodbye, Hadir cut in.

"Tell your friend not to have any ice in his orange juice."

Hadir turned the taxi back onto Avenue Mohammed V and they began to make their way north towards Rabat. Harry did not feel very hopeful but tried to take his mind off this latest delay by admiring the ever-changing scenery. 'God, I need a drink' he thought to himself as they left the city, following a line of mountains to the east, across the dusty barren landscape towards Rabat.

21.

Keith slipped his mobile phone back into his pocket. 'This was going to be a real long shot' he thought, as he walked through the gateway, amidst the pock marked terra-cotta walls of the Medina. He pulled his Ray-bans from his shorts pocket and wiped the lenses on a tissue. Donning his sunglasses, he looked the picture of a typical, yet affluent, Englishman on holiday. Dressed in a surfing tee shirt, customary baggy shorts and flip-flops, Keith continued to make his way around the square. He showed their daughters photographs, stored on his phone, to some of the orange juice stallholders, snake charmers, henna tattoo women, tour guides and a man with a monkey on a lead. The latter insisted on taking his photograph using Keith's phone with the monkey on his shoulder. Then he demanded payment, which Keith instantly agreed to, sensing the man was not going to give him his phone back if he refused.

Keith continued to wander the square for the next hour, asking passers-by to look at his photographs and see if they recognised the girls. After an hour of wandering in the intense heat and talking to anyone who would listen, he decided to take a glass of orange juice, with no ice, and sit at an adjacent table to collect his thoughts.

The approach was getting him nowhere. If Keith could even get them to concentrate long enough on the photo; and not on the quality of his phone, watch, sunglasses and clothes; he could tell from their blank expressions they did not recognise either Jade or Emma. He was feeling very dejected. Keith was normally an upbeat, resourceful and confident fellow. Relaxing his stocky frame, sipping his juice, he surveyed the scene. The square was bustling with people, vivid colours and exotic smells. This was truly a place to enthral and captivate the senses. The air was brimming with noise, haggling, laughter, traffic and heat.

Keith handed a few coins to some raggedly dressed children that were sitting begging beside him. This gave him a thought, a germ of an idea.

Maybe he had been going about this all wrong. Maybe, just maybe, he had been asking the wrong questions to the wrong people. The traders would barely remember who they had seen two minutes ago, let alone up to two weeks ago.

There was a shifty looking dark-skinned man, with mirrored sunglasses, white vest and khaki shorts playing cards outside a cafe bar. Taking a chance, Keith walked over to him.

"Ehrm excuse me sir."

Keith cleared his throat and sat down on a stool next to the man.

"Would you happen to know where I might find some girls?"

Keith thought he must have sounded very English, and maybe rather foppish. Asking a rough looking man for girls was not something that he had ever done before, and he really did not have a clue as to the etiquette of this particular situation.

"Girls? You English?"

The man took off his sunglasses revealing a nasty scar across one eye, the pupil of which was completely white.

"Yes, I am English." Keith shifted nervously on his stool.

"You have money?"

The man smiled.

"Yes, I have money," replied Keith shakily.

"You like," the man paused. "Young girls?"

The mans' smile broadened and Keith began to feel very uneasy. What was he talking himself into, and what was this man capable of?

"Maybe teenage, maybe younger?"

Keith felt sick to his stomach, and rose to his feet, but the man put a hand on his shoulder and pushed Keith back down onto the stool.

"Okay, you want ladies, I get you ladies. I see you are a man of taste, I get you nice lady."

The man stood, kicking away his chair, he grabbed Keith by the arm, and pulled him to his feet.

"Now we go to see the nice ladies," he said, gently pushing Keith alongside him.

Keith had no idea what he was walking into, so as they walked Keith began to hatch a plan.

Obviously, the chances of being taken to the exact girls he wanted, was at least one in a million, but at least he might get a feel for the places to search, when he could finally manage to shake off his new 'companion'.

They left the square and walked back through the gateway of the Medina he found himself back in the French built zone known as Gueliz, it was a bustling tourist area filled with nightclubs, bars and restaurants. It was dusk when they arrived; the daytime traders were heading for home, handing the reins of the city over to the night people. As they walked, they were constantly stopped by street traders and women, many looking and sounding as if they came from Eastern Europe, offering themselves for a handful of dirhams. The man gave polite but firm refusals as they walked on.

Suddenly Keith had a thought.

"Are there any new girls, maybe, English girls?"

Keith had a hopeful sound in his voice.

"Whatever you like we have them all here, and I know just the place."

The man thought for a moment and continued.

"Is right…"

He raised his hand and shook his head.

"… you don't want the old hags, I don't like them either, dirty old whores, you want new young flesh."

The man seemed almost proud of what he was offering, given that these were probably young women that had been cruelly trafficked into a life of despair.

After about half an hour of walking, doubling back and dodging down an uncountable number of side streets, Keith was feeling quite lost. They seem to have zigzagged across the whole of Marrakech and appeared to have entered the Souk from another entrance. The area was full of metalworking shops. Small furnaces stoked by young boys, as the teenagers and grownups hammered and shaped a multitude of metal objects. The work was frantic and basic health and safety was obviously something they had never heard of. On they walked, amongst the crowds and traders, a myriad of colourful items hung outside a multitude of shops. The tightly packed streets choked with tourists and traders and a constant flow of mopeds dodged and weaved amidst the throng. They finally came to a halt outside a tall, dark, intricately carved wooden door.

The man opened the door and gestured for Keith to enter before him. Keith paused for a moment and glanced up and down the street. There was movement everywhere, even at that time of day, the bustle and noise of the city had not abated. It seemed to Keith, that none of the passers-by had taken any notice of this pale looking Englishman, standing there, dripping with sweat, dry mouth, heart racing and desperately trying to keep his composure. Did these people know he was coming? Keith guessed that his 'guide' had taken the scenic route; probably to get him lost. Was he walking straight into a trap? Keith could feel his heart beating faster. He took a deep breath and stepped inside.

22.

The riad was dark and surprisingly cooler than the crowded market place outside. Keith nervously ran his hands through his hair as he scanned the room.

The reception, or what passed for a reception, was dark, with a damp, musty smell. An electric fan on the floor, in a corner, provided some welcome relief from the muggy oppressive heat. An old wooden table was cluttered with books, a paper spike full of what looked like receipts, some wooden bowls, a water jug and a small ornate Moroccan lamp. A tiny staircase rose steeply to the left and an arched doorway led through to what, Keith could only assume, were the living quarters. A few faded pictures hung from dirty mustard coloured walls and an old mirror was propped over a blackened fireplace.

"And now, you are here, someone will be with you in a moment."

The man held out his hand. Keith made to shake it, but the man shrugged, tilted his head, and held his hand flat. Keith immediately knew what he wanted and laid some dirham notes into the man's hand.

"Thank you, my friend. Enjoy."

He smiled a broad smile, showing off his teeth, some gold, some black. The man turned on his heels and was gone.

Alone in the room, Keith nervously cleared his throat, trying to attract attention. His heart beat faster. This whole, surreal experience was all so new to him, a world away from home and his safe relaxed English life. He fought the dryness in his throat, coughed and managed to utter a single word.

"Hello."

There came the sound of footsteps and a small dark-skinned man entered the room.

"Greetings my friend, you are English?"

The man had a slightly off-putting smile beaming across his lined rugged face.

Keith could clearly see he had some teeth missing, and the few that remained stained a dull dirty yellowy brown colour. A brief humorous thought crossed Keith's mind 'haven't any of these guys ever heard of toothpaste?' The hint of a smile flickered across Keith's face. He suddenly felt brave, after all he was the knight in shining flip-flops come to save his daughter Emma and her friend.

"I'm looking for a girl, a new girl."

Keith stammered, belying his newfound confidence.

"A new girl you say, we have fresh young girls from all continents, all across the world for you to choose from, I will pick a nice one for you."

"No, please, can I choose?"

Keith's hand shook as he held out the photograph of Emma on his phone.

"I'd like a girl that looks like this."

"I am sure we can accommodate you, I can see you like them young."

Keith had worked out that this whole 'liking them young' pitch was just another way of putting up the price. These people did not care how old their 'product' was, just as long as it brought them money, lots of money. And, the younger 'items' were probably easier to manipulate. The whole experience was giving Keith a very nasty taste in his mouth.

With a knowing wink, he motioned for Keith to follow him through the archway. Keith followed through into a small, empty courtyard, quite dark in the fading evening light, save for a brightly coloured lamp hanging from a metal hook in the wall above.

The man stopped.

"Now, you, I must search, please my friend, raise your arms."

Keith could feel the nasty taste become ever more intense, but there was an overwhelming feeling of dread, mixed with the forlorn hope that, in the next few moments, he may come face to face with Emma. Keith allowed himself to be frisked, and finding nothing of interest about Keith's person, the man waved for him to follow.

As they passed through the courtyard and further into the riad, a couple of large, dark and burly rough looking men appeared from a side room. 'They could be a problem' thought Keith as he passed them by.

With arms folded, they flexed their ample biceps in veiled threat. If they turned on him, he would be finished.

Keith was in dangerous territory, no one knew where he was. There may not even be any 'girls'. He may just be robbed and beaten or worse. All he could do was hold his nerve and see where the next few minutes would take him.

The man stopped outside a heavily built wooden door, Keith couldn't help but notice the large metal draw bolt on the outside of it. He may be stepping into a prison cell, or at worst, the last room he would ever see.

"She is in here."

The man gestured towards the door handle.

"What is her name?" asked Keith, the nervousness clear in his voice.

"What would you like her name to be?"

The man spoke softly, with an almost gleefully friendly manner.

"Might she be called, Emma?" Half expectant, half-terrified.

"If that what you want, then that what she called."

The man's English was becoming more broken as he spoke faster.

Keith stepped towards the door, but the man stood in his way.

"But first, we have the subject of the money."

The friendliness had drained from his voice; this was now very much a business transaction.

"How much?"

"One thousand Dirhams, half an hour, no more, you want more, you pay more."

The words poured out of his mouth, like water down a drain. It was just business, just paying for the use of a thing, a commodity for half an hour. There was no thought of the human being that waited behind the door; no comprehension, or care of what state she might be in or what she had endured. Somewhere she probably had a mother, a sister; maybe she was just a child. Maybe, he hoped, it actually was Emma.

"You pay the price, or you leave."

The man was getting agitated, and the two muscle bound men looked up.

Keith had taken the trouble of filling his wallet with local currency before he left the airport. Taking the wallet from his trouser pocket, he proceeded to count out ten of the one hundred dirham notes into the man's greasy palm and replaced his wallet back into his pocket.

"Enjoy."

The man slid the metal draw bolt back to unlock and stepped back from the door.

Keith took a nervous step forwards, 'just what or who would he find on the other side of the door?'

23.

Harry and Hadir reached Rabat and the British Consulate late that afternoon. They were both tired and thirsty and stopped to buy some bottled water from a small store just down the road. Harry drank quickly, trying quench his thirst, almost choking, as the cool liquid hit his parched throat.

"Thank you for getting me here," Harry croaked.

As Harry attempted to clear his throat, Hadir spoke.

"We must act quickly, we do not want the embassy closing on us. "

Hadir was right; they had come too far to lose this chance for the sake of a few minutes delay.

Hadir waited in the car while Harry entered the embassy. The air conditioning inside felt very cold and Harry shivered slightly as he approached the main reception. An attractive, longhaired Moroccan woman stood behind the desk. She was smartly dressed and greeted him with a friendly smile as he approached.

"I need to see someone urgently; my daughter has gone missing,"

Harry blurted out his story before she even managed to say 'hello'. She felt his urgency and knew there was not a moment to lose.

The woman picked up the telephone and made a call.

"Someone will be with you shortly," she said, beckoning him to a group of comfortable looking seats next to a low coffee table. Harry sat in a cosy leather chair and waited. There were a few magazines on the small table. He picked up one of them, thumbed through it and put it down without even registering its' contents.

What seemed like an hour, but was probably only a fraction of that, went by before a middle-aged English man approached and shook his hand.

"I'm Rogerson, I work for the Ambassador. He's out at the moment. Can I help at all?"

Harry relayed his story once again. Each version was getting shorter, as it became more urgent. Only the main points mattered. Rogerson tutted, and tapped the side of his face.

"Tricky situation, the best I can do is make a few enquiries, and see what I can find out. Leave your number with Yasmin over there and we'll be in touch."

Harry's confidence faded. Rogerson strode off and Harry sauntered slowly back to the reception desk.

"He says to leave my number with you, so he can let me know what he can find out."

Harry spoke slowly, his words jumbling as he tried to recount Rogerson's exact words. It was then, all at once, Harry began to come to terms with the thought that Rogerson really could do very little and he would never see his daughter again. He tried to fight back the tears, but it was no use. Yasmin offered him a tissue, which he took to dry his eyes.

"Have you some paper and a pen?" Harry asked, trying to keep himself together.

Yasmin handed him what he asked for and Harry wrote down his contact details.

As Harry turned to leave, Yasmin came from behind the desk and grabbed Harry by the elbow. Yasmin could see Harry was desperate and upset.

"Look" she began. "This may be of no use, but..."

Her voice trailed away slightly.

"Yes?" Harry's expectant eyes met hers.

"...I have an uncle, he works in Marrakech, he's, well, a sort of, investigator."

"Police?"

"No, not exactly, he's a sort of private investigator. He's a good man and well..."

She paused, as if she was not completely confident of what she was saying.

"... He may be able to help". Yasmin handed Harry a card. The card was a little bent and rather worn; she had obviously kept it in her purse for a very long time.

"His name is Mustapha."

Harry took the card but sensed that she scarcely believed in her uncle's abilities herself.

Slipping the card into his pocket, Harry returned to the taxi and asked Hadir to drive him back to Marrakech.

Harry felt a deep pain in his chest, the stress of the last few days was starting to take its' toll. He was living a waking nightmare and their chances of finding their daughters were fading fast.

24.

Keith gently knocked on the door. He really was not sure why he did, considering where he was, it was just a nervous reaction in an insane situation. He turned the handle and stepped inside.

The room was dirty, even worse than the entrance room he had first entered. The single low wattage light bulb gave the room a dim glow. The mustard grey walls were peeling with black mouldy patches. The floor was made up of bare wooden boards, suffuse with dirt and grime. There was one small window with bars on the inside, securely fastened to the wall with steel rivets. The room contained a small white sink, sitting on a cracked pedestal, that did not match, and the fragment remains of where a mirror used to hang.

In the corner of the room was a double bed. A single yellowing sheet covered a grimy mattress, with an uncomfortable looking pillow at the head of the bed. A small bedside table was next to it, on that was an empty plastic plate, a plastic cup and beside that was a plastic bucket with an old towel draped across the top.

Aside from the furniture, the room before him was empty.

He heard the door close behind him, the large bolt sliding back into place, Keith was trapped, a prisoner, a foolish prisoner, who had come here of his own volition.

It was then he heard her. She was behind him and had been hiding behind the door all the time.

Keith turned and saw her for the first time; she was crouched and had her back to him as she cowered in the corner, completely naked. At first glance, he could tell that she had not had a proper wash in a very long time. Her head turned slightly towards him, but the long, dark, matted hair completely covered her face. She was thin and most likely malnourished. She moved her hair slightly and Keith saw what he thought was a small red birthmark just below her hairline.

Stepping towards her, she immediately flinched away and as she did, he was able to see faded scars and bruises, probably from beatings she must have endured.

As Keith reached out a hand, she edged away and cried. The girl was similar in build to Emma, but it was not Emma. His heart sank in despair.

As he led her over to the bed, she bowed her head in submission. Keith motioned for her to sit next to him, and as she obediently did so, he wrapped the sheet around her fragile frame.

"I'm not going to hurt you…" he said and took her hand.

"…or do anything to you."

The girl continued to cry, and Keith could see what looked like needle marks in her arm. She was so young, and from her pale skin tone, he guessed that she probably was not from Morocco, or anywhere near North Africa.

Keith switched on his phone and pointed to a photograph.

"This is my daughter. Her name is Emma."

The girl lifted up her head and eyed the photograph.

"She has gone missing and I've flown here from the UK to find her and take her home."

The girl blinked, looked into his eyes, and quickly looked away, 'maybe she doesn't speak any English' he thought.

"Have you seen her at all?"

He spoke slowly, but quietly, just in case anyone was listening at the door.

The girl opened her mouth to speak, and the sound came out as a hoarse whisper.

"Help me, please help me."

She sobbed as the tears rolled down her face.

Keith could tell that the young woman was too traumatised to recognise anyone from any photograph.

To Keith's ears, she had a slight Scandinavian accent in her voice, but it was hard to tell as she started weeping uncontrollably. She began to shake. Keith thought for a moment that she might be having a fit. She gradually settled and as Keith wrapped his strong arms around her, she buried her head in his chest.

Somehow, he thought, he was going to have to escape with this girl and get her to a hospital, and then inform the police. But how? The room had bars on the window, so the only way out would be through the door; which had a massive bolt on the outside; along with three men who would probably kill him without batting an eyelid. He needed a very good plan and he needed it quickly.

At least a quarter of an hour had passed since Keith had been locked in the 'cell', and it would not be long before the door was opened when his half an hour was up. He scoured the room looking for some kind of weapon. The plastic plate and cups were useless. The plastic bucket just contained a small sample of the girl's urine. 'That may be useful' he thought if he could just throw it into one of the men's eyes. The bedside table was too heavy to lift, and then he spotted the large bolts that fastened it to the floor, the same applied to the bed. That left the sheet, which covered the young woman, the pillow, which would have been as much use as the plastic cup and plate, and the mattress. He could never lift the mattress, it was far too awkward, and he just would not have time to strip out some of the springs to use as a makeshift weapon.

Then his eyes lit up, the only other thing in the room was the washbasin and pedestal.

As Keith walked over to the basin, the girl stopped crying and eyed him curiously. He knelt down on the floor to work out how it was constructed. With a little effort, he could slightly move the basin. The entwined taps and pipes held it in place. If he had a hammer, then he could have broken it off the wall. But if he had a hammer he wouldn't have needed the basin.

The pedestal however, was a much better prospect. It had two screws attaching it to the floor, which were old and rusted. With a little force, Keith was convinced he could break them and release the pedestal from the basin above.

Quickly he went to work, pulling at the pedestal. Slowly the screws began to give, there was a slight creak as the first one gave way. Keith paused for a second, listening to see if he could hear anyone outside the room.

Nothing, just silence. Keith continued, twisting and turning until finally the second screw creaked its' way out of the floorboards. Some gooey glue substance joined the pedestal to the basin, and this provided no problem to Keith. As he peeled the pedestal free, the basin swung against the wall with a clunk.

The girl looked across at Keith a little bewildered, and a half smile registered on her face. There was no time to lose. The half an hour was nearly at an end and he was sure that the door would open early. He was right. Seconds later they heard the sound of the bolt sliding back.

"English man, your fun time is ended, you want more, you pay more."

The girl was still sitting alone on the bed as one of the muscle men entered the room. He looked surprised, expecting to see the Englishman hunched over her in some kind of sexual position. Keith appeared from behind the door wielding the pedestal in both hands. Keith had really misjudged the weight of the pedestal. He had hoped to hold it aloft and bring it down on the top of his adversary's head. The best he could do was to try to smash it up into his face. Keith swung hard. With surprise on his side, Keith swiped through the air and caught the man full force under the chin. His jaw cracked, and he fell to the floor with a crash. Keith was not sure whether he had killed the man, or just merely knocked him out. There was blood, but he did not want to wait around to find out.

Keith lowered the pedestal onto the bed, not wanting to make any more noise. Taking the girl by the hand, they slipped from the room, closed the door and slid the outer bolt back into place. They needed to tread carefully as he knew there were at least two other men around. They crept down the corridor, past some other rooms with bolts on the outside. Keith was making his plan up as he went, 'we'll get away from here and bring back the authorities to free whoever else is trapped in here' he thought to himself. As they reached the small courtyard, he could tell it was a lot darker outside; the gloom of the courtyard lit only by the glow of the solitary lamp. There was no one around, so maybe luck was on their side after all.

Keith took the lead and, hand in hand, they stepped through the archway into the 'reception' area.

Rough hands grabbed Keith from behind; it was the second muscle man. His anger fierce as he wrapped his arm tightly around Keith's neck.

Keith was forced to let go of the girl's hand; but as she made a dash for the front door, the small man stepped out of the shadows to block her path.

He tried to grab her arm, but she was too quick for him and he grabbed only air. As she darted towards the door, the girl tripped on the sheet she was wearing and tumbled against the wall. The small man grabbed for her again, and this time succeeded. Tightly in his grasp, she could taste his stale smokers' breath as his face met hers. He tried to kiss her, forcing his tongue into her mouth. Pulling away, she took a deep breath and spat in his face. As he wiped the mess from around his eyes and cheeks, he laughed and pulled her naked body tightly against his.

All the time Keith struggled as he watched the scene unfold in front of him, powerless to intervene. He was fighting for breath, as the stranglehold he was in was draining his very life away.

A rush of adrenaline overtook the girl. With freedom just a few feet away, just beyond the front door, she knew it could be her last chance. She bit the small man in the arm, sinking her teeth into his flesh and connecting with bone, he yelped with the pain and began to release his grip. But not enough. He grabbed at her again and swung her around, throwing her hard against the table. She clattered against it and the contents scattered about her. He was going to have his way with her. He was in no doubt. She deserved it. He shouted at her in English so that Keith could understand.

"I'm going to rape you, and then, I'm going to kill you."

The girl lay on the table, dazed. He dived on top of her and grabbed her hands so she could not fight back. Quickly unbuckling his belt, he started to undo his trousers. As he did so, he released his grip on her left hand. She reached amongst the table debris desperately looking for anything that she could use to defend herself. There had to be something. His hot breath on her face, his saliva dripping onto her lips. Her flailing right hand fell upon a bowl. Too light. She could smell his odour. His rancid unwashed torso had pinned her to the table. There was a jug, but it was just out of reach. The weight of his body upon her meant she could not even stretch far enough to touch it. She began kicking her legs wildly, screaming and crying as loud as she could.

The young woman felt something sharp digging in her back. She reached behind her and grabbed a fistful of papers. Receipts. And, running through their centre. A spike.

She gripped it tightly by the base with her free hand. He was on her now. Trousers round his ankles. Naked from the waist down.

Breathing hard. He was panting for his pleasure, pulling her hips towards him. She raised the spike, and thrust it forwards.

His right eye exploded on impact. The soft squelch drowned out by the man's terrifying scream. It was a scream to wake the dead. Blood spurted back in her face, but she continued to thrust, deeper, ever deeper into his skull. As the spike entered his brain, he fell silent. His lifeless corpse slipped to the floor. Her would be rapist was dead in less than a second, blood pouring from his eye socket. The girl, her body soaked in sticky red gore, wretched at the sight and the realisation of what she had just done.

The muscle man released his grip, as he looked on in horror. Keith's lifeless body fell to the floor with a thud. Now his attention turned to the girl, she knew there was no time to lose, in a moment, he would be upon her and there could be no escape. She jumped up, pulled open the door and ran.

Naked, bruised, and covered in her assailant's blood, she fled along the alleyway. The girl was a sorry sight, afraid, and running for her life. A few onlookers stared at her as she passed by. Barefoot, and sore, she ran, fighting through the pain. With her eyes streaming, it was hard to see where she was going; nearly colliding with a man on a moped, as he weaved his way through the narrow, covered streets. He swerved to miss her, and she slipped and fell sideways, into the arms of an attractive young man. His dark skin, mass of black curls and big friendly smile made her, for a split second, feel somehow at ease.

"Where are you going, sweet one? What happened to your clothes? Are you hurt?"

She could not speak. She just looked at him unable to move.

The young man slipped off his jacket and held it out to her; she grasped it gratefully and slipped it on.

"You look like you could do with something to eat. "

He spoke softly, not wanting to frighten her any more than she already was.

There was a food stall nearby, and the young man bought her some bread and a glass of fruit juice. Her eyes darted about her, worrying that her pursuer may be close. Seeing no one she recognised, she hungrily ate the bread, washing it quickly down with the orange juice. The young man instantly knew that she must be in some kind of trouble and tried to put her mind at ease.

"You are perfectly safe with me. Come; let's get you somewhere away from here, where you can get cleaned up."

The girl looked up at him, he was handsome, but not really her type. He could have been the most handsome man in the world and he still would never have been her type. But, he was kind, and the closest thing to a friend, since, the Englishman that had just tried to rescue her. Maybe she could get some help for him, or perhaps he was already dead. She had to trust someone and this well-dressed, handsome young man, with a kind face and nice smile would have to do for now.

She tried to speak, but the words would not come. She felt a little dizzy, and very tired. She wanted desperately to tell him her story. In her mind, she gathered the words, but her jaw was numb, her tongue was heavy and wouldn't move.

"My name is Liesel," she wanted to say. "I want to go home."

She could not. Her eyelids closed as her mind began to fade. She was just too tired. Within minutes, she had slipped into a deep sleep, and the young man gently gathered her up in his arms. The drug had done its' work.

"There, there, my pretty one, I'll get you somewhere safe," he whispered to her. "Somewhere where the nasty men won't find you. I'll take you to meet Mother."

Roman's unexpected bonus had come just at the right time. After that shambles when Tariq had killed a girl the previous week, they had been one short of their monthly quota. This gift from the Gods would do just fine.

25.

It was dark when Harry and Hadir returned to the 'Place de la Liberte' square. As Harry dejectedly climbed out of the taxi, clutching his rucksack and duty-free bags, he reached into his pocket and pulled out his wallet. Hadir shook his head.

"I will not take any money from you my friend, your sorrow is great, and I pray you and your daughters are reunited soon."

Hadir handed Harry a card.

"I am a father too, all I ask is, you let me know when you have found them."

Harry instantly choked up at Hadir's generosity. Two fathers from two different cultures sharing the same common bond. 'This was how the world should be' Harry thought to himself as he waved Hadir goodbye. There was no sign of Keith waiting, so he decided to make for the Medina.

As he walked, Harry reached into his pocket and pulled out his mobile phone. He tried calling Keith but there was no reply, so he left a voicemail message. As he wandered around the square, he could see the nightlife beginning to awaken. Bright lights and stallholders welcomed him at every turn. The vibrant colours of the fruit and vegetable stalls, amidst, the delicate aromas of food cooking in a vast array of spices, were enticing. For the senses, these were exciting surroundings but even though Harry was hungry, he was in no mood for celebration. Again, he tried calling Keith. Still no reply. Maybe Keith did not have reception where he was. Maybe his phone battery had run out. The evening drew on, and Harry began to feel very weary and depressed. He had been back to the square, where they had parted, about six times over the three hours to no avail. There was nothing else for it, Harry needed to eat and get a good night's rest, to recharge his batteries for the morning. He wandered back into Guilez and found a small hotel still serving food and checked in for the night.

As he began tucking into a lamb tagine, Harry tried Keith's number once again. He left yet another message detailing the name and address of his hotel. It was so strange, could Keith have discovered whatever had happened to the girls, and suffered the same fate? A million thoughts, worries and nightmares filled his head. His mind swirled. It was a bad dream, a cloud that filled his brain, a fog that would not lift, his every movement laboured, his mouth was dry, his voice tired and croaky.

And yet, there it was, he managed to find a piece of heaven, a place of safety, a refuge from the troubles of the recent days. He was happy, euphoric, this was all just a bad dream after all, and by the morning, he would awake in crisp white sheets, and this bad dream would all be forgotten.

Harry awoke two days later surrounded by a pile of empty bottles and a headache that would have floored an elephant. He had officially 'fallen off the wagon'.

26.

The morning sun streamed in through the hotel bedroom window as Harry stirred from his deep, troubled sleep. Gingerly, he opened his eyes to greet the day. He was still alive, which seemed little consolation judging by how ill he felt. He dragged himself to his feet and staggered from the bed to the bathroom, his head pounding. Falling to his knees, he was immediately sick into the toilet. Kneeling for a while, he gathered himself and crawled back into the bedroom. Hung over and dizzy, he grabbed a chair and pulled himself to his feet. Through his hazy vision, he spotted a small kettle on a plastic tray on the dressing table. Filling the kettle, with drinking water from a plastic bottle, he plugged it in and flicked on the switch. Harry sat on the bed and cursed himself for his foolishness. He had gotten himself drunk, very drunk, when so much was riding on his sobriety. He may be the only one that could save his friend and their daughters. And, he may have ruined any chance of doing so, by once more surrendering to his demons.

Steam rose and clouded the mirror on the dressing table before the kettle clicked itself off. The complimentary coffee was almost as bad as the muck he had tasted on the plane, but he took it anyway, strong and black. Harry gulped down the muddy liquid and poured himself another. He rushed to the bathroom and was again violently sick into the toilet. This may have at least cleansed his body of some of the poison he had consumed.

He turned on the taps, filled the sink and washed his face in semi cold water. Then he sank back onto the bed and, picking up a handset, switched on the television. He flicked around the stations and found the BBC World Service news channel.

He was horrified to see, by the date showing on the bottom of the screen, that he had lost a complete day. Apart from that, there was nothing really of note. More financial troubles in the Eurozone and more immigrants streaming into Europe from the troubled Syrian and Turkish territories. The little boy, Justin Hope, who had disappeared while on holiday, was still missing.

Nothing was mentioned about Morocco or either Keith or Jade and Emma's disappearances. Harry realised that he was the only person who could do anything about this mess. First thing he must do was go to the police, despite what Hadir had said.

Harry threw on his clothes and staggered out of his room. The concierge gave him a knowing smile as he teetered out into the street, just another drunken English tourist. He had to get himself together and with shoulders held straight back, he walked bolt upright, as if a wooden pole were propping up his back, into the town. After asking directions from a few passers-by and, stopping briefly to buy some bread and yet more coffee, he found his way to the police station.

The police, as expected, were not much help. They took his statement, he signed a few forms and left some contact details; and they said they would look into it and call him if they found anything. They could tell that he was still rather drunk from the night before, and his story was probably the ramblings of someone who was not of sound mind. They sent him on his way.

Harry sat on a wall not far from the police station. Bending over, he put his head in his hands and wept. Harry reached into his pocket and pulled out a napkin he had picked up in the hotel restaurant two nights before. As he did so, a small piece of cardboard dropped out of his pocket and landed on the ground in front of him. He reached down and picked it up. It was in English on one side and Arabic on the other. It read: "Marrakech Investigations."

There was an address and telephone number. The card was quite worn and had become even more creased and crumpled from being confined to Harry's pocket over the past few days, so the phone number was quite illegible. Straining his eyes in the morning sun, he managed to make out an address and the name 'Mustapha' next to the unreadable number. Through the mist of his brain fog, he had a vague recollection of the pretty woman in Rabat handing him the card. "He may be able to help," she had said.

Harry wiped his face with the napkin and staggered to his feet. This Mustapha fellow may be a long shot, but as things stood, he may be Harry's only hope. He wandered back into the Medina and spotted a tour guide leading a band of about thirty tourists across the main market square. The guide had stopped to give one of his rehearsed speeches about the history of the location, when Harry approached.

Harry explained a little of his story and that he needed to find the address on the card. The tour guide was sympathetic and said that it would probably be best if Harry joined the tour, as it would take him quite close to the location. The address was for a riad just beyond the souk and Harry knew he would lose his way trying to find it on his own.

Reluctantly Harry joined the tour, it would delay his meeting with the investigator for a short while, but he had little choice. The guide led the party through the streets, past the gaily-coloured shops, through the sweatshops of the artisan metalworkers, crafting their intricate jewellery. The party stopped to watch a man working on a most beautiful butterfly brooch. The man's eyes shone, smiling at the crowd, he knew there was a merchandising opportunity approaching. As the crowd watched in awe, the guide led Harry along a side street and out of another exit from the souk. This was a very different part of the city. It was more residential and where the buildings all seemed half built, mainly out of breezeblocks. It felt more like a slum. A sea of homes each with a satellite dish but no glass in their windows or render of any kind to cover the dull grey walls.

The guide led Harry to a few older looking streets and eventually to an old weathered wooden door. It was carved but no-where near as ornate and well cared for, as some he had witnessed since partaking of his impromptu free tour. The guide motioned to the faded rustic door and Harry gave him a few dirhams for his trouble. With a brief wave, the guide was gone and Harry stood alone.

He knocked at the door but there was no sound, save for a distant echo in the room behind the door. Harry turned the rusty ring that served as a handle and pushed. It was unlocked. The door slowly creaked open and he stepped inside.

In Marrakech there are riads, and there are riads. Some are frequented by the very poor and others by the extremely wealthy. They live side by side, and the casual passer-by would have no clue as to which class of person lived behind each door. The only clue was when you stepped inside. The riad, in which Harry stood, was not owned by anyone rich. The small entrance, containing an old wooden table, one chair and an old broken table lamp, led onto an open patio. There were dozens of plant pots, mostly containing dying or dead plants.

The owner of this particular establishment was neither rich, nor was he any kind of gardener, thought Harry. He cleared his throat.

"Hello."

Harry's voice echoed, bouncing off the walls that surrounded the patio.

There was no reply. Wandering through an archway, Harry spotted a set of stairs and carefully crept upwards. The walls were roughly plastered and coloured with a terracotta wash. Harry ran a hand along the wall, and some of the wash stained his fingers orange.

The tiled upper landing had a series of windows and balconies overlooking the patio below. Harry peered out of a window admiring the structure. 'This would have been quite a place to live about a hundred years ago,' he thought. Walking along the upper corridor, he spotted another door. This door had a sign next to it in English and Arabic, which read: "Marrakech Investigations."

Harry felt a pang of excitement as he reached out and knocked the door. There was no reply, so he turned the handle and entered. It was like stepping back in time, into a bygone age. An era that may have only existed in films or an author's imagination. Mustapha must have read every Sam Spade and Mickey Spillane novel and created his office accordingly.

A tall wooden hat and coat stand stood just inside the door, and the clanking of an old air-conditioning unit rattled close by. The room bore a stale smell of nicotine and coffee. It was quite dark, except for a tall Moroccan lamp flickering in the corner and a green shaded light that sat on a waist high plant stand. A small wooden desk, with evidence of a faux leather rectangle at its' centre, appeared buried under a pile of decaying papers.

Heavy curtains covered what Harry assumed must be the only exterior window. As he rounded the desk, he noticed a pretty face smiling back at him from inside a silver frame. He recognised the face in the photo immediately as that of Mustapha's niece from the consulate.

A filing cabinet stood open, and files stuck out above the drawers. Either they were details of old cases or maybe unpaid tax returns. Harry expected there would be a half hidden, half-finished bottle of bourbon somewhere inside one of the drawers; not for drinking, as the locals do not drink, but just to complete the effect.

The whole office lacked a woman's touch. Bookshelves stood full of ring binders and some files and folders lay in untidy piles on the floor. There were the obligatory metal blinds, covering an internal window; every pulp fiction private investigator should have such blinds.

A toilet flushed somewhere along the landing. Then footsteps. The door swung open and Mustapha stood in the doorway. He was a reasonably tall, middle-aged man, with a tired world-weary look about him. The dark rings around his eyes, probably from lack of sleep, or sunshine, were plainly visible against his wrinkled brown skin. The grey flecks of his worn-out suit matched those that glistened amongst his stubble and acted to highlight his short-cropped dark curly hair.

Mustapha muttered something in, what sounded to Harry, like Arabic, a greeting perhaps, as he extended a hand to shake.

"I'm Harry, I was given your name by…"

Harry could not remember her name, so he half pointed towards the photograph as a means of finishing his sentence.

"That's Yasmin, my niece", Mustapha continued, this time in English. "She takes care of me."

He looked like a man who needed looking after. In fact, a man just like Harry himself. Mustapha poured them both some coffee as Harry began to relate the fullest version of his story, being careful to miss nothing out. This may be the last chance to save the three lost souls and he wanted to give them his best shot.

After Harry had finished, Mustapha rocked back on his chair, carefully eyeing the notes he had been making on his pad.

"This is a tricky business," Mustapha said at last. "Most of my work is looking for missing people, and I would say my success rate is about thirty to thirty-five percent." His English was very good indeed.

Thirty to thirty-five percent did not seem to inspire much confidence, but before Harry could reply, Mustapha continued.

"People go missing all the time. In your country, in my country, all the time. Some people do not want to be found. They run away from unhappy lives, their parents, their spouses. Some people end up getting lost, or lose their memory, end up in prison and some just end up dead."

A trickle of sweat ran down Harry's back as he registered the word 'dead'.

"We do find some people, but it would be irresponsible of me to build up your hopes, and then we are unsuccessful."

"B-but, are you willing to try?" Harry stammered.

"I am willing to try, but this will not be easy, from what you have told me your friend was in Marrakech at least two days ago, and your daughters, maybe a week or maybe longer ago than that. Their trail will be much harder to follow."

"I, I can pay, whatever it costs, even if I have to sell my house, my car, everything, I just have to get them back."

Mustapha could see his new client was upset and feeling guilt for having stupidly delayed things by at least an extra day. He rose from behind his desk and reached out a hand to Harry.

"I will start to make some enquiries. It may take some time before I have any information for you, so please return to your hotel and get some rest. Just let me have your mobile phone number and I will call you as soon as I have any information."

Harry stood up to leave and shook Mustapha's hand.

"Oh, and one more thing," Mustapha added. "No more alcohol, drink water only and lots of it. If we are to succeed in this venture I will need you rested and sober."

Harry returned to his hotel, drank a full bottle of water, ate some dry biscuits and slept for the rest of the day.

Eight hours later, Harry woke to the sound of his ringtone. Expectantly, he grabbed his phone and clicked the answer button.

"Mustapha!" Harry shouted excitedly into the mouthpiece.

"This is the police," a stern voice replied. "I'm afraid we may have some very bad news for you...."

27.

Karim loved football; his dream was to be a professional footballer. His hero was the Portuguese footballer Ronaldo. He had seen him on the television. Karim's family was poor. Their house looked like it belonged on a building site. Half built, un-rendered, no glass in their windows and steel reinforcing bars sticking out above the flat roof. They did have a satellite dish connected to their television, and that was all that Karim cared about.

Apart from kicking his football about by himself, Karim loved to watch the great players from all around the world, kicking their footballs about. Best of all, he could watch them from the comfort of his own home. His father hoped that Karim might follow in his own footsteps and become a doctor, but Karim wanted to be a footballer.

The temperature was starting to cool, as Karim walked home from school. He enjoyed school and had many friends and most of them liked to play football too. Tonight, they were going to play a cup final. Every match was a cup final. He carried his football, proudly tucked under his arm, and arrived at the scrubland 'pitch', very early, long before the other boys.

Karim always did this, so he could 'soak up the pre-match atmosphere'. He expected there to be at least twelve boys, six a side, and grinned as he started laying out the rocks that were to be their goal posts. He imagined the crowds watching him play, cheering and chanting out his name, "Karim, Karim" they would shout. He ran the length of the pitch, the ball at his feet, flicked it in the air and volleyed it hard and fast between the goalposts. He ran in a circle soaking up the applause that filled his head. He collected the ball and amused himself with a quick game of "keepy-uppy". His skill level was good; he could keep the ball from touching the floor, using just his feet, for ages. He kept the ball up in the air for about twelve kicks, before it spun off the edge of his shoe and flew into the bushes. He scrabbled around in the undergrowth, trying to retrieve the ball, until he heard a noise.

An unfamiliar sound of car tyres crackled along the stony path beside the 'pitch'. Karim was a little scared, being out there on his own, so he ducked down behind the bushes and hid. After a few moments, curiosity got the better of him, and he peered out to get a look at what was happening.

The car was black and looked expensive. The sun glinted off the highly polished paintwork. It halted about thirty feet away. Doors opened, and two large men got out. One from the front passenger seat and one from the back. Karim held his breath as he watched them walk around to the rear of the vehicle. The trunk popped open and they lifted first one, then another large package wrapped in black plastic and dropped them on the ground.

Karim stifled a scream. The packages looked like they might contain bodies. He held his breath for nearly a minute, and slowly exhaled through his fingers. The men dragged the packages behind some rocks, completely hidden from the road, but in full view of Karim. A third man emerged, from the driver's seat, leaned into the trunk and pulled out a shovel.

The third man began to dig. The ground was hard, and the shovel bounced off the rocks and hard baked soil. For half an hour they worked, until at last, they slid the bodies into their shallow resting place and covered them over with the loose soil. Karim could only stare in horror.

A whistle sounded. It was distant, but he definitely heard a whistle. A referee's whistle! Karim knew immediately that it was his friends, coming to join him, and they were walking straight into danger. He looked up at the men; it was obvious they had not heard the noise. The voices of his friends were getting closer; soon they would be in sight.

Karim crawled along behind the bushes towards his friends, but as he did so, he knelt on a stick. The stick snapped. The sound echoed. Karim froze, not daring to breathe. One man stood up and the other two stopped what they were doing. They appeared to whisper to each other, standing back to back, they scanned the area around them. Karim could clearly see that one of the men held a gun.

Only the sound of the breeze filled the air. It seemed like an age before the men moved. Seemingly satisfied with their work the men got back into the car, turned the vehicle back towards the road and slowly drove away. Karim breathed a sigh of relief.

Once the car was out of sight Karim once again heard the referee's whistle, and three of his friends ran into view. Karim felt relieved and ran from his hiding place to meet them. They too had spotted the car and the men, so had ducked down behind some rocks, to hide until they had gone. Karim led his friends to the freshly dug mounds of earth that contained the two packages. The four friends took it in turns to stand as lookouts, constantly looking in the direction of the road, for fear the car might return.

There were two patches of soil, one quite large and the other a good deal smaller. The thin layers of earth barely covered the black plastic.

Karim got down on his hands and knees next to the smaller mound and started to move the loose soil away from where he thought might be a head. He recoiled as he hit plastic but recovered his nerve and began to pull at the tape that bound it.

His friend Safwah picked up a thin rock with a sharp edge. By using it as a makeshift blade, the plastic finally began to rip. The stench hit them first. The rotting smell of death rose up from the cut they had just made, making the boys gag and squirm. Before they knew what was happening, a mass of flies swarmed around their faces. The boys fell back as they wildly waved their hands about their heads, trying to drive the flies away.

After taking a moment to catch their breath, they approached the corpse again. The 'victim' had obviously been dead for a while, and, in the intense summer heat, decomposition had raged. Pulling the plastic, they saw it was indeed a head. First, they uncovered the nose. Then peeling back the covering, they found what was left of the mouth. The torn flesh was teeming with maggots and the remainder of the jaw and neck covered in a copious amount of sticky goo and dried blood. As they tore back the plastic a little further, they saw, to their horror, the victim's face. A face with one eye vacantly staring back at them, and a suppurating hole where the other eye used to be. All covered in a moving sea of flies and maggots.

Safwah dropped the rock and was immediately sick. Karim tried to use the ripped plastic to cover up the putrefying mass. The boys stood up as one and glanced nervously at the other mound. Could it be more horrific than the first?

All four boys wanted to prove how brave they were and carefully began to paw at the loose soil around the second body.

One boy screamed, there was blood all over his hands. Wet blood. The second body was still bleeding.

Karim, being a doctor's son, knew that wet blood might just mean the heart was still beating.

It could mean that this body was still alive. With all of the plastic wrapping, it was impossible to tell if the body was still breathing. Karim had been taught how to find a pulse when he was only five. He ripped the plastic from around the head and pushed his fingers deep into the folds of the tape, looking for a pulse in the victim's neck. It was hard to try to find a pulse in such circumstances. His own heart was beating so fast, it would have been easy to mistake his own heartbeat for someone else's, especially a faint one.

He quickly turned to his friend Dirar, who was a very small and slender boy.

"You are the fastest runner. Go and fetch my father he will know what to do."

Dirar ran as though the devil himself was chasing him. Within twenty minutes Karim's father Arib arrived in his small car, along with Dirar and his father Iyas.

Arib looked down at the second body and shook his head. He knelt and checked for breath and a pulse. The body was indeed alive. From the visible bruising and cuts, the man, it was quite clearly a man; had been brutally beaten, and most probably tortured, before being wrapped up and left for dead. Whoever had dumped the body could well be forgiven for thinking him dead, as the vital signs were so weak. The packaging looked hastily wrapped, which was probably the only reason the man was still alive, as the un-taped folds had allowed him just enough air to breathe.

Arib told the boys to run home and speak to no one about what they had seen. The man would need hospital treatment, and quickly, if he was to stand any chance of survival. Iyas was afraid.

"What if these bodies are of criminals, gangsters? What if the gangs find out and come after us. Maybe we shouldn't get involved."

In a second Arib had made his decision, he put his hand on his friend's shoulder.

"I cannot leave this man to die in an unmarked grave in the middle of nowhere."

Arib reached into his jacket pocket, pulled out his mobile phone and called for an ambulance.

28.

The grim voiced police officer could only tell Harry that two bodies had been found; and he should come to the hospital as soon as possible to try and identify them. Harry began shaking, he had a bad feeling in his stomach that either, the two bodies were Jade and Emma or that at least one of them would be Keith. Harry called Mustapha and asked if he would accompany him to the hospital, which he readily agreed to do. A few minutes later, they were on their way in Mustapha's, old Landrover.

On arrival, the police officer was waiting at the main reception; the pair were led to the mortuary where the police officer asked Mustapha to wait outside. Harry was shown into a small room where a single body lay on a cold stone plinth, covered with a sheet.

"Prepare yourself, this is not pretty," said the police officer quietly as he pulled back the sheet, Harry gasped, expecting the worst. It was a gruesome sight. Although the wounds had been carefully cleaned, the half-eaten face was still the stuff of horror movies.

"I do not know this man."

Harry sighed. It was a relief, all he had been told was there were two bodies, and he had not known if it would be Keith or their daughters he would be identifying.

"There is another we need you to try and identify, but he is still in intensive care."

"He's alive?"

"Barely alive," responded the police officer quietly as he led him from the room.

"It isn't the girls." Harry reassured Mustapha as he emerged from the mortuary. Harry was nearly in tears with the shock and relief that there was still some hope, no matter how slim that hope might have been.

They navigated several corridors before arriving at the intensive care unit. Again, Mustapha was required to wait; this time, in a small anteroom.

Harry entered the unit. It was very quiet save for the sounds of several heart monitors gently beeping. It contained a dozen beds all with patients on life support. Keith was in a bed near to a window that looked out over some trees. His breathing was being regulated and tubes radiated out from his body into all manner of machines. He would have been unrecognisable apart from his chin, which was larger than most.

"So, is this your friend?"

"It is. This is Keith Watson, my best friend."

Harry sat close to Keith, held his hand and spoke softly into his ear. There was no reaction. Not a hint of recognition.

Leaving Keith's bedside, they re-joined Mustapha in the anteroom. The policeman took Harry's statement and said they would liaise with the British Embassy regarding Keith's healthcare and possibly ship him back to the United Kingdom, when and if his condition improved.

Harry pulled himself together enough to call Keith's wife Andrea, but as he clicked off the handset, he broke down.

Mustapha put a hand on Harry's shoulder.

"How did she take the news?"

"I just can't..."

Harry's voice trailed away as he burst into tears.

"You need to dry your eyes and pull yourself together; we can do nothing for your friend here. That is up to the medical staff. We need to get to work to find your children and bring them home."

Mustapha was right, Keith was in the best hands, and all Harry could do now was focus his efforts into finding their daughters.

Back in the Landrover, it was Mustapha who spoke first.

We must leave Marrakech for a while. Best leave your things at the hotel, so at least anyone who may be looking for you, will think you are still in town.

"Looking for me?"

Harry was still getting his head around the sight of Keith in the hospital bed.

"Why would they be looking for me?"

"You have been to the police, and the hospital. People know you were Keith's friend and you may be trouble for them. We need to get you to a safe place, a place where we can work, and somewhere where there may be people who can help and away from anyone who may want to do you harm."

As they drove towards the edge of town, Mustapha began articulating his thoughts.

"Lots of people go missing. I've learned that even in your United Kingdom alone, every two minutes, someone goes missing. Some because they want to, and some because they are made to."

Mustapha turned right at an interchange.

"I believe that your young ladies have been kidnapped and trafficked."

Despite the warmth of the car's interior, Harry felt a shiver run down his spine.

"Trafficked?"

He repeated each syllable slowly and with amazement. It was hard to take in.

They both fell silent. Harry watched the world outside roll by, the road, the trees and passers-by, children played, traders haggled. The sun beat down on the dusty world that surrounded them as they drove. The snowy caps of the High Atlas Mountains lay ahead, far off into the distance.

"Did you know we have ski resorts in Morocco?"

Harry shook his head; he was in no mood for talking.

"Surprising for such a hot country but true."

They sat in silence, and for a while as the landscape began to change. There were now far fewer buildings and more wide-open spaces. The mountains loomed ever larger as they got closer to their destination.

"We are going to see my nephew Hassan, he helps me on some of my, ehrm, more, complex and technical cases. He is young, but he is skilled in his line of work."

"What does Hassan do?"

"He's a computer programmer."

Mustapha paused.

"A very good computer programmer and completely self-taught."

"What sort of things does he 'computer programme'?"

"Games mainly, he loves his high-tech games, but as a skilled programmer, his skills do include a bit of hacking from time to time. He learned his computer skills in Nepal, at a classroom in the foothills of the Himalayas and is one of the finest computer analysts in all of Marrakech if not the whole of West Africa."

'Hacking', Harry wondered how a computer gamer/hacker could help him get his daughter and her friend back from the hands of traffickers.

"These days..."

Mustapha paused as he negotiated a bend in the road.

"...your average criminals, traffickers, are smarter and more business-like than the thugs of the old times. They have bank accounts; they wear suits. Some have expensive tailors, cars, houses. They have staff and offices. True they still have thugs, doing their dirty work for them. But. They are more organised now. They employ specialists. Money is wired or transferred instead of being handed over in suitcases, or brown paper parcels. The coming of the internet has brought many great things, but it also has helped create criminal networks. Places where money can be hidden. There are ways that your average criminal can extort millions of pounds from an unsuspecting victim, right from the comfort of their own mansion, bedsit or internet café."

Harry was certainly aware of identity fraud, as it had happened to a friend of his. He had been duped out of thousands of pounds by an online investment scam that looked completely legit.

"But I am old, I don't even know how to switch a computer on, I've never been one of your silver surfers, but at least I know a young man who can."

The vehicle rode over a small ford and started rolling uphill. As the roads wound up and round the foothills, the scenery changed. They passed through small villages. The schools, being official buildings, all sported their customary bright red Moroccan flags waving gently in the breeze. The views were staggering, the beauty of the mountains, as were the host of crops grown by the Berber farmers.

"I am Berber and where we are going is a small village, where I grew up. My brother has a small farm up there, a few fields and some livestock, goats mainly; and sometimes he and his wife entertain the tourists in the Berber traditions to make ends meet."

After about two hours of driving, they turned down a small road, driving as far as they could before the track became too rutted and rough to drive any further. They parked and climbed out of the vehicle.

The buildings were old and ram-shackled, some had solar panels, and most had flat roofs. The village sat on the slopes of the valley, which gave way to a series of steep fields. An old man and three young boys approached, accompanied by about a hundred goats, some with bells clanking around their necks. Mustapha approached the old man and shook his hand.

"He is my brother, Ikrimah." Mustapha called across to Harry. Harry smiled and held out his hand as he walked to meet him.

Harry warmly shook Ikrimah's hand. The brothers then bade each other farewell and, with the aid of the three boys, the old man continued to herd his goats along the path.

Harry and Mustapha walked on towards the village. The sun high in the sky cast its' warmth upon them. Two small boys were sitting on a flat roof playing jacks with some stones, while another fired his catapult at a few old tin cans some distance away. The tin cans clattered as the stones found their marks.

"Wow! That kid can shoot." Harry uttered his first words for over an hour.

As they passed, the boy with the catapult walked over to them. Stripped to the waist; his dark skin glistened in the sun. With no sign of fear in his eyes, he looked up at Harry and held out his hand.

"Cigarette?"

"Pardon?"

"Cigarette?"

"He doesn't speak much English." Mustapha placed a hand on the top of boy's head.

"He just makes a little money selling cigarettes."

Harry handed a few coins to 'cigarette' boy, which he gratefully palmed and shoved in the back pocket of his shorts.

"And here it is…" Mustapha waved a hand towards a rough looking farmhouse.

"…our home for the next few days."

The investigator walked over to a side door and knocked. Harry could hear the bleating of the goats, and other animal noises in the distance. A group of about a dozen chickens were clucking and picking in the dirt around Harry's feet. The door opened and a young man, slim built, wearing gold-rimmed glasses, checked collared shirt, white shorts and bare feet opened the door.

"Hassan." Mustapha shook him firmly by the hand.

"Meet my new friend Harry, he's the man I was telling you about."

"Good to meet you Hassan." Harry shook Hassan's outstretched hand.

"Please come inside, it's a little cooler in here."

Hassan was young, probably in his mid-twenties, dark skinned with short curly hair, and a big smile. The tone and lilt of his accent betrayed the fact that he had obviously spent a few years in America.

Hassan led them through the old wooden door into his "den".

Harry was surprised as he entered, although he had not really worked out what he was expecting to see. Outside, the house looked like a plain, ordinary, rustic farmhouse. Inside was a different matter.

It was like walking into the Mission Control of some high-tech space station, albeit a very small one. Although the room seemed quite dark, banks of screens lit up the interior. Tiny green and red lamps radiated pinpricks of light. Workstations littered with keyboards, computer mice, laptops, a couple of ipads and the hum of computer fans from a bank of servers stacked in the corner. The room felt cramped and would have seemed small even if it did not house the multitude of IT equipment.

"Sorry, it's a bit messy."

Hassan cleared several piles of computer magazines off a couple of stools.

"I've just started setting up a dedicated link into the dark net, seeing if I could locate any recent activity that might give us a place to start."

"How on earth do you power all of this stuff?"

Harry seemed stunned and stood open-mouthed as he looked at the vast array of equipment.

"We have the sun, solar energy gives us quite a bit, and we do have our own generators. Plus, thanks to the recent investments in the telephone network, we have great wifi and internet connectivity up here. All this and we still use a well to get our fresh water."

Hassan smiled. He could tell the Englishman was impressed. Hassan loved to impress visitors with his passion for technology.

"So, what have you found?" Harry was impatient for news.

"First things first my friend." Hassan's softly spoken voice seemed to have a calming effect on Harry's nerves. "You have travelled far, and you must be tired and hungry. If you go up to the main house my mother will fix you something to eat. Do you like mint tea?"

"Ehrm yes, I'm sure I will." Harry did not wish to appear ungrateful.

"Then you will love my mother, she makes the best mint tea in all of Morocco, we grow it ourselves."

Mustapha took Harry outside and up the side stairs to the main house. It was quaint, and very rustic. The kitchen looked very basic, like it had been there for over a hundred years. Mustapha had said that they sometimes entertained tourists. And the tourists liked to see how things once were.

"The tourists like to think we are all simple people living the old ways. To them it may seem romantic, and who are we to shatter the illusions. In truth, we do like our old ways, but we also like to move with the times. We like comfort, but we are proud to be Berber."

As they entered the main living room, Mustapha embraced his sister in law; she did not speak any English so just smiled at Harry. She was good deal younger than Mustapha, and her pretty face, framed in her brightly coloured headscarf, gave her an air of innocence.

She motioned for them both to sit down and proceeded to prepare the tea. A young woman, Harry presumed must be her daughter, entered the room with a basket of flat bread and offered some to Harry. Harry was hungry, and the rumbling sounds his stomach was making could not deny it.

After they had eaten, Hassan sat with Harry and asked him a multitude of questions, making copious notes.

He needed the names and ages of the young women, the hotel they stayed in, the agent they booked through; even Harry's credit card number that he used for the payment. They talked of Harry and Keith's visit to the hotel and the brief phone conversation they had had with their daughters when they had first arrived.

Hours passed by and Hassan could see that Harry was getting tired.

"I have all I need to make a proper start, while you get some rest."

Mustapha led Harry to a guest room. It was simply furnished; with a single bed nestled against the far wall. Next to that stood a small set of wooden drawers and an old electric lamp with a slightly torn shade. A wooden framed picture hung from the wall, but it was so old and faded that Harry could not work out what it had once depicted. Harry flopped on the bed, fully clothed; and in a matter of minutes, he was fast asleep.

29.

Several days passed. Hassan busied himself with his technology and research, while Harry and Mustapha kicked their heels, waiting for news. Harry rose early each morning, hopeful that each new dawn would bring news of Jade and Emma. He would walk out in the fresh morning air, across the slopes, through the barley fields, watching the sunrise in the distance. The mountain people were hardy folk, but all seemed happy, happy to talk, as best they could. Happy to share, and happy to help. To Harry it was as though he had stepped back in time; to a long-forgotten world only talked about in fables. Apart from the tall new telephone pylons supporting fresh cables that snaked across the horizon, it could have almost been biblical times.

The walks helped keep Harry sane and focussed; they also helped his fitness too, which had been sadly neglected of late. One big advantage, towards Harry's immediate wellbeing, was no access to alcohol in the mountain village. In the afternoons, he sat for hours with Mustapha, on an old wooden bench, just talking.

Hassan was starting to make some headway. He had been trying to track movements of money that matched the dates of the disappearance of the girls and felt he was getting somewhere.

Hassan emerged from his 'den', which, to Harry, seemed more like a cave. He blinked as the bright midday sun bore down on his young face. Shading his eyes with his right hand, to take the glare from his reading glasses, Hassan walked purposefully towards the bench.

"I think I may have found something."

Harry and Mustapha quickly rose to their feet.

"I've been trawling the dark net looking for anything that might coincide with your daughters' disappearance, and I think I've found a money trail, and a pattern seems to be..."

Harry's mobile phone rang. The slick opening tones of Dire Straits "Money for Nothing" filled the air and echoed out across the valley.

Harry had completely forgotten it was in his pocket and even more surprised that the battery still had any charge. The number calling was unrecognisable. With trembling hands, Harry answered.

"Hello."

Harry listened carefully. He could hear what sounded like dozens of people chattering in the background.

"Hello." He repeated. This time louder.

"Ell-Oh."

A woman's voice filtered slowly into his ear, amidst the din.

"Is that Mister Turner?"

The voice sounded as if it might be of Asian origin.

"It is." Harry responded excitedly.

"Ell-Oh Mister Turner, I am calling about your claim?"

"What claim?" A puzzled frown crossed Harry's face.

"Mister Turner, it is about your claim for PPI."

The woman began talking, and Harry could tell she was reading from a script.

He sighed and clicked off the phone without uttering another word to the woman.

"Bloody PPI claim."

Harry gasped, just for a second he had raised his hopes that, somehow, it might have been Jade trying to call him.

"What is PPI?" Hassan was curious.

"It's some insurance thing, it's not important, just one of a million nuisance phone calls I get back home, that's all it is."

Hassan shrugged and continued.

"Anyway, before we were interrupted, I was telling you about the money trail. No scratch that, let me start from the beginning. I, no, we, need tea, this will take some time to explain."

As the three men ascended the stairs, Harry could not help feeling a deep sense of friendship and love developing for these two men. Men, who just a few short days ago, were complete strangers. He now felt he could trust them with his life.

They sat and talked, as Hassan's mother busied herself making them a fresh batch of mint tea. She and Hassan's sister carried in a delicious dinner of lamb and vegetables. As they sat and ate, Hassan related his news.

"I have traced your credit card as the first transaction to a website called Peachy Beaches".

"Peachy Beaches, yes I remember now." Harry's voice betrayed his excitement..

"Peachybeaches.com is, to all intents and purposes a package holiday price comparison site. It displays a selection of real holidays from real tour operators. When you book your holiday through it, you are actually booking a genuine holiday. They take a small commission, and that's how you assume that they will make their money."

Harry nodded, he had understood so far.

"The website encourages you to download an "app" which can be installed onto any computer, phone or mobile device and helps people to quickly find their dream holiday. Sounds good doesn't it?"

Hassan paused for effect and smiled.

"So, here's the darker side. Once you have downloaded the app, this helps them to get in behind your computer's firewall and security. You can try to uninstall it, and if you try it looks like you have; but it leaves some insidious tentacles behind that embed themselves into the computer registry, and its' work is totally unseen by the computer user. The only difference you may see is your computer is a fraction of a nano-second slower. Such a small difference that a human eye would never detect it."

Hassan took a sip of tea, cleared his throat and continued.

"Now these tentacles track your every keystroke, they can infiltrate into your online accounts, your social media, your photographs, so they know what you look like, Facebook posts and bank account passwords and transfers the information either back to a central server or somewhere in the cloud. It is so sophisticated, it makes identity theft almost seamless."

This was a lot for Harry to take in. He had never really bothered with computers or Facebook or that Twerking (or was it Tweeting?) thing that Jade had kept on talking about. But in light of his current situation, he wished he had paid more attention. Hassan looked Harry straight in the eye.

"Harry, you said that your friend mentioned that he'd spotted your daughter arriving back at Gatwick, but he was mistaken, then you said the authorities told you that your daughter and her friend had in fact left Morocco on that plane and arrived back in the UK and had then simply chosen to disappear for whatever reason."

"That's right, Keith did say that."

"Well this might explain it. If you happen to be an illegal trafficker or drug smuggler, and you happen to know what a visitor to a foreign country looks like. You know how old they are, and who they are travelling with, it would be so easy to find someone, among the thousands of asylum seekers, or illegals, that you want to ship into a chosen country, who looked like a certain passport holder. All you need to do then is kidnap the visitor and take their passport. Then your 'illegal', who may have paid a fortune, or one of your sex workers, gets a real passport and a real airplane ticket. The chances are if they keep their mouths shut and do not draw any attention to themselves they will get through the destination passport control unchallenged. Once inside the country they can destroy the passport; just in case the original person is reported as missing"

Hassan took a deep breath and another sip of tea.

"If you have enough time, especially if someone has booked up to a year in advance, you can arrange to get your 'illegal' some plastic surgery to make them look more like the person in the passport. All the time you are making money, from the legitimate sale of a holiday, to the illegal sale of a passport, ticket and traffic of who knows who, who knows where. The kidnap victim could either be killed or trafficked themselves."

"Yes," agreed Mustapha. "Europeans are now favoured by the sex traffic gangs, a Moroccan prostitute would probably work for herself, but would have to be very careful to avoid being stoned to death. These gangs used to just prey on runaways, but the quality, as they see it, could be poor. This way Facebook or Instagram photographs could be turned into an online trafficker's catalogue."

"The dark web has given up a few more of its' secrets."

Hassan scratched his nose and continued

"There also appears to be a trade of exporting women and girls across North Africa, if a woman is kidnapped in the east, she is moved to the west and vice-versa. At roughly the same time as your young women disappeared, I have found details of a money transfer and some emails relating to a haulage company collecting two young white women from Marrakech for onward trans-shipment to Egypt."

"Egypt?" Harry gasped.

Mustapha put a reassuring hand on Harry's shoulder.

"Morocco has just two external borders, Algeria and Mauritania. But, the borders between Morocco and the rest of the Western Sahara are locked tight and so, if they were travelling by road, they would probably have to pay bribes to get them safely through the militarised zone, into Algeria. The obvious route would then be Algeria across to Libya, Libya to Egypt."

They finished their meal and Hassan led them back down to his 'den'.

"So, what is our next step?" Harry asked.

"Let me see what else I can find out," replied Hassan, sitting back down at his terminal.

As he gazed at his computer screen, a look of horror washed across his face. Frantically he began typing as fast as he could.

"It cannot be, it cannot be." He started to panic. "I've been reverse hacked."

Harry felt a cold shiver run down his spine, he had no idea what 'reverse hacked' meant, but he could tell from Hassan's expression that it was not a good thing.

"When I entered the last company domain, just before dinner, I must have triggered a silent alarm that alerted their system that I was snooping. I had tried to cover my tracks bouncing my location across dozens of servers and satellites across the globe."

"That's good, right?" Harry was trying to calm himself, hardly understanding what it all meant.

"They've somehow tracked me back." Hassan frantically started to unplug the numerous pieces of equipment that adorned the room. Mustapha and Harry joined Hassan in switching everything off. Hassan was shaking as he broke his silence.

"I think they know where we are."

Hassan had indeed bounced his signal across many satellites and servers, to try and hide their physical location, but the trace he had put on the system when downloading and testing the app was now tracking back to him, unveiling and relaying their location.

The room fell into complete darkness, and the friends, along with the fans and flickering clicks of the servers fell into complete silence. Straining their ears, there was nothing, just silence.

And then it began, at first it was very faint, but then all too clear, the silence was broken by the whirring of a distant helicopter.

30.

Ikrimah was high on the hillside, feeding his goats, when he heard the noise. Gazing to the sky, he could just about make out a dark speck in the distance, travelling at speed. A faint 'chucka-chucka' resonated in the breeze. The shape approached. As it got closer, he could plainly make out the shape of a helicopter. With a roar it flew straight over his head and off into the distance, gradually banking as it disappeared into the sun. His ankle length grey tunic swished from the breeze of the rotors as it passed.

Ikrimah shielded his eyes against the brightness. His dark, heavily sun-lined face just visible beneath his white woollen hat. He squinted. The craft was turning, circling overhead. He was used to seeing the sunlight glint off large jumbo jets, high in the sky, or the odd light crop-spraying plane. This was different.

The helicopter had reduced altitude and was circling above the village, as if looking for a place to land. It hovered for a while and set down in a barley field close to his farmhouse. Skilfully guiding his herd over the rocks, he made his way back down the valley towards the village. Ikrimah sensed there would be trouble.

Three men jumped out of the craft as it landed, heads ducked under the spinning blades, fanning out as they approached the farmhouse. They were clad in lightweight dark suits, one pinstripe, the others plain black. Each wore a pair of designer sunglasses. They moved with a stealth and precision that suggested military training. The lead man, 'pinstripe', held what looked like a mobile phone out in front of him. Using hand signals, to communicate instructions, they approached the side of the building. As they reached the door to Hassan's 'den', they spread themselves flat with their backs against the outside wall.

'Pinstripe' put one hand on the door handle and in the same movement, drew a pistol from inside his jacket. The other two 'black suits' drew their weapons and, on a silent count of three, opened the door and darted inside.

The room was in complete darkness.

'Pinstripe' felt around for a light switch, waving his pistol in the darkness. He found what he was looking for and flicked the switch. The light bulb cast its' dim glow as they came face to face with three dishevelled looking men in a room full of computer equipment and cables in various stages of disconnect.

'Pinstripe' motioned for them to sit. Dragging three stools into a semi-circle, they sat despondently looking at each other, guessing what was about to happen next.

"Very clever, very clever, but not clever enough."

'Pinstripe' was in charge. His voice soft and confident with an Eastern European tone. He was in his mid-to-late fifties, with small flecks of grey amidst his thinning black, slicked back hair. His two companions were younger, one in his twenties the other in his late thirties, sat expressionless with pistols drawn and pointed at Harry and Mustapha.

"So why do you go meddling in matters that do not concern you?"

"They are helping me get my daughter back." Harry blurted out the words without even thinking. The youngest 'black suit' reached behind him and closed the door, deadening the sound of the spinning rotors.

"You," 'Pinstripe' pointed his gun towards Hassan. "What have you learned?"

Hassan struggled for an answer, he had loved the investigation, the uncovering of the truth, but coming face to face with the people he had been spying on was a completely different game.

"N-n-not much." Hassan stuttered. He knew that they knew he was lying.

"Enough, first I shoot your friend then you tell me what I want to know."

'Pinstripe' aimed his pistol at Mustapha's knee.

"O-o-okay, please do not shoot." Hassan rose to his feet.

"Please just let me show you."

'Pinstripe' eyed Hassan suspiciously.

"Just let me plug a few of these things back in and I'll show you what I did and how I did it." Hassan gathered up some of his cables and began to plug them back into the machines. Server lights twinkled as the computers began to warm up.

"It should not take long." Hassan's hands were shaking as he struggled to type a few commands into the keyboard. Several times he fumbled and red error messages appeared on the screen.

'Pinstripe' was impatient, pressing the muzzle of his pistol into Hassans' back. As he cleared his throat to speak, there came a knock on the door.

The second 'black suit' turned and 'Pinstripe' motioned to Hassan mouthing at him, not to try anything silly.

"Hassan, my son, would you and your friends like some tea?" Ikrimahs' voice, slightly muffled by the wooden door, had a nervous edge.

The younger 'black suit' motioned to Hassan to go to the door, and as Hassan passed 'Pinstripe' he whispered darkly:

"You say or try anything, and all of your family dies."

Hassan trembled as he slowly approached the door. The end may have come for himself, his uncle and the sad Englishman, but he must do something to save his father. With hands shaking, he pulled the door open.

"Pappy, I don't think…"

Hassan did not see it coming. The force hit him full in the face and as he fell backwards, his assailant was not a man at all, but a chicken. Clucking and fluttering, it had been thrown through the air, closely followed by two more chickens and three goats. Seconds later a flood of animals swept into the tiny room. Clucking, bleating and pecking as they came. 'Pinstripe' fired a shot at the first goat. The animal screamed in pain as the bullet struck home. A thick blood mist sprayed from the hole in its' neck.

Mustapha grabbed for the younger 'black suit' and wrestled with the gunman amongst the oncoming livestock. The pistol fell from his grip and smacked against the stone floor. The room became a chaotic sea of chickens and goats. Older 'black suit' wrapped his elbow around Mustapha's neck. He started to choke Mustapha, who was forced to release his grip on the younger man. From behind, Harry grabbed older 'black suit' around the face and dug his nails into his cheeks.

Hassan, his back to the floor, grappled with 'Pinstripe'. A pistol jabbed into his ribs. Hassan closed his eyes as he felt 'Pinstripe' begin to squeeze the trigger. A rock careered through the air. It struck 'Pinstripe' on the temple.

With a cry of pain, he fell to the floor, blood pouring from a gash just above his right eye. 'Pinstripe's' vision was a blur. He lifted his pistol thinking he was aiming at Hassan's face and, in the confusion, fired. The younger 'black suit' slumped to the floor. His face blown apart. Blood brain and bone sprayed across the wall and computer screens.

Amongst the goats, chickens and would be assassins, there were villagers entering the fray. Armed with rocks, sticks and agricultural tools, they attacked the two remaining men.

A villager struck the older 'black suit' repeatedly about the head with a rock. As he collapsed, blood bubbled out of his mouth.

'Pinstripe' made a dive for the door. On hands and knees, he crawled. Pelted by rocks. 'Pinstripe' half stumbled, half ran back towards the waiting helicopter.

As 'Pinstripe' approached the spinning rotors, the helicopter began to take off. 'Pinstripe' cursed the pilot and grabbed hold of the landing bar. He swung from the underside of the helicopter, and in doing so, unbalanced the craft. The helicopter rocked and a hail of missiles, thrown by the villagers, rained down on it and the defenceless 'Pinstripe'. Bleeding and shouting to the pilot, he hung on for his life.

All of the villagers were out of their houses, peppering the helicopter and 'pinstripe' with bricks and pebbles. The pilot spun the aircraft around, doing his best to dodge the projectiles. 'Pinstripe' flailed around like a rag doll. With one arm wrapped around the landing gear, just about managing to hang on.

Harry fought his way through the animals and fell through the doorway into the sunshine. It was then he spied the young "cigarette" boy. Standing a few feet away from the crowd, the youngster stood in a trance, carefully watching the scene unfold.

'Cigarette' bent down to pick up a pebble, never once taking his eyes off the helicopter. Gripping his catapult firmly in his right hand, he straightened up, closed his left eye and took aim. His actions were slow and deliberate. Holding his nerve, he waited for the precise moment. The helicopter spun round again. "Cigarette" timed his shot to perfection. The pebble whistled through the air like an arrow. He had waited for the side opening of the helicopter to come into view. The pebble entered the inside of the craft, just above 'Pinstripe's' head. The pilot, who was too busy trying to dodge the larger rocks, never saw it coming.

The pebble struck the pilot's temple with such force, he fell towards the windscreen, and in doing so thrust the joystick forward. The helicopter tilted in the air. The pilot's lifeless body fell forwards onto the cracked windscreen, which gave way under his weight. The craft flipped upside down in the air as 'Pinstripe' released his grip and fell towards the spinning rotors beneath him. A last look of horror crossed 'Pinstripe's' face as he knew his end had come; his body carved into pieces, as the rotors hacked through his flesh.

As the craft descended, the crowd scattered in all directions and Harry dived for cover back into Hassan's room. The blades dug into the earth below as the whole craft suddenly became motionless. A second later, with the sound of wrenching metal, it toppled over in a heap. "Cigarette" without moving a muscle, stared emotionless at the carnage he had caused.

There was silence, an eerie silence. Harry could smell something. A handful of villagers cautiously approached the wreckage, but Harry saw them and shouted for them to stop. He heard the soft trickle of liquid on metal. A small spout of fluid had sprung out of the fuselage. It was aviation fuel. Quickly, they ran, hiding behind the buildings and rocks.

The explosion rose majestically towards the sky. Flames and smoke engulfed the twisted wreckage with the smell of burning fuel tainting the air.

When the flames had died down, the villagers dragged the remaining bodies from Hassan's 'den' and tossed them into the blaze.

The helicopter had become a funeral pyre.

31.

Flames licked the burning bodies, as the crumbling wreckage blackened and twisted in the intense heat. Mustapha, his arms around Hassan and Harry' shoulders, led them back towards the 'den'.

"We need to move fast, we may have won this round, but, once they find out their helicopter has not returned, they will be back."

Hassan, his face bloody and bruised, turned to Harry.

"It would not be safe for you to return to Marrakech or try to fly by normal means to Egypt."

Harry knew that Hassan was right. He had to get to Egypt but could easily be picked up at the airport or at any of Morocco's seaports. He sat on a stool with his head in his hands. Mustapha gently put his hand on the top of Harry's head.

"I know a man who might be able to help."

Harry looked up.

"He's a little unconventional, but he has the heart of a lion; and best of all…"

Mustapha paused; there was a mischievous glint in his eye.

"…he has a plane."

Hassan motioned to his uncle as he began to un-plugging his computer equipment.

"You must leave now, and so should we."

"Hassan is right, the longer we linger here, the more dangerous it will be."

Hassan paused to shake Harry by the hand.

"My friend, I hope you find your daughter and soon we will all again drink tea together to celebrate."

There was a tear in Hassan's eye as he spoke, the young computer expert was a good man and Harry, with a lump in his throat struggled to utter the words:

"Hassan, thank you for everything."

Harry hugged the young computer expert. Hassan had provided the only clue that might yet rescue Jade and Emma, and Harry was eternally grateful.

"I have your number and will call you as soon as we find out anything," Hassan added.

Mustapha turned to his nephew. "I will be back soon to help you, we will relocate back to the city where we can continue our work hidden away amongst the crowds."

As Hassan continued his frantic dismantling, Mustapha and Harry took their leave.

Minutes later, the two comrades were speeding through the staggering scenery of the High Atlas Mountains. Harry stared out of the car window deep in thought.

The snow-capped mountains in the distance appeared as a mirage against the scorching heat of the afternoon sun. They spoke little on their drive, the incident with the helicopter and the enormity of task that lay ahead weighed heavy in their hearts.

The vehicle wound around many bends, with views down into steep valleys. They crossed streams and travelled through many small villages.

'Morocco is such a beautiful place,' thought Harry. '…and in different circumstances would be a fabulous terrain to explore.'

After driving for nearly an hour, they came to a small outcrop of land, where Mustapha stopped and applied the handbrake.

"Here is the airfield." Mustapha announced proudly.

Even to Harry's untrained eye it did not look like any airfield he had ever seen before. It was a flat patch of dry ground sitting amongst the scrub. The only reason Harry could discern that it could be called a 'field' at all, was that it contained a few less rocks than some of the surrounding areas.

They got out of the car and marched towards a mud brick shelter next to a large barn with a badly rusted corrugated iron roof. A handful of colourful chickens were picking in the dust. Two large solar panels glinted just beyond the building. As they approached the shelter, the front door opened and there stood a suntanned giant of a man.

Mustapha smiled, and gestured towards the giant with his open palm.

"I'd like to present you to my very good friend Leo Zettler."

Leo Zettler, stood tall and proud. A bear of a man. Stripped to the waist, grey chest hair flecked his dark brown leathery skin. A big beaming smile lit up his face as he recognised his friend.

"Leo!"

"Howdy Mustapha!" His loud American accent boomed. "What brings yer to these parts, and who's yer friend?"

Leo outstretched a hand as Harry approached. They shook hands. Zettler's grip was firm and could have easily crushed Harry's hand had he wanted to.

"We have a great favour to ask of you, my friend," ventured Mustapha.

"This is Harry, his daughter Jade is the victim of traffickers and we believe she and her friend are being transported to Egypt."

"That's real bad," replied Zettler, "and they could be anywhere in between here and Egypt I guess. So where do I fit in?"

Zettler had a glint in his eye, he knew what was coming; and with that big smile across his face, Mustapha knew he knew.

"I need you to take me to Egypt," stammered Harry adding, "I can pay, whatever it costs."

"Egypt is pretty far, I guess you can't go the legal way?"

"It's going to be too dangerous to travel that way," explained Mustapha. "We had a close shave back at Ikrimah's farmhouse; and I'm sure they will be looking out for any of us if we tried to get out through the regular airports."

"Okay I'll do it, it's been a while since I had an adventure, and as it's in a good cause, and a favour for a friend of Mustapha I'd be glad to help."

"How soon could we leave?" Harry was keen to keep moving.

"Well it'll be sundown soon, so I guess we'd better leave it 'til first light, that'll give me a few hours to fuel her up and get her ready, you stayin' for some chow Mustapha?"

They could both sense that Leo Zettler was quite looking forward to his new adventure.

Mustapha shook his head. "Sadly no, I have to go back to help Hassan pack his equipment, and then relocate us to somewhere safer. Another time for certain. There is one thing I forgot to mention Harry. I have a friend who works for the Egyptian military his name is Guryon. I will let him know you are coming. He may be able to help when you arrive."

"Well, ah wish you a safe journey Mustapha," said Zettler. "Such a shame you'll be missing out on some great tucker."

Mustapha turned to Harry, who opened his arms wide and hugged him, as he would have done his own brother.

"Be safe my friend, you have my number in your mobile phone, and I have yours, we will continue our work to find your young ladies. Keep the faith and we will keep in touch."

Harry, feeling tired and emotional, felt the tears start in his eyes. He had not known Mustapha for long, but in him, he felt he had found a true friend and kindred spirit. Someone who would help a stranger in need and risk so much for nothing in return, Mustapha was a good man.

"Thanks to you and Hassan for all you have done."

As Mustapha turned to go, Harry stopped him.

"We will find Jade and Emma and we'll all be back for some more of that mint tea."

Mustapha smiled, and he hoped, above all else, that it would be so.

In the dark days that were to come, the 'mint tea promise' would prove to be more difficult to keep than any of them could ever have imagined.

32.

They waved as Mustapha's vehicle turned away and disappeared in a cloud of dust. Harry's attention turned to Leo Zettler, his new companion. The big American was quite a character and as loud as he was broad. He stood approximately six feet five inches tall. On his feet, a pair of old brown leather sandals; on top of his head sat his fake designer sunglasses; and below his tanned belly he sported brightly coloured Hawaiian shorts, the legs of which hung down just below his knees.

Harry guessed that he must have been about fifty years old, judging by his ruddy complexion and the creeping swathes of grey amongst his dark brown curly hair. With a big beaming smile across a suntanned face and bright blue eyes that glinted in the sunlight, Harry somehow felt immediately at ease with this stranger.

"Mustapha is a good man."

Zettler's accent was strong and had a deep southern drawl.

"I first met him when I came out to Morocco for some R and R after serving in the Gulf war, Desert Storm they called it; back in the nineties. We got talking, in some restaurant that he used to part own, over a tagine or two. I thought he was just keeping me talking because I was spending money in his joint, but it turned out he was really interested in hearing my stories. I was going through a rough time, what with battle stress an' 'all. Mustapha must have took pity on me or sumpt'n', and he let me stay rent free, in his spare room. I must have put him through hell though, with all that waking up screaming."

Harry listened as they stood looking out over the mountains. The sun warmed their faces as the chickens scratched in the dirt around their feet.

"Things were going bad for him with the restaurant, and he had to sell, and somehow he got suckered into doing that private investigator thing. I think he just likes helping people.

He got me set up here as he knew I could fly a plane, and I also flew choppers back in Desert Storm, so he knew some of them Berber people up here, and them being farmers an' 'all, what better for a pilot helping farmers doing a bit of crop dusting for them."

Harry already knew that Mustapha was one of the good guys, and now he was getting a feeling of how good he really was. Then there was this big American, Leo Zettler, war veteran, maybe even a hero, mentally scarred by whatever he had been through; but another seemingly good soul. This was all a far cry for Harry, and his home back in Lichfield, his safe, sad, boring little life. This was the start of the adventure of a lifetime, trekking across North Africa into who knows what or where. Even with the sadness of the reason for the trek, under the surface there was a glimmer of excitement. Harry was finally living again, he might just be the knight in shining armour, all he needed was to rescue his beloved daughter Jade and her friend Emma, and his life would be transformed.

"Do you want to come see her?"

Zettler strode off towards the barn, obediently, Harry followed.

They entered the ram-shackled barn that doubled as an aircraft hangar. Harry could see an old rusting truck; random pieces of metal strewn around the floor; an old fibreglass canoe; an array of tools cast upon old wooden workbenches; and in the centre of the barn stood a small plane where a huge tarpaulin; with about a dozen ropes dangling over the side, covered most of the wings and cockpit.

Zettler grabbed one of the ropes and motioned to Harry to grab another and they hauled aside the covering to expose the fuselage.

"It hasn't been out in over a month," said Zettler, "it ain't really crop spraying season right now, especially since I ran out of spray."

He laughed. A big booming laugh that echoed around the barn.

The plane was white and quite compact, with a small propeller on the nose cone. The cockpit sat below the wings and the spraying mechanism fastened below the wings and underbelly. The windscreen and windows were tinted black, so from the outside no one could actually see who was flying the craft.

It was old, but not so old to give Harry any fear of it getting off the ground. But, Egypt was a long way. Even with Harry's schoolboy knowledge of geography, he knew they would have to fly across several mountain ranges and worst of all, the Sahara Desert and Libya to get there.

Zettler moved around to the side of one of the workbenches and pulled out a long hosepipe, which he fed into a large tank at the back of the barn, then climbed up onto the plane and undid the fuel cap.

"This is the bit I don't like."

Zettler sucked the end of the hosepipe. He must have had a huge capacity in his lungs to suck the fuel from that distance. Zettler coughed and spluttered as the fuel entered his mouth. He pushed the hose into the plane's fuel tank and spat out the contents of his mouth at the same time.

"I'll get her filled up and then we'll need to take some extra in those cans as we'll never make it on one tank."

Zettler pointed to a small pile of jerry cans in the corner, and Harry collected them, two at a time, and brought them back to the plane.

Once the plane's fuel tank was full, Zettler handed down the still running hosepipe and trying to spill as little as possible, Harry duly began to fill the cans. Zettler fastened up the plane's fuel cap and jumped down from his perch.

"While you finish off here I'll go and get us something to drink and get this bad taste out of my mouth."

Zettler moved towards the barn doorway, paused for a moment and turned his head slightly back to his new assistant.

"Harry, how do you take your coffee?"

"White with two sugars."

"Well son, that's a pity."

Zettler shrugged.

"I was hoping you'd say black, no sugar, you see I ran out of sugar a while back and I don't have a goat for the milk, so how's black, no sugar grab ya?"

"That will be fine."

"Glad to hear it, anyways that's at least one good thing about this country, the coffee is great."

Zettler returned to the shack to make the coffee, leaving Harry to finish off fuelling the cans. Once the last can was about full Harry pulled the hose from the big tank and dribbled the last of the fuel into the final can. After screwing the tops up tight, Harry made his way to the shack to find Zettler pouring the coffee.

As Harry sipped on the warm brown liquid, the coffee aroma filled his nostrils, he closed his eyes and, just for a moment, his mind drifted back in time. It was a Sunday morning and Vicky was brewing coffee in the kitchen. The smell of the coffee beans ran through the entire house. Jade was doing her homework at the kitchen table and all was good with the world. He opened his eyes; the big American was staring at him, as if waiting for Harry to say something. Zettler moved his head to one side.

"Well what'd you think, good ain't it?"

Harry nodded, and the big American moved his lips towards his own mug.

Harry drifted back from his dream.

"Yes, it's really good coffee, it reminds me of home."

That evening they sat down to a hearty feast. Zettler had brought some goat steaks on a recent visit to the market in Marrakech, and with vegetables and some eggs from the chickens, they supped on strong coffee and ate well. They talked for hours about their situation, about their lives. Harry learned of the wartime traumas and the resulting nightmares that had led Zettler to split with his wife and come to live in a remote spot in the Atlas Mountains.

Harry spoke of his family and their own personal tragedies. The events of the past few days finally caught up with Harry, and despite the worries and danger he had faced, and the overdose of caffeine he had consumed, sleep overcame him in a huge wave. As he sank into a deep slumber, Zettler laid a thin blanket over him as he would his own son.

The next morning Harry awoke to sunlight streaming in through the living room window and the crackle of eggs frying in the adjacent kitchen. The sofa that Harry has slept on had been quite uncomfortable, but despite this, he had slept remarkably well.

The eggs and brewing coffee smelled so good. Zettler whistled "Sweet Home Alabama" as he cooked the breakfast and seemed positively excited about the adventure to come. This gave Harry at least a morsel of confidence in his new companion. Zettler certainly appeared to be a man to have on your side in a scrap.

Zettler paused his whistling when he saw Harry in the kitchen doorway.

"Howdy young feller!"

"Good morning Leo."

Harry yawned and simultaneously breathed in the divine coffee aroma.

"Most of these local dudes drink mint tea, all the time it's mint tea. Now, I don't mind it, but you can't beat that strong shot of Java first thang in the morning."

He re-commenced his whistling, this time it was Rick Danko's "Java Blues" and not a song that Harry was familiar with; he was more of an Elton John/Beatles fan; but the fact that Zettler seemed confident helped to settle Harry's nerves a little more.

They sat and ate their breakfast, chatting about lighter things, mostly about the weather, sport, TV shows and Zettler showed Harry a few of the souvenirs picked up on his many travels, including a fancy crystal flower formation he called a desert rose.

The journey they were about to make was foremost in both of their minds but sitting down to a 'normal' breakfast raised their spirits immeasurably. As Harry began to clear away the mugs and plates, Zettler stopped him.

"Just stick those critters in the sink; I'll wash them up later when we get back."

It was as if they were going out for an hour's joyride in his plane, then back for an afternoon's chilling out; and not setting off on a perilous journey over some of the most dangerous countries in the modern world, where the desert was probably the least of their worries.

Within twenty minutes, it was time to set off. Zettler had already taxied the plane out of the workshop and loaded the fuel cans, blankets, water and food. There was no room for anything else in the small cockpit; in fact, there was only just enough room, as the two of them had to clamber over the provisions to slide into their seats.

"Survival purposes only."

Zettler flicked his head towards the bottles and bags of food. Harry noted that clothes, shampoo, soap and the like would only add extra weight and therefore would have needed extra fuel to transport.

Harry had not managed to wash or brush his teeth in days. When they got back, he vowed to treat everyone involved to a hotel break at a luxury spa. He would even sell his car back home to pay for it. He mentioned his thoughts to Zettler who roared with laughter.

"Son, you got yourself a deal."

Keys in the ignition, Zettler fired the plane into life. The engine roared and the plane trundled along the rough ground. Zettler knew the best line to take to avoid the rocks on the ground, and although they bumped across a few, they were soon picking up speed.

"Hold onto your hats, here we go."

Zettler screamed to make himself heard above the rattle of the engine. Harry sat back in his seat quietly. There was so much to think about. First, they had to get to Egypt; then with the aid of Mustapha's friend Guryon, find out where the traffickers had taken Jade and Emma. Then they somehow had to rescue them. Maybe the Egyptian police would be more helpful than the Moroccan and British authorities had been. He had little doubt that Zettler would also have some ideas when they got there. Obviously, Egypt was a big country and the girls could be anywhere. First stop they agreed would be Cairo and then see what help the British Consul would afford them.

33.

The Atlas Mountains stretched out ahead. Somewhere below was Ikrimah's farmhouse and the wreckage of the downed helicopter. Harry hoped that Hassan and Mustapha had managed to clear out and get to somewhere safe before anyone else found them.

On they flew, across mountains, small towns and villages, they followed dirt roads and large stretches of sand and scrub. Zettler explained to Harry that they could not fly too high as the first thing they wanted to avoid was coming into contact with the Algerian air force; and keeping reasonably low should keep them out of their radar contact; plus, his plane was a crop duster and not really designed for higher altitude flying.

"The only thing we need to be wary of is being shot at from the ground," said Zettler, "...so we need to keep our eyes peeled for any sign of movement down there."

Harry had begun to feel quite confident up to this point, but now he began to feel a wave of panic wash over him. His eyes scanned the ground below looking for the enemy. He had no idea who that enemy might be, but then it really could be anyone, anywhere.

On they flew, across the Algerian Maghreb, below them a barren landscape as mountains gave way to desert.

"Hey Harry!" Zettler shouted to be heard above the noise of the engine.

"Did you know that Algeria is the tenth biggest country in the world, and the biggest one in the whole of Africa?"

Zettler was trying to put Harry at his ease and forget a little about the deadly threat that lay below.

"...and they reckon there's a ton of oil down there somewhere."

The sun was shining brightly, it was a good day for a flight, visibility was good and there was very little in the way of wind, perfect conditions. They flew on into the sun unchallenged.

They crossed over what looked like a main arterial road; it was busy with quite a few trucks heading North and South along it.

"Just a little way up there…" Zettler pointed to their left.

"…is Ghardaia, beautiful architecture it's one of those UNESCO world heritage sites."

"Maybe I'll take Jade there one day." Harry tried to sound interested, but he knew that Jade would have probably hated it. She never much liked museums. Jade. Harry tried to picture his daughter's face, but it would not come to him. Just like Vicky's face had faded from his memory. He reached into his pocket and pulled out his wallet. There was a photo in the little clear plastic slot in front of his credit cards. His two women grinned back at him. A silly little photo taken in one of those passport photo booths when Jade was ten. Harry wiped a tear from his eye and slipped the wallet back into the safety of his pocket.

They sat in silence for a while, save for the roar of the engine. The heat of the day was upon them and they each drank several bottles of water as the dripping sweat coated their clothes.

"We're not far to the Libyan border now, just to the left there's Ouargla. I stopped there in the eighties, where I bought that 'desert rose' thing from the old rock market there. Quite a fancy thing, don't you reckon?"

The constant attempt at small talk was having no effect on Harry, maybe it was the heat, the worry of the dangers ahead, the thoughts of Jade, or maybe it was the fact they were about to cross into Libya. From what Harry had seen on the television news, Libya was one of the most dangerous countries in the world, lawless and terrifying, ever more so since the fall of Muammar Gaddafi in 2011.

Another hour passed by as Zettler glanced at the fuel gauge. "We're getting a bit low on juice; I think we're going to need to find somewhere to land."

Skilfully, Zettler lowered the craft towards an outcrop of barren scrubland.

"This will do."

As they gently touched down, the plane bounced slightly. The rocks and boulders below the wheels made it shudder before coming to a halt on the dry cracked soil. Harry looked about him expecting to see the enemy all around. There was nothing, just a haze from the heat of the day heading off into the distance blurring the horizon.

"Best stretch your legs it's going to be a long next leg."

Zettler stretched his arms and clambered out of his seat. Harry jumped down and hobbled slightly as his feet and legs once again became accustomed to his body weight.

Zettler whipped out a couple of the jerry cans, climbed up, unscrewed the fuel cap, and quickly began pouring the fuel into the tank.

"We don't have a lot of time son." He called down to Harry. "Keep yer eyes peeled for bandits."

Harry shaded his eyes. Even with his sunglasses, the brightness of the sun was making it very hard to see any distance. Then he thought he heard something, it sounded like an engine, it was far off. Yes, it sounded like the engine of a truck or something very similar.

"Time to leave," shouted Zettler, "I think they're on our trail."

"Who are they?"

"I'm not sure but I don't want to hang around to find out."

Both men scrambled back into the plane and took their seats. Zettler turned the key, the engine stalled. The sound of the approaching engine was getting closer, and they could hear the faint chatter of the men in the approaching vehicle. Harry glanced over his shoulder. The approaching men were very close, dressed in long dark robes and they had guns, their hands waving they gesticulated towards the plane.

"They don't look very happy." Harry's, voice was shaking.

Zettler turned the key again, and the engine burst into life.

"Let's get this sucker in the air."

Zettler shouted, as he began the run up to take off. A host of bullets spun through the air; luckily, the chasing truck had struck a boulder and bounced, sending the spray of bullets off course skimming alongside the cockpit narrowly missing the spinning propeller. On the plane rattled, picking up speed, the open-backed truck still chasing, trying to keep up with the taxiing crop duster. Another salvo of bullets. This time their aim was better. The bullets thumped into the side of the fuselage.

"If they hit the fuel tank it would all be over."

Zettler fought with the controls as more bullets zinged past the cockpit.

"Here we go, hang on to your hats; this is going to get hairy."

Zettler was in his element. In his mind, he was back flying missions in the Gulf. As he pulled back the column, the airplane left the ground and nosed skyward. Zettler breathed hard, that was a closer call than he had wanted to make so early in their journey.

Harry looked below as they finally crossed the border into Libya. Zettler had never set foot in this country, so he had no tales to tell or small talk to deliver. He looked out at the scenery below, sand, sand and yet more sand.

They were deep into Libyan airspace and skating above the endless dunes of the Sahara Desert. Mile after mile they flew. Harry's head dropped and lolled around for a second as he began to fall into an unintentional doze. He forced his eyes open, and before he had chance to lift his head, he noticed a dark pool underneath Zettler's seat.

"Leo! You're hit!"

"Yup, I think you're right." Zettler's voice betrayed the pain he was feeling.

"I felt the pain, but I reckon I just need to keep flying, we can't stop. I'll take a look at it when we get there I reckon."

Looking up at Zettler's face Harry could see that the big American was indeed in a lot of pain and was starting to look quite pale.

"Where does it hurt?"

"I think it's my leg."

Zettler pulled back his leather jacket and Harry could see that Zettler's shorts were steeped in blood. Zettler tried to keep the plane steady as Harry frantically opened the first aid kit and wrapped some bandages around the injured leg. The bullet had entered through his thigh, it seemed to have missed taking out the main artery, but there was still a lot of blood. The bullet had not gone straight through, so was still embedded somewhere in his leg. That would have to wait. Harry was no doctor, so someone else was going to have to take care of the wound. The blood flow seemed to cease, although the bandages were completely soaked, as were Zettler's shorts. Harry hoped the bandages had been applied well enough to get them to Egypt.

They flew on. Zettler winced every now and again but stayed steady at the controls. Mile after mile they covered, until the engine started making a strange noise. It sputtered and coughed.

"Now that ain't good." A worried frown crossed Zettler's face.

"I have a feeling that one o' them bullets must have pierced a fuel line…."

Harry listened in horror.

"…and our aviation fuel is now pouring on them dunes down there."

The fuel gauge had dipped to show tank was depleting very quickly. All they could do was to try to land somewhere safely; get help for Zettler's wound; and find another means of making it to Egypt.

The sputtering stopped, as did the propeller. The aircraft was gliding and rapidly losing height. Using his years of experience, Zettler guided the plane down as gracefully as he could. The landing was rough. They skidded along the tops of the dunes to slow them down, coming to rest in a cloud of sand and dust with the nose and propeller embedded in a sand dune.

The Sahara is one of the most extreme places in the world. Its' harsh dry climate with soaring temperatures and strong winds that helped to shape its' landscape, conspire to make it one of the most beautiful and deadly places on earth.

"Where are we?" It was Harry who spoke first.

"In trouble and we have two choices, stay put or start walking…"

Zettler grimaced as he tried to move.

"…and neither of them is a great plan."

"Do we even know which country we are in?"

Zettler could see Harry was starting to panic.

"I think we managed to cross the border back there, so my guess is, we must be in Libya."

Zettler tried to get up from his seat, and collapsed, howling with pain.

"Looks like I'm not walking anywhere."

"What are we going to do?"

Harry was shaking.

"All I reckon we can do is hunker down here for the night. My leg has at least stopped bleeding for a while. Let's get some rest. We have enough food and water in back for a few days. Maybe just see how things look in the morning."

Harry agreed. He clambered down to the sand below. Looking up to the big sky above he felt the sun burning his face and remembered he hadn't used or even purchased any sun cream since landing in Morocco. His face was dark red and sore from exposure to the sun from the past few days. Harry had not really noticed the pain. He was more concerned about how he was going to rescue his daughter and save his new comrade. How could he do this now they had crash-landed in the desert?

For what remained of the day, they sat in the half buried and slightly shaded cockpit. The blistering heat of the day gave way to sunset and the cool night air. As the evening temperature plummeted, Harry managed to start a fire using some sacking and matches from the plane's survival kit. The embers flickered and danced seemingly alive, giving off a primeval and raw, yet at the same time, pure energy.

They huddled under the blankets that Zettler had thoughtfully packed. Harry dozed in a fitful sleep and Zettler sat restlessly, struggling with the pain. Morning and the new day could not come soon enough for them both.

34.

There were horses, beautiful white winged horses. Jade and Vicky were riding them on a sea of cloud. Vicky reached out a hand towards him, their fingers almost touched. She looked above. There were storm clouds approaching. Small droplets of water rained down like tears. She withdrew her hand. The white winged horses had changed into large black stallions. Teeth snarled as they whinnied, their hooves raised, and as the breeze sharpened, they drifted away from his outstretched arms. Then all was black. Lightening and sheet rain. It was raining so hard he could feel the pain. Sharp pin pricks on his face, his clothes torn and soaked.

"Help me Daddy."

Jade sat in her prison cell all alone, dirty matting for a carpet, blood and tears streaming down her face. With pleading eyes, she cried:

"Please help me Daddy."

A sudden pain in his stomach. The blow was violent, then another to his back.

Harry opened his eyes. The sun's rays burned into his eyes. It was so bright. There was another kick, this time to his side. Instinctively, Harry curled into a ball and, as his mind began to clear from the haze of his nightmare, came face to face with a pair of booted feet. His eyes strayed upwards, combat trousers, black coverall. His rising gaze ended at the barrel of a rifle pointed directly at his face.

Zettler lay next to him, moving awkwardly with the pain in his leg. He leaned towards Harry and touched his arm.

"Put yer hands up son, so they can see you ain't carrying."

Slowly, Harry uncurled his body and raised his hands above his head. Lying on the ground it was hard for him to count them properly. 'Maybe a dozen, maybe more.' All armed with rifles or automatic weapons and only their eyes visible through their black balaclavas. The remnants of the fire smoked on the broken piece of fuselage.

Harry cursed to himself, 'the fire must have given their position away'.

"God damn!" Zettler let out a roar of pain as they tried to drag him to his feet.

"You American?"

Their leader allowed himself a broad smile through brown decaying teeth. He could see that Zettler was unable to walk so signalled to several of his comrades to help him to his feet. He turned to Harry.

"You American too?"

"English, I am a British citizen."

Despite the soreness in his midriff, Harry got to his feet and stood as tall as he could. He tried to look brave, but his look fooled no one. A further punch in the stomach sent him reeling back to the ground. Two men took his arms and dragged him again to his feet. Harry's stomach ached, he felt sick and dizzy with the pain. Powerless, Harry and Zettler, hands tied behind their backs, were bundled towards a waiting truck. There was no use trying to fight back or attempting to escape.

Two trucks and a jeep made up the small convoy. It weaved its' way along a dust road, before finally turning left onto the main road. Harry and Zettler sat in the back of the truck facing each other, with two armed guards eyeing them intently.

"Lucky they didn't just shoot us where they found us."

Zettler tried to raise Harry's spirits stating the obvious fact, but deep inside Zettler knew that being shot there and then might have been the preferable option, compared with what might happen when they reached their destination.

For two hours, the convoy rattled along the road. Doused in sweat, as the sun beat down on the canvas roof of the truck, they sat in silence.

Zettler had his eyes shut. Harry's eyes darted constantly around him, first at Zettler, then the floor, then out of the back of the truck and the heat haze of the road behind.

Miles and miles of nothing but road and sand. The occasional bird appeared as a tiny speck in the vastness of the pure blue sky. It was then he saw the body.

By the side of the road, hanging from a gibbet, was a headless corpse. It had been there for days. Despite the heat, a chill ran down Harry's spine.

There were a couple of birds feeding off the carcass, pulling the entrails from the hole where his head used to be. Harry's gaze was transfixed. As they drove on, it got smaller and smaller, until it completely disappeared from view. Even then, Harry could see it, indelibly imprinted on his mind's eye.

An hour later, they approached the outskirts of a town. The sound of prayer radiated from a distant minaret. The vehicles turned off the main road and down a dusty track. The houses on either side of the track were in a poor state of repair. Some had rudely cut wooden planks covering their windows; while others had slates missing from their roofs; in fact, one barely had any kind of roof at all, with a ripped tarpaulin stretched across the void. Other buildings looked more like disassembled rubble.

The vehicles came to a halt a few yards from the end of the houses. As they climbed out of the back of the truck, made all the more difficult with their hands tied behind their backs, their eyes beheld the 'stadium' for the first time.

There were two large wooden gates in the centre of the high white walls of the arena. A large faded sign, in Arabic, fixed above the gates. The gates were open, and as they were pushed closer, they could see row upon row of tiered seating, all around a central arena, which would at some point in time have been a pitch. Zettler was breathing hard; the pain in his leg was causing him extreme discomfort.

One end of the stadium, beyond the arena, was home to a few trucks and jeeps, a couple of old looking helicopters, some metal cages and some large metal shipping containers.

"I wonder when they release the lions?" There was a grim tone to Zettler's 'joke'. Pushed and shoved, they approached a large white building within the compound. An armed man, next to an opened steel doorway, beckoned them inside.

The room inside had no windows and was a few degrees cooler than outside; the shade offering small respite from the full heat of the sun.

Harry shaded his eyes. As he started to become accustomed to the dimness of the room, he saw a desk in from of them and a black flag with white Arabic writing hanging on a wall behind it. Their captors began talking in a language that neither Harry nor Zettler could understand apart from the odd word such as "American" and "English."

The knots in Harry's stomach were causing him a lot of pain. Whether it was the result of the earlier kicks and the punches, or the nervousness he felt, he did not have time to ponder. Within two minutes of their arrival, they were bundled from the office, down a corridor and confronted by a steel door with large bolts on the outside. The bolts were drawn open, before the pair were pushed inside. The door slammed shut.

The room was very spacious, had it not been for the two hundred, or so, inhabitants. It had the appearance of a sports hall, with partial wooden flooring, the remainder of which, Harry surmised, had been ripped up for firewood.

The first thing that stuck their senses was the smell. Men, women and children all shared what had become a very large prison cell. The first thing Harry noticed was the row of buckets along one wall, where a woman was stooping, in full view of the rest of the hall. Most people looked unwashed, some probably for weeks. As they stood and stared a fight broke out, seemingly over a small piece of bread.

"Where the hell have we come to?" Zettler shook his head. It was like a scene from Dante's Inferno.

They moved amongst the throng. Some slept on piles of rags, others sat by the edges of the floor wailing and crying. A dark-haired woman, with her back to them, knelt on the floor, bandaging a woman's hand. Her patient was crying with pain.

"Excuse me Ma-am." Zettler touched her lightly on the shoulder, as she finished treating her patient.

"Do you think you might take a look at ma leg?"

She swivelled and with dark brown tantalizing eyes, looked up at them.

"I got ma-self shot yesterday, and this sucker hurts like hell."

Zettler dropped to the ground beside her. His shorts and leg caked in dry blood.

"Tis very bad." Her soft French accent played like sweet music against the backdrop of misery.

"I will have to rip these." She took hold of Zettler's leg, unwound the hasty bandage that Harry had applied and pushing her fingers into the hole in the fabric ripped the leg of his shorts apart. The wound was messy. Matted blood and hair mixed with particles of skin.

"We need to clean this properly."

She reached over to a bowl of water, dipped a clean rag into it and began to bathe Zettler's bullet wound. Zettler winced with the pain but did not cry out.

"The bullet is still in there, no?"

"It sure is little lady."

"This will hurt."

She looked up at Harry.

"Please brace your friend."

Harry did as he was told. He took both of Zettler's arms and held him tight.

Her slender fingers dipped into Zettler's leg. He writhed and grunted in pain, but still did not yell out. In a few moments she stopped.

"I feel it, if I can just…"

Zettler let out a roar, and the inhabitants of the hall, as one, fell silent.

"I have it."

She pulled the bullet from the wound and with a triumphant smile held it aloft for all to see.

Zettler's body sagged and Harry released his hold, lowering the dazed American flat to the floor.

"Thank you." Harry held out his hand for her to shake. Instinctively she lifted her hand to his but paused.

"No wait, the blood…"

She wiped her hand clean on another piece of rag.

"I'm Harry and your new patient here is Leo."

Harry held her hand for a second; noticing the softness of her skin.

"Zettler," Zettler stirred, "people just call me Zettler, there were two Leo's in my platoon, so it was easier just to call me Zettler."

"Bonjour 'arry and Zettler." She smiled at Leo's name, and shook him by the hand.

"Je m'apelle Francois."

Harry watched Francois carefully clean Zettler's wound and wrap it tightly. She had obviously been allowed to keep some medical supplies, so he guessed that their captors must have felt they were all more valuable alive than dead. Zettler moaned and lay back on the ground, his eyes closed.

Harry sat closer to Francois and spoke just loud enough to be heard above the din that echoed around the hall.

"So, what brought you to this place?"

"I came to Benghazi with my friend Jean-Claude as aid workers. We were only here distributing medicines to the needy of the town."

Tears began to trickle down her pretty face.

"Jean-Claude was murdered, and I was arrested for witchcraft or spying or something and brought here."

"Your friend was murdered? What happened?"

"There were three young boys just playing in the street. Everyone else around had gone to pray, but these boys, so engrossed in their game, had not noticed. They must have been about seven years old, harmlessly playing."

Francois wiped her eyes with a tissue.

"All of a sudden, five men all dressed in black, appeared with black hoods covering their faces. They took the boys. They were screaming with fright. They tied their hands, strung them up on a bar by their wrists and began beating them with sticks. There was nothing we could do."

Francois burst into floods of tears; Harry put his arm around her shoulder.

"We just hid behind some tall dustbins. Then without warning, a jeep pulled up behind us, and three men got out. They had automatic weapons. They arrested us and confiscated our medicine. As they took us away, we saw the boys being cut down. I think they were alive. I hope they are okay."

Francois sobbed as she nestled her head against Harry's chest.

"They tied our hands behind our backs and marched us down the street like criminals, pushing and prodding. They took us to a rough building.

There was lots of shouting and pointing at us. Jean-Claude told them we were just aid workers and had come to help their country. They struck Jean-Claude at the back of the head and he fell to the floor. They called him something, but I don't understand the language, and started kicking him."

She took a breath, sat up and sipped some water.

"Then they took us both around the back of the building to a small square. In the middle of the square was a metal cage.

They pushed Jean-Claude inside and locked the door. He came to the bars and started shouting for them to let him go. One of the men picked up a canister. He walked calmly over to the cage and threw its' contents over Jean-Claude. I could smell it. I knew it was petrol. As the man stood back from the cage, another man lit a match and threw it at Jean-Claude."

Francois cried uncontrollably, Harry held her for a while until he calmed down.

"He did not stand a chance, he did nothing wrong. They forced me to watch as if it was a warning, then they hit me a few times before they brought me here."

She paused and collected herself a little.

"They are just animals, I have spoken to some of the women in here and it seems I am one of the lucky ones, so far. "

Zettler stirred and propped himself up on his elbow.

"How do they work that out?"

"They have not raped me yet."

35.

Surveying the large room, Harry noted that the occupants were a mix of nationalities. Some looked like Europeans, who could have been tourists, aid workers and adventurers or locals who did not believe in the same things as their captors. Most could speak at least a few words of English, so they managed, to a degree, to communicate with him. The horror stories were many. It seemed that the punishments metered out for even the most minor of offences, or what they deemed to be offences, were, at the very least, severe and brutal. Alleged crimes were for spying, apostasy, witchcraft, fornication, blasphemy, listening to music and smoking. The sentences ranged from being strung up by the wrists and being whipped and tortured; to having jump leads attached to their nipples and genitals and being electrocuted using car batteries, with the worst punishment being amputation and the ultimate being decapitation.

A scraping noise reverberated, metal on metal. Harry looked up. The lower shutter section of the door opened; and a few stale loaves of bread hurled into the room. A few desperate people scrapped for their share of the meagre ration. Harry was not hungry, he still had a pain in his stomach from the beating, but he was thirsty and noticed a trough of water next to the wall. He signalled to Zettler and Francois.

"Do you think it's safe to drink?"

"It has to be," replied Francois, "it's all we have."

Harry limped over to it, picked up a ladle and took a sip. It appeared to be drinkable, so he took a long gulp of the warm liquid.

For the remainder of the day they rested. Zettler's leg still pained him, but as the day went on the pain eased, and he slipped into a long and noisy sleep.

The following morning, the ritual began. The stinking, overflowing toilet buckets emptied, food thrown into the room, gathering dust before being pounced upon; and the trough refilled with water from jerry cans, that were brought in by the guards.

Every morning, a handful of people were chosen. Some were summarily punished, beaten or raped, then thrown back in the room. Some were taken away and never seen again. From their faint distant screams, it was clear to see they had met with an awful fate.

On the fourth day, the guards took Harry and Francois, along with four others. They did not resist, as they knew there was little point. With their hands tied behind their backs, they marched outside into the bright sunshine. Two men held a large black flag with white Arabic lettering. A video camera stood on a tri-pod facing it. Forced to kneel before the camera, a masked guard stood behind each of them. A tall man in long flowing robes, Harry assumed he must be in charge, stepped in front of the camera.

"Here are more infidels ready to face punishment."

Harry's ears pricked up, the man was English. Sickened at this new thought, Harry listened on to the tirade. He shouted for about five minutes about God, Western oppression and vengeance. Then he came to his main point.

"Your governments must pay, and release our brave brothers that are being held captive, or we will kill all of these..."

He waved his hand towards the six still on their knees.

"...and their blood will be on your hands."

Each of the six had their heads pulled back by their hair, so that their faces would be clearly recognised. Harry could feel his heart pounding in his chest. He had seen this scene played out many times on the BBC News broadcasts. It hardly ever ended well.

Francois knelt next to Harry. The guard behind her began to stroke her shoulders then moved his hands down to her breasts. He bent his face close to hers, took a deep breath in through his nose and whispered:

"You smell so good."

With his breath hot on her cheek, she began to shake. Harry felt a rage shudder through his tired body. He had nothing to lose. He was probably going to die anyway. Struggling against the guard behind him, he found enough strength to get to his feet.

"Keep your dirty hands off her."

Francois' guard rose to his feet to face Harry. Harry looked deep into his eyes, then head-butted him in the nose. The guard yelped in pain as he desperately clutched his bruised nostrils.

Tottering backwards for a second, the guard regained his footing, turned back to Harry and punched him in the stomach and then full in the face. Harry crumpled to the ground. The leader laughed.

"The English one, bring him to me."

The commanders' English accent unmistakable. They half dragged Harry across the ground, blood pouring from his split lower lip and forced him to kneel at the feet of their commander. Harry, covered in blood, knelt on the dusty earth, staring up at him defiantly.

"There's not much chance of anyone paying for you now is there, 'me old mucker'?"

The commander picked up a large brown petrol canister and unscrewed the lid. Harry felt like his heart had stopped as his whole world went into slow motion. All he could think about was Francois' story. The Cage and Jean-Claude. The commander lifted the petrol canister and began pouring the contents over Harry. Francois cried out. Harry could not hear her scream. The clear liquid rained over him. His clothes covered, soaked to the skin. The commander took a step back. Pulled out a box from his pocket. A matchbox. He took out a match. Struck it. Wood scraped on powdered glass. A sulphurous flame burst into life. The bright orange flicker danced. Beautiful and pure. It blurred before Harry's eyes. Hypnotised, in a trance he watched it fall. Slowly descending. Rotating as it fell. The match landed on Harry's soaking jacket.

A small wisp of smoke replaced the burning sulphur. Harry could not believe his eyes. He had cheated death.

"It was only water, you daft bastard."

As Harry knelt on the ground, he lowered his head and burst into tears. The commander roared with laughter. His open mouth exposed yellow teeth, peppered with brown nicotine specks.

"Take them back to the hall."

Francois felt rough hands grope her body as they returned to their cell. A cold shiver ran down her spine, she had a bad feeling that she may be next on their rape schedule.

Reunited with Zettler in the hall, Harry sat on the floor with his arms wrapped around his knees. The shock of the last hour overcame him and he started to shake uncontrollably.

Francois knelt down next to Harry, gently stroking his face.

She kissed the side of his temple and with both arms, held him tightly to her. 'This is a good and brave man,' allowing herself a light thought amid the horror 'and not bad looking either.'

Francois had decided she would like to get to know this Englishman a little better.

36.

For Emma and Anja, the days were long and monotonous. Weeks and months went by, each day the same routine. The ever-growing conveyor belt of 'customers' continued to grace their beds as the establishment grew in popularity.

The busiest times usually began in late afternoons, after prayers, and on into the evenings. Long queues formed, and the waiting areas were always full of expectant 'clients', who would then be returning to their homes and families. Their wives and children unaware of their activities, and the diseases they were inevitably bringing home with them.

Some clients were young, keen, and over in a matter of minutes. The older ones often wanted a little more, and in some cases much more. Depravity became the norm and nothing they were asked to do surprised them.

The food was as monotonous as it was dreadful. A sombre mix of brown and beige, completely devoid of nutrition. Stale bread, water and some runny kind of porridge became their staple diet. Emma remembered reading about 'pottage' in her medieval history lessons. A soup of boiled vegetables, fish, meat, whatever was available; and thought that must have been a hundred times better than the daily slop they were currently faced with.

Malnutrition had started to work its' way through the women. Tiredness, weight loss and rashes plagued them, with some finding clumps of hair on their pillows in the mornings when they woke. Many had loud phlegmy coughs that barked and rattled through their insides, keeping the others awake at night.

Constantly trapped within four walls, the lack of sunlight to their bodies sapped their strength and willpower. Their skin became pale. When anyone became too weak to work, they disappeared, probably sold onto more unhealthy surroundings and new women would be found to replace them.

Anja and Emma grew closer. A deep bond of friendship forged between them as they faced endless adversity together.

Each had to stay alive and alert to help protect the other. Anja acted like a big sister to Emma, and Emma in turn watched out for Anja. Their only respite was when they huddled together at night under a thin blanket. They worked out a signal, something Anja suggested. If either of them were with a 'client' and he started to, or looked like he might, get rough, they would knock on the wall in three short bursts. One, one-two, one-two-three. On hearing this, the other would run and fetch Malek, Nassim's son. He would always 'resolve' the situation, and often called on a couple of his men to have the disruptive 'client' beaten up and thrown out into the street.

Although Malek was definitely one of 'them', he was not their enemy. In many ways, he tried to act like a brother. He was tough, but also had a softer side. Sometimes Nassim's guards would beat them, but often Malek would intervene if he felt they had not deserved it. A swift word from Malek and they would desist. Emma guessed he was saying 'don't damage the goods' or 'my uncle will be upset if you harm his property'. He brought them extra bits of food whenever he could and often guarded them as they slept.

He never appeared violent, until one day he proved himself very capable when a client refused to pay for his 'extras'. A fight ensued and Malek punched the man hard in the throat, shattering his windpipe, very nearly killing him.

Some days were slower than others. On the slow days much of their time was spent waiting around or cleaning. The waiting was the hardest part. Would they have clients? Would the client be nice and not hit them? Would they be clean? Would they safely make it back to their night-time huddle unscathed? Sometimes even the doing was better than the waiting. The anticipation was often terrifying; the doing was just a process. Stand in line. Get picked. Lead the client to the room. As the money had already changed hands, the clients were free to do pretty much what they wanted. The process was always the same. Undress, then the thing, whatever it was they wanted, degrading practises after a time became just part of a normal day. Terror gave way to numbness, thanks in part, for most of them, due to the crack and alcohol.

Then the client was gone, followed by the clean-up. It was always an icky task getting clean of the mess, sweat and stench the client had left behind. A quick wash, then onto the next, and so on.

Some of the girls became hollow inside. Shadowlike zombies, they would just sit and stare at the walls with vacant dead eyes. Some clients preferred two girls. This made the process a bit easier as they could share the burden. "When he's on top of her, he's not on top of you," one woman had once said to Emma. It also gave them more protection in case the client wanted to beat one of them. Their masters certainly did not like them to be beaten, as that made them damaged goods, and they would often need recovery time before they could work again.

Emma found one of the worst things was not knowing what time it was. Was it day or night? The date, the month? So, Emma used her own internal calendar. 'If it felt like a Tuesday, then it was a Tuesday.'

Privacy was another issue. Emma longed for a toilet door with a lock on the inside, and the ability to go in alone. After Sabine's suicide, their captors would never let them go to the toilet or bathroom alone. There was always a man present, and usually watching, while they were relieving themselves.

Anja tried to comfort Emma as much as she could. She would plait her hair for her, and every night Emma would cuddle in with Anja and they would hold each other until the morning. Anja felt an immense guilt. She would keep Emma safe. She had not been able to help Liesel, but determined, Anja was going to get Emma out of there.

They had been at the 'establishment' for several months when truckloads of trafficked young women, girls and boys started arriving day and night.

They were of all ages, from many different countries, but most seemed to be European. An ever-increasing number of boys arrived, probably to cater for every taste and fetish.

One day one of the boys sat alone in the kitchen. He looked very pale and traumatised. One of the other women had heard that he 'must not be touched' by anyone, as he would be fetching a very good price. Anja sat near to him and offered him some chocolate a client had given to her. He did not respond, just stared into space. He was probably just terrified or numb like the rest of them.

It was a Thursday according to Emma's calculation, when a very large client arrived for his usual 'massage'. He was morbidly obese and of Arabic descent.

He sported an unkempt beard, and a deep odour of someone who either has very bad personal hygiene or was extremely unwell.

He staggered along the line as usual, inspecting each of them, smelling their hair, touching their faces. They had been encouraged to 'smile at the gentleman, plenty of eye contact.' Sweat trickled down his face and onto his dirty vest. Curly black hair tufted out of his nose and ears. They could almost taste his odour. His asthmatic breath rattled as he wheezed in the heat. He paused at Emma, her mouth fixed in a fake smile. He grabbed her roughly by the elbow. The relief in the room, from the others in the line-up, was almost audible. It was Emma's turn.

Emma's heart sank. Ten minutes earlier, Anja had taken a client through, so Emma led her client to the room next door. As he closed the door behind them, Emma heard the outside bolt sliding into place. He moved over to the bed, sat down and beckoned her to him.

"Please." He paused, trying to catch his breath; reached for an inhaler from his pocket and took a puff. "Undress me."

His accent was strong and hard to understand; his body language did most of the talking for him. As Emma undressed him, she noticed the sores under his folds of fat. The smell was the acrid, putrid stench of puss-filled abscesses. It was disgusting even by the usual standards, and Emma had to hold her breath as she got near him. After removing his dirty boxer shorts, he made her undress and lie on the bed. He wheezed heavily as he took his place on top of her, pounding like a walrus moving across mud. The folds of his fat slapped around like waves on a beach.

Emma made no sound. She had learned to make no sound, no matter what happened to her. If she screamed, he might have beaten her; or possibly killed her. He was sweating with the exertion. He moved faster, stepping up the pace. His vile grunts and breath getting louder with each thrust. Beads of sweat dripped down his face onto hers'. He made a loud noise. He climaxed. That noise usually marked the end of the hellish ordeal. He flopped back down on top of Emma. The beads of sweat ran from his temples. He did not move. She could not move.

A few moments later Emma realised, to her horror, he had stopped breathing. She raised her right hand to the side of his neck and felt around for a pulse. Nothing.

Frantically she dug her fingers deeper through the fat of his collar; seeking out his jugular vein. Still nothing. He was dead. The fat blubbery monster was dead, and he was still inside her. The weight of his corpse was so incredibly heavy. Emma found it hard to breathe. 'Short breaths', she thought 'take short breaths'. She started to panic as silence engulfed the room.

Emma completely trapped between him and the bed, felt her chest ache with the pressure. Her breathing constricted, she could not even shout for help. Winded, afraid, disgusted, with her one free hand Emma reached out and gently knocked on the wall next to the bed. She prayed that Anja might hear.

Tap, tap-tap, tap-tap-tap.

Fearful thoughts raced through her mind, 'what if Anja's client had finished early and the room next door was now empty?' She tried again.

Tap, tap-tap, tap-tap-tap.

Emma listened. Silence. Desperate, she tried again.

Tap, tap-tap, tap-tap-tap.

Silence again. Emma held her breath for a few moments more.

Tap-tap-tap.

The reply came. Emma's heart jumped with joy. Anja had heard her.

All was quiet except for the distant sounds of sexual fulfilment from the adjoining rooms, some real, some obviously faked. Emma heard the bolt on the outside of the door slide gently across. The door creaked open and Anja's head peeped inside. Anja gagged at the sight and the smells that filled the room. Anja quickly slipped inside the room, closing the door quietly behind her.

Anja ran over to the bed and heaved at the corpse. With all her strength, Anja pushed the body upwards, and off Emma's chest. Emma took a grateful gulp of air. A vile squelching noise broke the silence. Once Emma had an arm free, she added her strength to Anja's and between them rolled the enormous flaccid body across to the other side of the bed.

'So here they were,' thought Anja, 'the two of them, alone in a dirty stinking room with a massive putrefying corpse'. The main points suddenly hit Anja again like a bolt from the sky.

'Two of them, alone.'

'They were never alone.'

'Never Alone. But, yet here they were'.

Anja turned to her friend, and with both hands took hold of her face and spoke quickly.

"We have to act fast. This could be our only chance."

Emma was shaking and still traumatised by the events of the last half hour.

"I-I can't do this, I can't do this anymore."

Emma began to cry. Anja pulled her close for a moment, whispering gently trying to calm her nerves.

"Come on Emma, get dressed, we have a lot of work to do if we want to get out of here."

Emma dutifully put on her dirty slip. Anja looked down at her friend, looking so pale and thin. Emma had barely eaten anything for days. She looked dazed and a little confused; shock was beginning to set in.

"Come on Emma."

Anja shook her friend by the shoulders. As Emma fought the hazy mist that filled her head, she started to realise that this could be their best and only chance to escape. Anja quickly searched through the man's clothing, looking for anything that might prove useful. Amongst his oversized clothes, they found a wallet, keys, penknife and a belt. They knew he had paid for at least another half an hour; so, they would not be bothered for a few minutes at least.

It was lunchtime, and they knew that some of the guards would have gone to prayers. This, they thought, would give them their best chance. Anja wrapped the belt around her hand, with Emma taking charge of the penknife. Slowly Emma opened the door and peered out. There was a guard named Farid a little way down the corridor; he was young and strong. He may not have been the best choice, but he was their only choice.

"I need some help." Emma whispered.

She held the penknife tightly behind her back in her nervous, sweating hands, as Farid walked towards her.

"What is the problem?"

"I think he must have passed out."

Farid entered the room, and to his horror saw the body, flat out on the bed. As he walked calmly over to the body, Emma quietly closed the door. The guard covered his mouth and nose, gagging at the smell, before bending over and reaching down to touch the lifeless form.

Anja moved quietly from behind the door. The belt pulled tight between both hands.

"I think he's dea…"

His voice trailed away as he caught sight of Anja out of the corner of his eye. Anja dived on top of him, trying desperately to wrap the belt around his neck. He fought back, lashing out with both arms. They landed against the bed and he pushed Anja's face into the corpse. The ripe smell of death, stale sweat and semen filled her nostrils. She kicked back, hard, her bare foot landing in his stomach. Farid doubled, and as he did, grabbed her around the waist and they both tumbled onto the floor. Anja let go of one end of the belt and lashed out. Her nails scratched deep into his face. Farid recoiled at the pain and let out a yelp. This was Anja's chance. She jumped on his back and looped the belt around his neck, pulling it tight. He tried to shout. Tighter and tighter. He managed a low gurgle. Struggling for his life. Arms flailing. Choking. Fingers pawing at the belt. Desperate to breathe. Using his weight, he threw them both backwards and landed on the floor, on top of Anja. The back of his head smacked Anja in the nose. The blow made her lose her grip and the belt loosened. Farid took a deep breath, turning over as he did. Body to body, he pinned Anja to the floor. Blood pouring from her nose, she started to lose consciousness. A wide grin flickered across his face. He licked his lips as he stroked his hand across her breasts and down past her stomach. He began to lift Anja's slip. He was going to enjoy this. He felt something. It was sharp. In disbelief, he looked down. Anja's body was soaked in blood. It was pouring. No, it was gushing. It was his blood.

Emma took a step back, the penknife in her hand still dripping with the dark crimson fluid. He put a hand to his throat, but it was too late. He tried to call out for help. No words would come.

He felt panic. He fell on his side, his eyes looking straight up into the eyes of Emma. She froze. She had never killed anyone before. He reached out a hand towards her, then a second later, fell backwards onto the floor, body convulsing, eyes wide open and blood spurting from the deep wound in his neck.

Then he was still. Dead eyes stared at the ceiling.

Anja coughed and held her nose as she sat up, covered in blood. Emma opened her mouth wide in silent scream, shaking violently she dropped the knife.

37.

As Malek returned from prayers, he stopped at a market stall to buy some bread and fruit. He was tired. Tired of the job he was doing. Tired of his uncle Nassim. Sure, Nassim had taken him in when his parents died; but, this was not the life he wanted. His uncle scared him. He was a violent and angry man, given to fits of rage over the slightest little thing.

With his purchases tucked safely under his arm, Malek made his way back to the 'establishment'. He entered the reception and was surprised not to see Farid, as he had left him in charge while most of the other guards had gone to prayers. Two other guards sat talking and smoking.

"Said, where is Farid?" Malek enquired.

"He's probably in with one of the whores." Said smirked, it was one of the 'perks' of the job.

A few of the women milled around reception returning with clients. Malek pushed past them and marched purposefully along the corridor. He was angry with Farid. He should have been on reception making sure the clients had paid. He looked in several of the empty rooms. Nothing. There were a few bolted doors; these he could ignore. The final door was closed, but with its' bolt drawn back.

Anja looked up from Farid's body as the door opened. She had just pulled the pistol from his belt, turning she pointed the muzzle towards Malek.

"Come in and close the door."

Malek could not believe the scene that met his eyes. There was blood everywhere. Anja pointing the gun at him, soaked in blood; Farid, on his back, staring at the ceiling and obviously dead; a large naked man on the bed, probably dead; and Emma, kneeling weeping, spattered with blood.

"What the hell happened?"

His words were more in disbelief than anger.

Anja rose to her feet and circled him, slowly pushing the door shut. Malek felt his heart beating faster.

"You are going to get us out of here, or I will kill you, here and now."

Anja's words were slow and deliberate. Malek nodded that he understood. He was confused; he had been good to them, given them extra rations, watched over them when they slept. He had even just brought them some bread and fruit.

"Now we go to the washroom."

Anja sounded as though she had it all worked out. In fact, she was making it up as she went along. She secreted the pistol in a dirty bedsheet, and still pointing it at Malek, carefully opened the door. Anja glanced down the corridor. Some women were walking back and forth with 'clients', and there were two armed guards stationed just at the end of the corridor, listening out for 'troublesome customers'.

"If you utter a single word, you will be dead before you hit the floor."

When the coast appeared to be clear, they stepped out into the corridor and crept towards the bathroom. Emma shivered as they entered, the memories of Sabine lying in the still pink water, came flooding back.

Aside from the bath, there was a locked cupboard on the far wall. Anja motioned to Malek to pull out his keys and open it, which he did. Anja knew the contents before he opened it. This was where they kept the cloaks. They had arrived in cloaks and when they left, they would leave in cloaks. Anja and Emma each slipped one on.

Anja spoke in hushed tones that only Emma and Malek could understand.

"The story is that your uncle wants us to work at another of his places and you are going to take us there."

She paused so Malek could take in this information.

"Understood?"

Anja looked deep into Malek's eyes, the gun pressed against his stomach. Malek nodded, he was not ready to die just yet. They stepped slowly out of the washroom. There was no time to wash, but at least, their long cloaks covered most of the tell-tale bloodstains. As they walked to the end of the corridor, Said looked up.

"Where are you taking those two?"

"I'm taking them over to the other place, my uncle called earlier, we have some VIP's visiting and we need the best girls for them."

Malek was thinking on his feet. He had his arms around the two of them, with Anja pointing the gun, hidden under the cloak, into his kidneys. They entered reception, with Said following closely behind. The reception was quite full, with clients and women mingling, and a few other guards carrying out price negotiations. Then their luck ran out. Nassim walked in from the street.

Nassim not in the best of moods, flanked by three of his armed guards, he saw Malek immediately and shouted at him. "Why are they dressed in cloaks, where are you taking them?"

Nassim's voice was accusing and angry at the same time.

"We need them at the err…"

Malek stammered, he was never confident in front of his uncle, and, with a gun pointed directly at his vital organs, he was even more nervous. He was sweating profusely and Nassim could tell straight away that all was not as it seemed. Said, walking behind them looked confused.

"Malek said it was you who ordered it."

There were two choices. Surrender or fight. They could not surrender, there were two corpses lying in a bedroom, and for that, they would surely pay with their lives. Anja whipped out the pistol and shot the closest guard in the stomach. He screamed, falling to the floor clutching his midriff. The recoil forced Anja backwards and accidentally fired off a second shot, which narrowly missed Emma, thudding into the wall behind her. Anja had never fired a gun before and the recoil had taught her an instant lesson about the power of the weapon.

"Kill those filthy bitch whores." Nassim barked out his order as he took cover behind the reception desk.

Malek had to make an instant decision. Follow his uncle's order and face punishment for his treachery, or, help Anja and Emma try to escape. Malek chose the latter. As the second shot rang out, he grabbed a pistol from Said and fired a bullet into his thigh.

Said fell, clutching his leg, blood pouring from the wound. Women and clients scattered, some running for the door, others back down the corridor to the safety of the rooms. Two guards fired warning shots, which ricocheted around the room.

A woman screamed as a bullet struck her arm. A client fell to the floor with a bullet hole in the back of his head. There was noise and confusion. More shots rang out.

Malek made an awkward grunt as he fell forward but managed to regain his footing. Emma made a break for the door but dived under a table as another guard tried to grab her. Anja got up from the floor and, using a chair for cover, she fired towards another, the bullet glanced his cheek, ripping the side of his face open. Nassim took aim and fired; the bullet spun through the air; missed Anja by a whisker; but struck one of his own men in the neck.

"Now run." Malek shouted pulling Anja by the arm and firing a couple of bullets above the reception desk, forcing Nassim to take cover. Emma scrambled to her feet and ran for the door. Running out of the front door, they collapsed into the street.

"This way."

Malek shouted to them as he led them through the myriad of market stalls that spread out opposite the doorway.

In the early afternoon heat, the streets were a chaotic blend of shoppers, tourists, traders, mopeds, bicycles, some men with donkeys, some pushing handcarts and children playing. Ducking down an alley draped with washing lines, they blindly followed Malek. Without him, they would have been completely lost. Twisting and turning through the tight knit alleyways it seemed impossible that Nassim and his men could have followed them. Eventually they reached a doorway, parched by the sun its' paint peeling.

"This is Farouk's house, the client you killed. We can hide here for a while."

Malek tried the handle. The door was locked. He looked up and down the alley. It was busy, but no one was paying them any attention. He put his shoulder to the door. It was old and weak and the lock crumbled at the first attempt. Disappearing into the house, they quickly closed the door behind them, propping a chair under the handle to secure it.

The building was cool and dark. Making their way through the sparse living room to the kitchen, they sat down on some old wooden chairs.

Anja and Emma's feet were sore; covered in cuts and bruises from running barefoot through the streets. Malek staggered to the sink, and with a grimace, he doubled up in pain. He reached his hand out from under his shirt. His hand was covered in blood. Malek collapsed on the floor.

Emma ran over and knelt down next to him, putting his head in her lap. She looked up at Anja."We must do something; he's just saved our lives."

Emma pressed on Malek's wound while Anja looked for anything that would stem the flow. She returned with towels and parcel tape. They wrapped the towels around him and bound them with the tape. The bleeding appeared to stop. For nearly an hour, the three of them sat in the kitchen exhausted, barely saying a word to each other, each trying to come to terms with what they had just been through. Malek needed medical attention, but he seemed out of danger for the moment. Eventually Anja broke the silence.

"Where are we?"

"Bechar." replied Malek, he winced as he tried to prop himself up on his elbows.

"And where is Bechar?" Emma asked.

"You have been here for months and you don't even know which country you are in? We are in Algeria."

They were all very hungry, so Anja began to search for food. For such a large man, Farouk did not keep his kitchen cupboards very well stocked. Anja found bread, some sweet spread that looked a bit like dates and some biscuits and crackers. She also found a few unopened bottles of water, so they made a meal up of what they had.

Emma began leafing through a newspaper that was lying on the table. Unable to read Arabic, she just looked at the pictures. Some military looking men in some, some men in suits in another. As she turned a page, Emma took a deep breath. She put her hand over her mouth and stared at the photograph in front of her.

"Anja look, look who that is."

Anja pulled the newspaper round and glanced down,

"It's a boy." Anja replied casually.

"That's right, but not just any boy, look closer, don't you see who that boy is?"

A light went on in Anja's head.

"It's that boy they brought into the 'establishment' a few weeks ago, the one who never speaks."

"That's right I thought I recognised him, he was on the news back home," said Emma "His name is Justin, he was on holiday in Tunisia with his family and he just disappeared. The whole world is looking for him."

"I knew he was important," said Malek. "They say he is worth a lot of money. That is why we never let anyone harm him. But, there is a customer; he is coming to collect him tomorrow, big money."

Emma looked at Malek and then back at Anja.

"Anja you do realise, only we know where he is, and tomorrow he will be gone."

Emma paused for a moment, barely believing what she was about to say, her voice trembled as she spoke.

"We have to go back."

38.

Escaping from the 'establishment' had given them renewed hope of seeing home again, but the realisation that they had to return filled them with dread. They knew that if Justin were 'collected' by the rich client, he would be gone forever. A rescue attempt was Justin's only hope.

Anja devised a plan. Noticing that some of the Algerian women wore white veils to cover their faces, the veil would make a perfect disguise. Anja searched Farouk's bedroom and found some large garments, obviously worn by him, but there was no sign that a woman had ever lived there. Under cover of darkness, Anja crept out of the house. She found some suitable items hanging from a washing line that draped across an adjacent alleyway. Anja climbed up onto a ledge and pulled at them. They gave way with a snap as the clothes pegs that secured them flew into the darkness.

She slipped into an alcove and leaning on a parked moped, put on one of the white robes. It was the cleanest garment she had worn in months. Then an idea crossed her mind, she looked down at the moped. It was old and dirty, but to her joyous surprise, the owner had carelessly left the keys in the ignition. She silently rolled the moped away from the alcove and back towards the house.

Anja and Emma had hardly slept as the sun rose on the new morning. In the bright sunlight, Malek kept watch as they stepped out of the door. Anja started the moped, to make sure it worked. After a couple of attempts, the engine fired into life. She checked the fuel gauge. It was half-full. They thought it best to conserve as much of the fuel as possible, so Malek pushed the vehicle as he directed them back towards the 'establishment'. Emma noticed him limp and wince with the pain, but he never once complained. As they got nearer, he parked the moped against a market stall.

It was early morning. The market traders were setting up their stalls. Anja and Emma, dressed in their white robes and veils, pretended to examine the wares, while keeping a watchful eye on the 'establishment' door.

Malek was in obvious agony and Anja spoke softly to him. "It's time for you to leave us."

"I'll stay with you and..." He faltered with the pain.

"For all of our sakes, you must go," whispered Emma. "Thank you for helping us. Now go and save yourself."

Wearily he nodded in agreement, and as he regained his composure, he took them each by the hand and softly said:

"I'm sorry for how I have wronged you. I pray you may forgive me for everything, even though I do not deserve it."

He kissed them both on the hand and, with a backward glance, disappeared into the crowd.

Anja kept her hand firmly on Malek's pistol, carefully hidden under her white robe. The market, opposite the main door, was the perfect vantage point to watch the comings and goings. Nassim would never have suspected that they would return. Taking it in turn to watch the door, they pretended to examine the merchandise on sale in the market. Feeling the cloth and admiring the bright colours, shopping was the furthest thing from their minds.

They knew the building opposite intimately. It represented pain, humiliation and death. Emma held back a tear as she remembered Sabine and then Jade. It all seemed so long ago.

A shiny black car stopped outside the door, the motor remained running as one man, talking on his mobile phone, escorted two young women into the building. He reappeared with another man and the boy. Justin. His eyes blinked in the bright morning sun. Justin was bundled into the back seat and the man on the mobile phone got in beside him.

Emma kept a watchful eye on the vehicle as Anja ran behind the corner market stall to collect the moped. She fired up the engine and rode around the corner. Stopping briefly for Emma to jump on the back, Emma clung tightly to Anja's waist. The car moved carefully around the streets and Anja chose to stay a safe distance behind, for fear of being spotted. Eventually the car came to a stop in a rough street. The man in the rear got out and entered a doorway of a two-storey building. Justin sat motionless in the car.

Anja parked the moped and both girls slipped alongside the car. Anja drew Malek's pistol and, as one, they each opened a door, Anja the front passenger, and Emma the rear door. Anja thrust the gun barrel into the driver's stomach, and, with a no-nonsense voice, she commanded him.

"Drive."

He looked at Anja. The thought processes evident in his features, it was confusion, he was only a driver, what was she doing pointing a gun at him? He was innocent. Yes, in his own mind he knew he was innocent.

Anja and Emma knew differently knew that he was far from innocent. They remembered him as a client from the 'establishment'. He had raped both of them several times, and even with their veils still covering their faces, he knew their smell. As he took a deep breath, he recognised them, and fear spread across his face. He looked deep into Anja's eyes, as he had done on so many other occasions, and this time he knew she was in charge. The driver did not try to escape, he just turned the steering wheel, and the car moved slowly forward. Anja pressed the barrel of the gun even harder into his midriff and he winced at the pain. Trying to avoid rocks and potholes, for fear of it shaking Anja, and her accidentally pulling the trigger, he gradually began to speed up. Glancing in his rear-view mirror, he noticed his colleague step out of the building, along with two other men, as they stared about them in desperation, the vehicle had already melted amongst the city traffic, and become invisible.

In the back seat, Justin stared ahead. Obviously drugged, his big eyes looked up at Emma like saucers. Emma hugged him to her, as she had done with Jade. She had not been able to save her friend, but she had to help save this boy.

They left the outskirts of town and headed north. The landscape gradually changed giving way to mountains, scrub and desert. Emma reclined in the back seat, surrounded by the aroma of new leather. The car felt like it had come straight from a showroom.

The jet-black paint and bright chromework glinted as the sun's rays shone down from a cloudless sky. At Anja's bidding, they turned off the main road and along a dusty track.

With her arms gently cradling Justin, Emma stared out of the windows, almost admiring the scenery, the desert was such a large, beautiful place. The sun was shining. Her guardian angel sat in the front seat, with a gun trained on the driver, their 'hostage'.

After about half an hour, Anja motioned for the driver to pull over. He eased the car into a layby at the side of the dirt road. Dust billowed as the wheels crackled to a halt.

They sat for a few moments, stationary with only the steady whir of the engine and air conditioning to break the silence.

The driver turned to look at Anja. He stared straight into her eyes and smiled. He assumed that Anja would never have the guts to pull the trigger. He also knew that to try anything in the close confines of the vehicle would be too risky. He might accidentally get himself injured or worse. He would bide his time and wait for the chance that would inevitably come his way. Anja pressed the muzzle of the pistol into his stomach and with her free hand, reached towards him. Their eyes fixed on each other as if waiting for one of them to make the first move. She was so close. He could smell her. Their lips were almost touching. He felt aroused and wanted to taste her. Running his tongue along his thin lips, she knew he wanted her again.

As she moved slightly nearer, he almost licked her face, but immediately thought better of it. He remembered every inch of her, her slender figure, her beautiful breasts. The way she screamed when he hit her and made her beg for his manhood. He inhaled her perfume.

It was an animal smell. He loved that smell of fear, mixed with dirt and sweat. Anja nearly gagged at the thought of him enjoying breathing in her fragrance. With a jerk, she pulled the keys from the ignition and pulled away from his lecherous gaze. The engine died in an instant and a peaceful quiet fell upon the occupants of the car.

Anja clicked her passenger door open and a blast of warm air filled the vehicle. Waving the gun at the driver, she handed the car keys to Emma. Never taking her eyes off the driver she spoke calmly but with menace.

"Out."

One word was all she spoke, the driver fully understood but sat there in silence, reliving his memories of Anja. 'This stupid little whore will never make it out of here alive' he thought to himself. Anja slid from her seat, keeping the gun trained on the driver. Emma climbed out of the back seat, tightly holding onto Justin's hand, as Anja circled the car and slowly opened the driver's door.

"Out," she screamed.

The driver sat defiantly with his hands on the steering wheel. Anja edged closer and pushed the muzzle into his ear.

"Get out or die here, you choose."

He felt the muzzle shake in Anja's hand, and even if she did not intend it to, the gun could easily go off. It would make a mess of the car, and he would be dead, that was not an option. Slowly he took his hands from the steering wheel and slid round on his seat to face Anja. She took a step back; worried that he might try and jump her. He moved slowly and deliberately, his intention was to keep this power play going for as long as possible and wait for her to make a mistake. Then 'she and her silly little friend would pay'. He rose to his feet and took a step towards Anja. She moved her free hand around her flowing robe and looked like she was going to remove it, but she did not. She flicked the gun, and he did not understand. She looked again like she was going to disrobe, and again she did not. Then she pointed the gun at him. He realised what she wanted. She wanted him to take off his clothes. He looked around for anything that might help. All he could see was rocks, scrub and sand. Nowhere to run. The only weapon being in Anja's shaking hand. She held the gun in both hands to steady herself.

He glanced down the dirt road. They had not seen any traffic on the drive and the likelihood of anyone driving past, out there, in the heat of the day, to that remote place, was very unlikely. The best thing to do was to continue to bide his time, do what she asked and let her play her little game.

Slowly he unbuttoned his shirt. 'This was a game he was going to enjoy'. 'Look at this hunk of man' he thought to himself 'you will wish you were mine again, when you see what I have waiting for you, little bitch'.

He untucked the shirt from his trousers, slowly undid the buttons, slid it from his back and arms and tossed it onto the sand. His hairy paunch flopped down over his waistline. 'You want more? I will give you more'

The conversation raged in his head, outwardly calm, but inside his anger was brewing. Seething with hate and passion. He wanted to beat them, rape them and then let Anja watch while he slowly killed the little one, before causing her such pain that she would beg for her own death.

Anja waved the gun, pointing to his trousers. Slowly he began to undo his belt, the belt he was going to whip them with. He threw the belt to the ground and slowly undid his trousers. They fell to his ankles and he stepped out of them, kicking off his shoes as he did so.

The heat of the sand rose up through his socks and he winced, hopping from foot to foot. Anja could not help but smile. She could tell what he was thinking; he was a shallow, small-minded man. He had forcibly taken her many times, so she knew him probably better than he knew himself. As he got down to his underpants, he began to feel a little more uneasy. The heat of the sun burning into his hair covered flesh. As he placed his thumbs into the waist band Anja stopped him.

"No."

She waved the gun again, this time pointing to the ground.

"Down, you beg, now."

'This was her game', he thought, 'I made you beg, and now it's my turn is it? Just come a little closer, you little bitch and we will see who ends up begging'. He got down on his knees and looked up at her. He was a pathetic sight, balding and middle aged, with ape-like hair covering his overweight body. He was now completely at Anja's mercy. She levelled the gun at his head. At last he spoke.

"You don't have it in you, do you, you stupid whore?"

His English was clear, obviously his second language. He tried to stand. Reaching forward as he did, he tried to grab the gun. Anja squeezed the trigger. The bullet hit him full in the centre of his stomach. He doubled and fell to the ground. Anja tottered from the recoil, and just about kept her footing. He was bleeding badly from the wound, but he was still alive. Standing over him, she aimed the gun at his face. He cowered pathetically, naked, save for his underpants and socks, pain rifling through his body, knowing his life would soon be over. He just prayed it would be quick and relatively painless. Emma touched Anja's arm and looked across at Justin.

"He doesn't need to see this, he's traumatised enough."

The driver was bleeding quite badly, and Anja knew the wound was more than likely mortal and if they just drove off and left him he would be no threat and just bleed to death. Anja spat at the man and turned back towards the car. Slowly he staggered to his feet and shouted something in Arabic, it sounded like a curse.

With a last gasp of adrenalin, he ran towards Anja, arms outstretched, screaming at the top of his voice. She turned and fired. The bullet whistled past his head by a whisker. Unbalanced she fell over backwards, and as she fell, dropped the gun. It skittered across the dusty ground for several feet. Anja scrambled on all fours trying to retrieve it.

Emma could only watch rooted to the spot in fear. The semi-naked driver got nearer and launched himself through the air. Anja reached the gun first. As he dived onto her back, she fumbled the pistol in her grasp. She tried to flip herself over. Face to face, she instinctively squeezed the trigger.

Another shot rang out, this time at close range. The bullet tore into his leg, shattering his kneecap sending blood and bone fragments flying into the dust. He stumbled and grabbed her by the waist. Screaming with pain and rage, he tried to bite her face. His gnashing brown teeth narrowly missed her nose and she managed to head butt him on the chin. Anja grappled wildly trying to escape him. He tried to punch her in the face. His fist flew past her temple. He caught her hard on the cheek. Dazed, she thought she might lose consciousness.

The blood poured from his stomach and leg wounds with every heartbeat, but still he fought on. It all happened in an instant. Emma picked up a rock. He was on top of Anja. Her cheek ached. His face pressed against hers. Beads of sweat dripped from his forehead and nose into Anja's eyes. She blinked hard to try to see. Through the salty tears that were clouding her vision, she made out a shape behind him. He raised his fist high above Anja's face. It began to fall towards her. With both hands, Emma brought down the rock and his skull cracked with the impact. His fist fell limply onto Anja's face. His body now dead weight across hers.

Justin was screaming. Anja found herself, not for the first time, covered in blood and brain matter. Anja lay panting and it was Emma's turn to drag a naked overweight corpse from on top of her friend.

They sat for a moment panting. Justin walked slowly over to Emma and wrapped his arms tightly around her. It was quite a scene, Anja's beautiful white robes covered in the driver's blood, her cheek bruised and sore from the impact. Emma took his left hand and Anja his right and, straining, they dragged his lifeless heavy body behind some scrub. Anja searched the car as Emma searched through the driver's clothing. Her eyes lit up. He had a mobile phone. Emma tried to turn it on, desperately waiting for the screen to light up. If she could just get a signal, she could phone home and summon help.

Anja discovered a bottle of water in the boot of the car. Resisting the immediate urge to wash herself, she took a handful of sand and rubbed it into her face to wipe away some of the mess that smothered her.

Anja winced as the pain shot through her gradually purpling cheek. It was heavily bruised, but hopefully not broken. The sand was warm to the touch and seemed to soak up much of the blood. Anja surrendered her robes and used the cleanest part of them to towel her face and hands.

The mobile phone came to life. Emma clicked the button marked zero and nearly burst into tears when she saw that the phone was asking for a six-digit PIN number, which they didn't have. Anja could see Emma wail in desperation and the three of them wrapped their arms around each other in a huddle. Emma slipped the mobile phone into her underwear, just in case. She still had her robe, and Anja put the driver's clothes on. They were a terrible fit, far too big, but there was no other alternative. Anja looked at the road behind them.

"We have to move."

39.

They returned to the car. Anja sat behind the wheel and started the engine. She had found a baseball cap in the boot and with it on her head, pushed her long hair underneath. With the assistance of the tinted windows, she hoped that anyone passing would think she was a man driving the car, and with Emma in the back seat still wearing her veil and Justin hidden below the window line, no one would stop or suspect them.

Malek had told them they had been in Bechar, which, by the position of the sun, meant the dusty track they drove on, must be a little north of there. Anja reached into the glove box and looked for anything that might resemble a map. She found one. Bechar, as far as she could tell, was about half way along Algeria's western border, with a main road that could take them to the north and onwards to the coast. Algiers was an obvious place to head for, as it was a tourist destination. If they could reach it, they thought there might be some European tourists that could help them, or at least find a way to get a message home. Scouring the map, Algiers was going to be a long drive, and looking at the petrol gauge, they were not at all sure whether that amount of fuel would get them that far. They settled for Oran.

Traversing the mountain tracks and unsure of their map reading skills, Anja tried to avoid the main roads. Neither of them had ever heard of Oran, but as it looked like a large coastal town, there could be tourists or perhaps a boat across to Spain. The route to Oran would take them through the high plateaus of the Saharan Atlas Mountains and therefore be less likely to run into any of Nassim's men on the hunt for Justin.

With Anja in the driving seat, Emma, with her arm around Justin, had a glazed look in her eyes. She was in a daydream. Her mind drifted away from the events of the past few months.

She was at home, her mother and father were going about their normal Sunday routine, Mom preparing the vegetables for dinner, Dad was outside mowing the lawn.

She gazed at them, how she loved her parents, such a safe place, the warm sunshine rolling in through the open patio doors, the birdsong, the soft whir of the lawn mower, the radio playing soft love songs filtering through from the kitchen.

"Baszd meg."

Anja cursed as she glanced up at her rear-view mirror. Emma was back in the moment and turned to look over her shoulder. She saw it too. Another car. Black. Dark windows. Driving at high speed towards them. Anja put her foot down as far as she dared. As the speed increased, she used all her concentration to stay in control and keep it on the road. To their left the sheer sided ravine, with only the flimsiest of barriers between them and a fall of hundreds of feet. To their right, rocky mountainside rising as high as they could see above. The track had only room for one car, with the odd passing place dotted here and there. They climbed. The car behind closed in and nudged their rear bumper. Anja fought to keep control as their bodies jolted forwards. Another bump.

At a sharp bend to the right, Anja skidded the car around the corner, the other car locked in tight pursuit. Emma noticed a man's arm reach out of the passenger window. There was a gun in his hand. Emma ducked as the first bullet shattered the rear window, showering them with tiny fragments. A second bullet whistled through the gaping window, and straight through the windscreen. The windscreen shattered but held in place, with just a small bullet hole providing the only clear view of the outside world. Anja could barely see where she was going. She leaned forward. With one hand on the steering wheel, punched the windscreen with her free hand. The windscreen crumpled around Anja's fist, up to her elbow.

Anja fought to pull her hand free, while simultaneously steering around the sharp bends with her free hand. The black car bumped them again. Another shot rang out. The bullet thudded into the passenger headrest, narrowly missing Emma's head. She dived into the rear foot well for cover dragging Justin down beside her.

Anja managed to shake her hand free and sped on. Justin was crying with fear. The car rocked back and forth, swerving on what little road there was. Anja was determined, trying not to let the gunman have an easy target. The road widened, and the other car began to pull alongside.

The chasing car sideswiped Anja's driver side crumpling her driver's door.

The locking mechanism failed, and the door began to flap open and shut as Anja tried to pull in front.

Emma glancing up from her hiding place, caught sight of the driver, through the open window. With a determined look on his face, he swerved and bumped into their car once again.

The rear of Anja's car skidded sideways and glanced off the barrier, sending loose rocks down into the ravine below. The driver shouted at them, it was something in Arabic, probably asking them to stop. The chasing car finally managed to draw level and slammed into the side again. Anja had tensed herself expecting the jolt and turned her steering wheel back towards the chasing car, giving it a clout in return. Her driver's door swung open and hung lifelessly from its' damaged hinges. Anja had become an open target.

The road became more dangerous as it curled up the side of the mountain, there were sections of road where the banks had eroded, and crash barriers no longer existed.

Anja tried to be extra careful, any mistake would have sent them straight over the edge and to certain death. Justin was crying, uncontrollable sobs as Emma tried to comfort him. Anja held their lives in her hands as she fought to stay in control. The road became more of a track again, so Anja put her foot down, as there would have been no room for both vehicles side by side. She knew she needed to stay in front. Anja turned hard right at the next bend. A truck piled high with wooden crates of noisy chickens, was in the middle of the road heading straight for them. The truck swerved with just enough room to pass and Anja skidded towards the edge of the precipice. Anja bounced the car off the barrier. Bolts skimmed down the mountainside, as the end of the crash barrier unfastened.

The chasing car slammed into the back of Anja, and as she tried to avoid going over the edge, her vehicle flew into a spin and smashed its' front-end against the mountainside on the opposite side of the road, Anja's car came to a halt and stalled.

The truck driver, not wanting to get involved, continued driving, chickens clucking and fluttering in their wooden cages. The pursuing car came to a halt alongside the damaged barrier. Anja could see them in her rear-view mirror. Another second and they would be out of their car and the chase would be over. She had one last plan. She shouted at her passengers.

"Get out now."

There was no emotion in her voice, just a stern order. Emma pushed open the rear door, and she dropped to the dusty ground, dragging Justin out on top of her. Anja dropped into reverse gear. She frantically turned the ignition key and floored the accelerator simultaneously. The man in the passenger seat levelled his pistol, through the open window, and began firing. It was a split-second decision. The rear of Anja's vehicle struck the side of the pursuers' car, at full speed. The flimsy barrier gave way. Desperate bullets shot through the air. There was a loud creak of scraping metal as the barrier swung out over the ravine and both cars disappeared over the edge.

Emma and Justin lay in the road transfixed by the scene not daring to move. It was all over in an instant. The only sound was the distant clatter of metal against rock as the two vehicles hurtled down the mountainside to the valley below. Then silence.

Emma could barely realise what had just happened and burst into an uncontrollable wail.

"No! No!" Emma screamed it at the top of her voice. If felt as though her lungs would burst.

Justin was the first to hear the noise. The grinding of metal. He put a hand on Emma's arm; she stopped screaming and began to wipe her eyes. Justin pointed. The broken barrier that dipped over the edge was creaking, and straining. It looked and sounded like it would fall away at any minute. Emma thought she could hear a muffled cry.

"Help!"

Emma rushed to the edge of the road to see Anja dangling from the swinging barrier by just one hand.

The metal creaked under her weight, and Emma could see that the bolts securing it to the side of the road were loose. Justin peered over the edge. The gaping chasm greeted his scared saucer-like eyes. It was a long way down. No one could survive a fall of that distance.

Emma could not reach Anja's flailing hand, or the fingers that clung to the barrier in a fragile grip. Anja tried to swing. With a stretch, she managed to clutch the barrier with her free hand and began to drag herself along, inch by inch. Her arms were so tired. A thought crossed Anja's mind 'it would be so easy just to let go and all of this would be over.' 'But what of Justin and Emma? They may never make it without her'.

The barrier began to groan even more as Anja pulled herself along. The barrier and its' frail mountings were separating from the crumbling road under Anja's weight. One bolt fell and then another, bouncing down the mountainside. With more urgency and panic, she scoured the edge of the cliff looking for something more substantial to hang onto. Another bolt fell, and so did Anja. She jolted as the barrier dipped again. Another bolt fell. Anja desperately tried to swing towards Emma's outstretched hand as the last of the bolts began to loosen. Finally, the barrier cracked under her weight, and Anja began to fall. She bumped against the rock and her right hand fell against a protruding tree root.

Anja's fingers locked around the root. Desperately she held on as the barrier clattered past her head and down towards the rocks below. The root appeared to be strong, and held Anja's weight, but as she had fallen a little further, she was completely out of reach of Emma's despairing fingers. Anja tried to pull herself up, but it was no use. She was completely exhausted. It took all her strength to hang on where she was. Justin was crying uncontrollably. In desperation, Emma looked around for something she could use. All Emma could see, beyond Justin, were rocks, scrub and dust. Then looking down she glanced at her robes.

"Hold On," cried Emma. "I have an idea."

Quickly Emma stripped, down to just her slip. The white silk felt strong in her small hands. She lowered one end to Anja. Anja reached over and grabbed hold of the fabric with one hand, with the other still clinging to the root.

"Come over here Justin," said Emma, "Hold onto this."

They both grabbed the silk and steadied themselves.

"Justin, when I say pull, I want you to pull on this as hard as you can."

Justin nodded that he had understood. Emma prayed that, between them, they would have the strength to lift Anja up, and that the silk itself was strong enough.

"Anja, grab a firm hold; we're going to start to pull."

Emma shouted, and Anja wrapped her arms and legs around the silk. For her, the robe was a little slippery, but she managed to intertwine herself enough into the fabric, to not just slide off the end. With her left hand, she still held onto the root. As Emma felt the weight of her friend she knew it was now or never.

"Now pull."

Emma could feel the robe starting to slide through her fingers. She gripped as tightly as she could; knowing that to slip now was not an option.

"Pull Justin, pull." Emma encouraged the young boy, who did as he was told.

Emma was in charge; her friend's life was completely in their hands.

"Come on Justin, we can do this, pull."

Their arms were tired, but they did not give up.

"Hold on Anja!" Emma screamed to her friend.

Anja was silent, too tired to do anything but hang on, trying to gain traction against the rock and dirt with her dangling feet. Anja thankfully hugged her silken lifeline as they pulled her to safety.

Thirty seconds later Anja's head peeped over the edge of the road, managing to drag herself the last foot and scrambled to safety. Anja lay in the middle of the track, breathing hard and looking up at the clear blue sky, the bright sun beating down on them.

"How many more dangers must we face" she whispered to herself.

Reunited with Emma and Justin, they scrambled to the safety of the scrub and rocks at the other side of the road. Anja held her two companions in a warm embrace.

"I love you...."

Justin had never spoken a single word in all the time they were with him. His little voice timid and afraid; his big eyes looked up at Anja, arms hugging her knees. Three simple little words that meant so much.

"...and I love you."

He gazed at Emma. They had risked everything to help him escape. They all burst into tears, relieved. The release in tension was exactly what they needed. There was still a long way to go. They had no vehicle, no food or water, no map and no weapon and they were hopelessly lost in the Algerian Atlas Mountains. As Emma put on the, now dirty, robe, Anja considered where they should head for next. A thought occurred to her.

"How did they know which road we were on?"

"Could it be this?" Emma took the mobile phone from her underwear.

"Maybe they tracked us with the driver's phone?"

"It's possible. I suppose it would be best to throw it away, just in case," replied Anja.

Emma hurled the phone as hard as she could over the edge, and they watched as it disappeared from view far below. They began to walk, Emma wrapped in her dirty robe, Anja in the driver's ill-fitting clothing. As day turned into night, the temperature began to drop. They had hardly seen any traffic all day. In the distance, out of the darkness, came a set of dim headlights. At first, they were afraid, but as it drew nearer, they could see it was an old farm truck. The truck stopped, and the driver got out. He was an old man in a checked shirt and jeans, sandals on his feet.

"Could we get a lift somewhere?" enquired Anja walking towards him, hands outstretched to show she meant him no harm.

"Lift, yes, you need food? My wife cook. Good food. Come."

He spoke in broken English, but enough for them to understand. He waved them to climb into the cab of his truck with about a dozen goats bleating in the back. They squeezed into the cab. The clutch and gearbox rattled as he forced the gear stick into the slot. The truck shook as they pulled away. They sat in silence, appreciating the gradual warmth as the engine heated up.

About half an hour later, they arrived at an old farmhouse. There were lights on inside and smoke billowing out of the chimney. The man opened the door and led them inside.

The house was sparsely furnished. In the middle of the main room was a large wooden table, with four wooden chairs and a series of small rag rugs covered the stone floor.

A middle-aged woman stood at the stove stirring a large metal pot, while an older woman sat in a wooden rocking chair, a blanket over her legs. A roaring fire in the hearth, surrounded by logs was so inviting and the three companions gratefully warmed their hands.

The middle-aged woman spoke to the man in a language Anja could not understand. Then she addressed them all.

"Hello, I am Nadira; this is my Mamma and Papa."

Mamma and Papa nodded and grinned.

"You look hungry, would you like some? It is Jwaz"

Emma peered into the pot; it looked like vegetable stew.

"Yes please," Emma's stomach was rumbling. Nadira served the Jwaz into six dishes serving it with couscous and some freshly baked flat bread. Hungrily and in silence they ate.

Once the meal was over, they sat around the fire telling the family about their troubles with Nadira translating for Mamma and Papa.

Nadira told them a little about herself. As a young woman, she had travelled to Spain, and then Gibraltar working as a cook in restaurants and hotels, which is why she could speak Spanish and English, as well as a smattering of a few other languages. When Mamma had become ill, she returned home to the Atlas to look after them. She had never married, although there had been a young Spanish man who had captured her heart, but it was not to be.

"So how are you planning to get home now?"

"We were hoping to make it to Algiers and find some European tourists that might help us." Anja said confidently.

"You wouldn't have a telephone would you, by any chance?" Emma politely inquired.

Nadira shook her head.

"Unfortunately, we do not even have electricity up here. I looked at us getting solar panels, but they are too expensive. We barely make any money from the farm as it is."

As evening turned to night, they sat in front of the fire, watching the shapes in the flames dance. Papa began to play, what Emma thought looked like, a Lute.

"This is an Oud," Nadira explained, "Papa is one of the most accomplished Oud players, in all of the Atlas region."

Listening to its' haunting melodies, their minds imagined the old times; the tones of this instrument would have reverberated across the North African and Arabian world for many centuries past. Faces warmed by the fire's glow, and with tiredness washing over them, one by one, they drifted off to sleep on the floor, where they had sat listening to the ancient lullabies. Nadira laid blankets over them and eased soft pillows under their heads.

They slept until the light of dawn, when the strong smell of coffee awoke them from their slumber.

Nadira was making breakfast. Eggs, flat bread, homemade jam, honey and deep-fried 'Makrout El Assel', which looked, to Emma, like doughnuts. They sat at the table and devoured the feast.

"Papa can give you a ride into Oran, and here…" Nadira reached into her apron pocket "…here is some money for food."

"We cannot take it from you, you have done enough."

Emma, extremely touched by the family's generosity, shook her head.

"You can, and you must, the troubles you have been through in our country are dreadful, you must be free to get home to your families. Here I also have these."

Nadira handed Emma a bundle of old clothing.

"These should serve you, until you get chance to buy some new ones."

Anja and Emma gratefully accepted the gifts and put on the clothes. Papa started up his old truck and waving from the cab the three travellers, bade Nadira and Mamma goodbye.

40.

The journey to Oran was bumpy, but the companions were in good spirits. Papa sang happily to himself; a song that none of them could understand the words to. The morning sun was warm, and after a good night's sleep and full bellies, they were feeling better than they had for many months. They were nearing journey's end. They just needed to get to the ferry terminal, and even without passports, they could explain their situation and the officials would surely help them. Papa's truck entered the city driving along the wide modern roads following the signs for the ferry terminal.

Emma could tell straight away that Oran was a modern city. Traditional buildings of Spanish, Ottoman and French influence sat among the high-rise hotels, shops, bars and apartment buildings.

Anja let out a deep sigh as the large white ferry, stating "Algerie Ferries" in large blue lettering on the side, awaited them at the dock. They felt pleased with themselves, having evaded capture, using their wits and determination, they would soon be on their way home.

Papa dropped them a short walk from the terminal building. Anja and Emma both kissed him goodbye and Justin gave him a hug. He waved to them. A big smile beamed across his face, as the truck headed back towards the terminal exit and the road back to his home in the mountains.

They walked with a spring in their step, Justin holding onto Emma's hand, Anja in a slight lead. Up ahead they could see an armed police officer, in deep conversation with two men in dark suits. Anja halted and held up her hand. She turned to Emma and Justin, pointing over her shoulder. Anja voice trembled as she spoke.

"Those are Nassim's men."

They had come so far, endured so much, and Nassim's men guarded their only means of escape.

"We have to get out of here before they see us."

Emma had tears rolling down her eyes. A second earlier, she had felt happy, for the first time since the nightmare had begun.

Now she was crestfallen.

"How could they know we were coming here?"

Emma started to sob uncontrollably.

"Come on Emma, we're not beaten yet."

Anja was determined, there had to be another way. Anja put a hand on her friend's shoulder as they hurried away from the port and back towards the town. The streets were busy, full of shoppers, so they opted to remain where there were many people. They needed to blend in, until they worked out what they were going to do. They still had the small sum of money that Nadira had given them, so they purchased some coffee and a glass of milk for Justin, in a small café, and sat at a small table while they planned their next move.

Emma was watching the passers-by through the café window, when she felt her spine run cold.

"It's Nassim, he's here."

Nassim had walked past the café, with three of his men in tow. Emma's hands started shaking. Anja got up from her seat and moved towards the doorway.

"Which way did he go?" she whispered.

Emma raised a shaky finger and pointed.

"Then we go the opposite way."

Anja led her two scared companions out towards a group of market stalls, bedecked with rolls of material. They pretended to be feeling the quality of the cloth for sale, taking it in turns to glance around them for fear Nassim's men may be closing in. Emma led Justin to another stall that sold carved wooden animals, standing behind him, to try and shield him from view.

Anja turned to walk towards them, when suddenly; arms grabbed her from behind, wrapping tightly around her waist in a bear hug. She tried to scream, but the grip was so tight, and coming as such a surprise, it had completely winded her. Anja glanced across at Emma and Justin in desperation. After all they had been through, their bid for freedom was finally over.

41.

For Harry and the rest of the prisoners, most days began the same. The captives queued while a guard poured water into the trough. Given the hot stuffy conditions, they were all thirsty, most of the time. There were no drinking vessels, so they had to either cup the water with their hands, or drink like animals on all fours. The food was sparse and consisted of mainly stale bread, rice and beans. They became immune to the smell of sweat, body odours and bodily functions. Fresh air circulated through the cracks in the walls, more from lack of building maintenance than design.

Around the middle of each day, groups of prisoners were taken outside, forcibly washed and paraded in front of a video camera. Some were handed scripts to read, while others, who refused to read, were beaten. By mid-afternoon, most of those taken, had usually been returned to the sports hall. Those that were not, were never seen again.

It was a Thursday, Harry had been trying to count the days and decided that the day in question was probably a Thursday; and 'probably' was close enough for Harry. On this particular Thursday about a dozen Egyptian prisoners, men and women, had been taken earlier in the morning. All was quiet for about an hour. That all changed when the captives heard shouting, then a volley of gunshots. All went silent for about five minutes. Then they heard the screams. It sounded as if the Egyptian prisoners were being slaughtered one by one. No gunshots, just the tearing of flesh and splintering of bone. The whole sports hall fell into a hush as they listened. One by one the screaming stopped. The last man merely whimpering before he too was silenced.

A deathly quiet hung over the prison cell for the rest of the day. There was less squabbling over the mouldy bread after that. For a few days the beatings stopped, and there came a sense that all was not well with their captors and that something big was going to happen, and that all the prisoners may play some part in whatever it was they were planning.

Three days after the massacre of the Egyptian prisoners, so to Harry's reckoning must have been a Sunday, the beatings and filming began again. It was not a return to normal, but an escalation. More prisoners were arriving, and many were younger, with more girls and young women among them. The captors seemed to prefer the younger girls as their playthings, and although it gave little comfort to Francois that she would not be top of their rape list, it just meant she had moved higher up the expendable list.

Apart from squabbling over the meagre food there was little to do. Harry and Francois spent more time in each other's company, deep in conversation about home and family. They discovered that, although each had lived very different lives, they had many things in common. Harry had a passion for history, art and music and Francois had visited, in the course of her work, many of the historical sites that Harry had only read about.

It is in darkest moments, when everything seems lost, that a little light can sometimes fall. The small alpine flower growing in the harshest of mountain climates, sweet birdsong in a bombed-out warzone. As Francois looked deep into Harry's eyes, for the first time in years he felt something. His one and only love had been Vicky and, try as his daughter Jade might, with her date night set-ups, he had never fallen for anyone else. He looked away from her gaze, but an invisible force kept drawing him back. Those deep brown eyes, enticing, inviting. He was lost in thoughts of her. Francois. Her unwashed hair, hands dry and cracked, clothes shabby, dishevelled and torn. And her pretty face. When she smiled, she beamed, her eyes lit up, like diamonds glinting against her grubby tanned skin. Looking at her, even in that state, she was nothing less than beautiful. Probably the most beautiful woman he had ever seen.

"'Arry?" she whispered. "Are you okay?"

Harry found it hard to find the words but shuffled closer to her on the cold stone floor.

"Francois, I, I, just wanted to tell you…"

Harry faltered, he wanted the words to be right, but just could not bring the right ones to mind. She knew what he was about to say. She had felt it too. Without a word, she lifted her hand and stroked his cheek with the back of her fingertips.

Francois drew closer. Her breath on his lips. His heart pounded. Tilting her head slightly, it was the gentlest kiss. The lightest touch. Brushing her lips gently against his. She drew closer.

The tip of her tongue traced the edges of his mouth, sending erotic tingles of excitement throughout his body. They embraced, holding each other as though they were the last two people on Earth.

"Oh, Francois I…"

"Sssh" Francois, whispered quietly, as she held him for longer than he could ever remember being held. He breathed her in, as she breathed him. They could feel each other's heart racing. Tears welled in Harry's eyes, so strong was their connection.

That night, they lay in each other's arms, bodies entwined, beneath an old ragged blanket. There was danger all around. The ever-present threat of death. 'Harry needed at least a few fleeting moments of happiness', thought Zettler to himself, as he sat quietly on watch nearby.

Harry awoke early the following morning with Francois still asleep, her head resting softly on his chest. He stroked her hair, kissing the top of her head. She awoke and turned her eyes to his.

"Bonjour 'Arry."

She smiled. Her sweet French accent was like music to his ears.

The metal door opened, and three armed guards entered. As usual, they selected twelve people. This time, all western and white. Having picked the first nine, they approached Harry, Zettler and Francois. It was the usual drill. Hands tied behind their backs, then bundled and pushed into the bright morning sunshine. The sunlight glinted off the camera lens, which had been wired to a laptop computer. They approached the line of masked gunmen in the centre of the 'pitch'. They each stood in front of a guard facing the camera before being forced roughly to their knees.

The commander approached looking relaxed, he had a coffee in one hand and a revolver in the other.

"This is just a rehearsal…" he shouted merrily, "…there will be no executions today."

The red light on the camera blinked; the guard behind it pressed a button and the red blinking light turned solid. The commander took a deep breath and began to spout his rhetoric in clear tones. Harry cringed as he listened to how the West was the oppressor, something about infidels, someone must pay, the release of brothers and large amounts of cash and gold to be deposited somewhere or other.

The people of the West were kept fat, stupid and compliant, fed an addictive daily dose of fast food, alcohol, fake news and loose morals and were blind to the evils their governments were perpetrating. It was the same old thing. Harry counted at least a dozen times, when they had been dragged out in front of the camera for this spectacle. The only benefit was breathing the fresh dusty air and feeling the sun on their faces for the short time they knelt there. It was always too soon before they were cast back into the dullness and stench of the 'sports hall'.

On this particular day, something was different. The commander seemed to be more and more agitated and excited. He talked of money in exchange for prisoners. At this point, he produced a mobile phone from his pocket and began to read out the phone number on camera, to the 'supposed' audience. Harry began to wonder, 'is this a live broadcast?'

In his excitement, the commander announced, they would start the bidding or start the killing. Although this was only supposed to be a rehearsal, a shiver ran down Harry's spine, he glanced at Francois and then at Zettler. All of them knew that their governments would let them die rather than give in to terrorist demands.

The commander waved the mobile phone in front of the camera, but there was no response, no one rang. He shouted again at the camera, but still no answer. He walked over to the line of kneeling prisoners and dragged a young woman by the arm towards a wooden block in front of the camera. Harry suspected she was from Eastern Europe, probably in her mid-twenties. Once in front of the camera he forced her down to her knees, her chin resting on the crudely made block.

"Last chance."

He glared at the camera, looked down at the phone, then back to the camera. None of them had any idea whether there was anyone out there watching, or was it just another rehearsal or scary bluff to keep the prisoners in their place? As the commander stuffed the phone into a pocket beneath his robes, the camera lowered to get a full view of the woman.

The commander walked over to a long wooden table. On it lay a long ceremonial sword which he withdrew from its' sheath. It had been highly polished and glinted in the sun. He carefully examined the blade, as if in a trance.

He walked across to the woman, on her knees, her head bowed to the floor, with hands tied behind her back. She was crying. Frightened, she had wet herself, a pool of bright amber liquid spread out across the ground beneath her, soaking her legs. As he stood behind her, the mobile phone rang, the stock iphone ringtone sounded out against the soft breeze. He answered. Immediately his face turned red and threw the phone to the floor.

"Fucking PPI!"

His eyes were crazed, he began to lick his lips as he approached the woman, cowering and begging for her life. She could sense that this was no rehearsal. Her time had come, and her life was to end right there. Right then. The commander raised the sword above his head and took a long look straight into the camera. He winked, smiled, relaxed his arms to his side lowering the blade. He smirked. The woman glanced to her side and breathed a sigh of relief that it was a rehearsal after all. The commander took a deep breath. With a swift movement, he lifted the sword above his head, and brought it down with full force onto the back of the poor young woman's neck. She died instantly. Blood gushing from her neck, her decapitated head fell from the block and rolled across the dry, dusty ground.

The kneeling prisoners all gasped in horror. The commander roared with laughter as he reached down and lifted her head up by the hair, showing it as a prize to the remaining prisoners before posing with it in front of the camera.

Harry was sure he saw the young womans' eyes flicker in shocked realisation, as if her brain was still alive just for a few moments after her decapitation. Francois looked away as the blood dripped to the ground. The commander hurled the head aside like a toy as he strode back towards the table. Flicking and then wiping the blood from the sword, he laid it flat and returned to face the camera. Picking the mobile phone from the ground he began waggling it and smiling at the camera once more. He bowed and the guards behind the prisoners applauded. Then, as two guards dragged the woman's headless body away, with hands on hips, he proudly inspected the remaining prisoners.

"Who will be next?"

The commander laughed as he repeated the phone number twice straight into the lens. He scanned the prisoners, looking for his next victim.

He walked up and down the line, stopping for a second then moving on to the next. He moved to the end of the line, turned and pointed to the middle. He pointed at Francois.

"Bring her to me."

Harry felt sick, hands tied behind his back, a guard's hand on the top of his head, he was helpless. Zettler flexed his muscles, but he too was helpless to assist. Two guards, one on each arm, dragged Francois towards the pool of blood and urine and forced her to kneel at the commander's feet. The commander knelt beside her and touched her face gently. He moved to kiss her, but Francois spat straight in his face. He slapped her hard and she fell heavily to the floor. Harry squirmed under the force of the guard.

"Take me, take me next please I beg you."

The tears rolled down Harry's face. He knew he had fallen completely in love with her, and now someone else he loved dearly, would be mercilessly taken from him, albeit for a few moments before his own demise. Zettler was struggling too, but it was no use.

The commander laughed, ignoring Harry's plea, waved the phone at the camera.

"Last chance."

He strolled slowly towards the long table, he was going to enjoy this, and drag it out a bit longer, so that he could inflict a little extra suffering on the Englishman. He lifted the sword and carried it, glinting, towards his stage.

He held the sword to the sky, watching the blade in awe as he turned it into the sun, sending its' bright reflection in different directions around the stadium. It was pure theatre.

The two guards pulled Francois to her knees and forced her head onto the now blood soaked block, as the camera was adjusted and fixed in place.

Hey English, he mocked, "say goodbye to your girlfriend."

His triumph was almost complete. The commander turned, his feet right next to Francois' knees. Gleefully, and slowly, he raised the sword. Francois, shaking with fear, just managed to cry out a last few words.

"Je Taime 'Arry."

The life they had lived for the past few months was about to end, in the most dramatic way possible.

# 42.

The first explosion ripped through the stadium wall. The ground shook as if an earthquake had gripped the land. The commander toppled backwards as the camera hit the floor, smashing the lens and breaking its' connection to the outside world. A second rocket exploded into the stand, sending wooden seats flying and splitting its' masonry asunder. Dust and rubble engulfed the stadium, with only the sounds of high-speed aircraft coursing overhead, punctuating the blasts.

A third salvo struck the main building. Huge pieces of falling concrete and steel lurched through the air, projecting shards of debris towards prisoners and guards alike. Dead bodies lay with the injured and dying, pinned by sections of rubble; their screams drowned out by the overhead screech of the planes as salvo upon salvo rained down on the stadium.

Harry lay flat on the ground. The guard that had stood over him had been struck in the head by a flying piece of wood. Harry dragged himself out from beneath the corpse. Zettler lay amongst a heap of bodies. He groaned as Harry approached. Harry dragged his friend to his feet, and back to back, they managed to untie each other's hands. The old building rattled as each missile found its' target.

"Where's Francois?" Harry cried.

"I think she's over there." Zettler pointed and they hurried through the dusty fog. Another rocket struck the building and the wall began to rock. Prisoners and guards ran into the compound, and as they looked back, the roof of the building caved in, trapping whoever was left inside. There were prisoners and guards running in all directions trying to avoid the continual rocket attack.

Through the dust and debris, Harry saw them. The commander was dragging the defenceless Francois towards the helicopters.

"There they are!" Harry shouted as he broke into a sprint.

Zettler joined the chase; he was much slower, his damaged leg still bothering him as he ran.

All around the flames rose higher amidst the burning wreckage. A missile struck one of the large metal containers, and its' contents exploded like an out of control firework display. A section of the container skidded through the air and struck the commander square on the back. He tumbled to the floor, with his arm still curled around Francois.

As Harry caught up with them and slowed to a stop, the commander lay on the ground, his one hand wrapped tightly around Francois' jaw, and a pistol in the other, pressed into her cheek. Zettler, out of breath and in pain, caught up with his friend. The commander smiled at them.

"You let me go and I promise I'll free her when I land."

The commander was desperate and knew that Harry had the upper hand. But, he had Francois, and that was all he needed to make good his escape. Harry and Zettler both knew it was an empty promise, if he escaped he would never let her live. Francois also knew this to be true, and he would also surely kill Harry and Zettler before making his getaway. They both stood back unsure of what to do, that was when Francois made her move. The commander had one hand around her mouth and one on the gun. Her lips were close to his thumb. With all her strength, Anja bit his hand. Her teeth cut into his flesh like a knife. As the commander shouted, Harry jumped for his other hand just as he pulled the trigger.

The gun made a loud click. The mechanism must have jammed in the blast. Harry was on him in a second. Wrestling the pistol from his grasp, he struck the commander across the face. His head fell to one side, and Harry struck him again. Repeatedly, Harry beat him, smashing the useless gun into the commander's face until it was just a bloody pulp. So severe was Harry's rage, Zettler had to drag his friend off the lifeless body and slapped him across the face to bring him to his senses.

"Come on!" Zettler screamed.

The helicopters were still a few hundred yards away, and about a dozen guards were running towards them. Francois was on her knees in pain. She tried to stand but collapsed.

"I cannot walk." She cried.

Harry could see the pain obvious in her face, and as he glanced at her foot, he could see it had been shattered into a bloody mess.

There was no time. The guards would soon be upon them. Zettler had already begun running for the chopper, as Harry turned, Francois looked him in the eyes.

"You have to leave me. I'm not going to make it."

Harry ignored her plea and managed to lift her into his tired arms.

"I'm not leaving without you."

The enemy was closing in from all directions. Francois felt heavy as Harry half limped, half staggered towards the helicopter. From the pain in his shoulder, he realised that he too must have been injured, but he was not going to give up.

In front of them stood the helicopter, Zettler ran around the side and pulled open the door, it was quite a sizeable chopper.

"I've flown one of these suckers before," he shouted gleefully, "and they've even left the keys in the ignition."

He quickly scanned the interior. There were a few boxes of munitions and a machine gun. He grabbed the machine gun, locked in a magazine and, as Harry and Francois approached, sprayed a volley of bullets over their heads. Two guards keeled over into the dust, while others dived for cover.

It had bought them enough time, Harry lifted the now unconscious Francois up to Zettler, and clambered into the helicopter beside her, cradling her head as Zettler attempted to start the engine. A rain of bullets hit the side of the chopper as the guards returned fire.

Zettler clicked the ignition and the rotors burst into life; starting their gentle spin, then faster, ever faster sending clouds of dust towards the guards. Zettler had performed his magic, the helicopter eased into the air. As they rose, Harry's first thought was for Francois, she was in pain but alive, he quickly checked her over for other wounds but found none. Zettler was more concerned whether the fighter planes in the air would see them as friend or foe. A single rocket could simply blast them out of the sky.

He waved a white handkerchief in front of himself. He prayed they would see it and not fire on them. It seemed to work. Zettler nosed the helicopter out into the sky and away from the chaos on the ground.

Zettler noted that there seemed to be a reasonable amount of fuel on board; and after Harry had tended to their wounds; he turned his attention to the contents of the hold. There was the machine gun. It looked like Zettler had exhausted the ammunition for that in his earlier burst. There were a few empty sacks, a winch with a large length of rope attached, a metal box which contained a couple of grenades and a can of engine oil; and, apart from a few pieces of bread and a plastic bottle of water, there was nothing else of any real interest. They shared the water and hungrily, ate the bread.

Zettler flew as high as he dared; and they reached the Libyan coastline a lot sooner than they anticipated. Small boats littered the near shore, as they flew out over the sea.

"We'll head for Malta; they should give us safe haven."

Zettler shouted above the noise of the rotors, clearing his mouthful of bread. He radioed ahead and contacted Maltese Air, requesting somewhere to land and for an ambulance to be on standby for when they arrived. For the rest of the flight they sat in silence, exhausted. Harry with one arm around Francois shoulders, her head gently bobbing against his chest with the vibration of the chopper. As the Maltese coastline came into view, Zettler finally breathed a sigh of relief.

43.

In Marrakech, for the past few months, both uncle and nephew had been busy. Following the raid on Ikrimah's home, they had relocated to the city. Mustapha knew of a small office a friend of his owned, which had been empty for months, not far from his own. They had gradually wheeled the equipment, from Mustapha's vehicle to the new location, in a handcart, topped with fruit, vegetables and some old sacking, so as not to arouse suspicion.

They were pleased to find that the electricity and water were still connected. As Hassan began setting up his new control centre, Mustapha set about organising the coffee. It took Hassan about half a day to be back online, with his collection of servers and terminals. Small green and red lights flickered as the screens came back to life.

Mustapha sipped his coffee and made a phone call to his friend Guryon, who was a senior officer in the Egyptian air force. Mustapha explained about the missing Jade and Emma, and that Harry and Zettler would be arriving in Egypt the following day to begin looking for them.

"Of course I will help," Guryon was a father too, he had a boy and a girl, and if he lost either of them, he would be devastated. Mustapha said he would be in touch as soon as his friends had landed, so they could meet and discuss their plans.

Two days went by, and with no message from Harry or Zettler; Mustapha was worried. Hassan searched for sightings across the entire internet and came up with nothing. He also searched for traces of Jade and Emma, and that trail had also gone cold.

Hassan did not give up. For months he searched, using all of his connections from the dark web. He investigated the scores of people smugglers and was amazed at how widespread the problem had become. Some people were making fortunes from the misery and enslavement of others.

Several months on from Harry and Zettler's disappearance, Hassan was perusing a technical chat room when the screen before him froze.

Hassan prepared to reboot his servers, but as he did so, a video of a black flag suddenly appeared on his monitor. It was as though someone had taken control of his screen and was streaming a live feed directly to him.

Mustapha came into the control room from the kitchen, a steaming mug of coffee in one hand, his mobile phone in the other.

"Hassan, something's really odd with my phone,"

Hassan looked at the phone. Mustapha's phone was also streaming the same feed.

"How can this be?" Hassan was puzzled. "We have two separate devices, on two different networks, yet we are picking up the same video."

"That neither of us were searching for," replied Mustapha.

Hassan tried to change his screen, but it would not clear. Nothing, apart from powering off his system, would stop the stream.

"It's as though someone out there has hijacked the internet?"

They both sat and stared at Hassan's screen. The black flag cleared, and the scene changed. It was outside, a shot of bright blue sky. The camera angle was changing. They could hear some background chatter as the camera adjusted. The voice was muffled, but clear enough to make out the words:

"This is just a rehearsal. There will be no executions today."

It directed to a man in a hood and black robes. He was ordering some people to line up. A dozen prisoners knelt in a line and the camera angle settled as if it had finally been secured on its' tripod.

"This doesn't look good," Mustapha murmured.

Hassan shifted nervously in his seat, as the camera panned down the row of captives.

"Wait, look," Mustapha pointed at the screen, "that man there kneeling, that's Leo, Leo Zettler."

The camera focussed back on the face of the man in the robe and hood, he seemed to be the one in charge. He started delivering his rhetoric followed by his demands. Mustapha and Hassan sat transfixed to the screen. After spending the past few months looking for their friends, here was at least one of them. But, where were they?

The leader read out a phone number, which Hassan hurriedly noted.

"Maybe I can trace the number from the satellites."

Hassan's brain was in overdrive, this could be their one and only chance to save their friends.

He switched on another computer. Row after row of machine code filled the screen, a flashing prompt appeared at the bottom. Hassan typed into the machine as fast as he could.

"I think the phone is located somewhere in Libya, although it could be a false number that's been cloned then bounced around the world a few times, it all depends how smart this man is. The only way I can know for sure is to call it."

A young woman was dragged to the front and fell to her knees.

"Last chance," said the voice on the screen.

"What on earth are you going to say to him?" Mustapha sounded bemused.

Hassan thought for a second, before recalling the conversation they had had when Harry's phone had rung unexpectedly. He dialled the number. It clicked, and the tone rang out. The figure on the screen answered. Hassan took a deep breath and cleared his throat, his knee shaking beneath the table.

"I am calling to discuss your PPI claim..." Hassan paused staring at the rows of code, rolling down the screen.

"Fucking PPI!" shouted the voice on the screen, which echoed through Hassan's handset. They watched the screen as he threw the phone to the ground. Hassan looked up at the machine code spinning into overdrive. It suddenly stopped.

Hassan turned to Mustapha.

"I think the idiot is using his own phone, and he's forgotten to re-route it."

"Which means?" said Mustapha expectantly.

"I know exactly where he is."

Hassan wrote down the coordinates, while Mustapha hastily called his friend Guryon.

"Guryon, Mustapha here, there is no time to talk, we know where Harry and Zettler are, is there anything you can do?"

Guryon explained that, after the recent atrocity when some of his countrymen had been brutally murdered, Egyptian military fighter planes constantly patrolled the Libyan border.

Mustapha read him the coordinates and warned him that they also needed to look out for Harry and Zettler.

Guryon, clicked off the call with Mustapha, immediately putting a call into the Egyptian air force commander.

Hassan looked back at the screen; the leader was holding up the girl's decapitated head and laughing. They saw Harry, in the background, being restrained as another woman was led forward and forced to kneel. The man waved his phone, with a huge grin on his face.

"Last chance," he cried, before stepping back into position. They could just about hear the faint sound of the approaching aircraft in the distance.

As he raised the sword above his head, a loud whoosh emanated from Hassan's speakers.

Then the screen went black.

44.

Liesel sat on the front step, inhaling the smoke from her cigarette. It was another hot and dry day in Oran. Her next client would be along soon. He was nice enough, and at least she knew he would be clean. He was a regular, she knew what he wanted, and she was confident that he would not beat her.

After her last client of the day, Liesel had the rest of the afternoon off, she was a good girl, all her clients said so. She was popular and her "Patronne" liked the fact that there were never any arguments. Liesel did as she was told, and because of that, she was allowed a little freedom. Today she was going to spend a few hours walking around the shops and market. The "Patronne" gave her a little pocket money, and sometimes the clients gave her a few extra dinar for being a good girl.

As she wandered through the streets, she paused for a second and sat down on a low concrete wall. She closed her eyes and lifted her head towards the sun. The warm rays danced upon her face, and for a short while, she was free. Her mind could dream, of what might have been, and maybe what still could be. Her thoughts flickered to the past, back to when she was a cleaner in a dreary hotel, with awful bosses, bosses who sold her into this life. Her mind drifted, and as she journeyed back over the memories and events of that last year; she thought that no matter how bad this life might be now, it could never be as bad as it had been just a few short months ago.

She had been drugged, sold, drugged and sold again and transported for many miles in the back of a stinking bone shaking truck; huddled together with many other women, girls, and a handful of boys. The ride had been interminably hot, and she had been so very thirsty. Liesel had expected to die in that truck, and sadly, some people did.

The claustrophobic heat, the stricken inhabitants, choking on the smell of sweat and excrement. It was a wonder that any of them had survived at all.

Liesel had originally arrived in Marrakech in the middle of the night and immediately put to work. She had been so tired from the journey, but despite this, they had stripped and prodded her; checking the state of her teeth, hair, and various orifices like a vet might examine a dog. Scrubbed within an inch of her life, she felt as if the skin was going to be ripped off her back.

A rough towel draped round her neck and dragged, naked into a small bedroom. They had injected her again. Her head swam as she had tried to fight the feelings that stirred within her. Whatever the injection contained had made her weak and compliant. It was then the first man raped her. It had been horrible. Liesel had never been keen on men. She had always shied away from them and had never really found them physically attractive. There had been a few boyfriends back home, but never "serious" boyfriends. No boy had ever done 'that' to her.

The rape was over quite quickly, Liesel did not even believe that the man who had done that to her, had enjoyed it either. It was more about control than enjoyment, breaking her spirit rather than anything physical. It was at that moment, as she started to clean herself up from that first encounter, she had decided, very calmly, that she was going to survive. Whatever it took, there would be a better life beyond this. She just had to live long enough to see it.

Then there was that man. That nice English man that got her out, albeit for a few minutes. She wondered what might have become of him. During the escape, she had killed a man; he had really deserved it. A nasty, odious little man. Then completely naked, she had run, run as fast as she could to get away. What bad luck, she had bumped into that Arab, what was his name? "Roman" that was it. He had said something about meeting his mother. He seemed nice, at first, until she met mother. Then it was all the same. The same old story, drugged, raped, drugged again, raped again, thrown into a truck, more rapes, more drugs and then on into another truck.

Liesel was empty inside, there was no love, just sex, and lots of it, constant, unfeeling and occasionally brutal, sex. When it was happening, she put on an act, her survival mechanism. She had been quite good at drama at school and treated every encounter as a role she played. When it was over she removed her costume, her mask, and became Liesel again, or at least a more tired version than she had been just a few months earlier.

On arrival in Algeria Liesel was bought by a gang who gave her crack cocaine. Within a month, they sold her to another gang who had taken her north to Oran. She felt like a piece of meat, just another girl with pale soft skin traded for profit.

They thought they had broken her, but she found an inner strength, she managed to kick the crack habit on her own. Liesel had gone through all the withdrawal symptoms of a recovering addict. She was not an addict; it had not been her choice. She was stronger now, wiser. Her future was sealed and she accepted it. She had food, shelter and cigarettes, plus, there were even doctors that checked on her once in a while. Amazingly, she had not contracted AIDS or any of the other deadly viruses that had befallen some of the other women she had encountered in this business.

Her current owners seemed kinder than the rest; they appreciated the money she made for them. For the first time in many years, Liesel actually felt like she belonged somewhere. It was certainly not the life she had imagined for herself, all those years ago when she was growing up. At least she was still alive, healthy, drug free, well fed, trusted and relatively safe. The sex thing was just a job, a means to an end. She was even allowed to buy her own clothes and dressed as well as she could with the pocket money they allowed her to keep.

Liesel opened her eyes and got up from the wall, brushing the dust from her dress. Turning towards the town, she could hear the distant throng of the market traders. She walked slowly towards the market, savouring every step. Here she could melt into the background like any other tourist. Liesel felt at home amongst the colours and bustle, the smells of the food stalls enthralling her senses. She breathed deeply, this was heaven, or as near to heaven as she was ever to find in this world.

The atmosphere of the market enthralled and enveloped her, just as a warm fuzzy quilt might comfort on a cold winter's night. Here she could feel alive. Liesel slipped another cigarette from her pocket and a helpful stallholder struck a match and offered her a light. She knew the stallholder. He was another of her regulars.

One of the secrets of her success was building up her regular clients. She knew that if she had enough nice, clean, semi-decent clients, there would not be time for the "Patronne" to send her any of the less savoury men.

They would go to the others, the new ones, the ones the "Patronne" had to keep an eye on. Liesel treated her clients with the utmost respect. She would always 'go the extra mile' to please them, and they in return always tried to please her. They did not please her. They could never please her. She had become so used to the process now, and, as part of the process, made them believe that they also pleased her.

Taking a puff on her cigarette, Liesel reached into her pocket again, feeling around for some loose change. She needed a new lighter, and the next stall had a few brightly coloured ones she liked. Liesel bent over as she fumbled around looking in her purse for a few dinar to buy a pretty pink lighter she had spotted. As she straightened to her full height, she looked past the stall and saw a face she thought she recognised. Her eyes widened, could it be? Could it really be? It must be a dream.

Relief, disbelief, a myriad of mixed feelings and confusion filled her head. This truly was heaven; would she wake in a moment to find this was all just a dream. She was walking on air, no, she was running on air. This was real. Standing there, just a few feet away, was Anja.

As Liesel ran around the stall, Anja turned and appeared to be walking towards a young woman and a small boy. Anja hadn't seen her, Liesel, with a huge sigh and tears in her eyes, the first tears she had cried since leaving Egypt, grabbed Anja tightly from behind, around the waist, and hugged her with all her might.

Liesel felt Anja tense and ducked, as Anja's elbow swung round, as she tried to escape.

"Anja, it's me."

As Liesel relaxed her hold, Anja turned, and their eyes met for the first time, in so many months. "Liesel. Oh my God Liesel!"

She pulled her friend close to her.

"Liesel, I thought I'd lost you forever."

Emma and Justin stood and watched as Liesel and Anja embraced, holding each other so tightly, fearing to let go.

"Anja, I thought you were dead."

Tears streamed down Liesel's face.

"I never thought I'd see you again," Anja spoke through her sobs.

There were people in the crowd starting to take notice.

"We cannot stay here," whispered Liesel.

Taking Anja by the hand, with Emma and Justin close behind, Liesel led them away from the market stalls and back towards her accommodation.

Liesel's room was small but tidy. She had a separate toilet with a washbasin and shower. The main room contained a small table, two wooden chairs, a neatly made double bed, and a bedside cabinet upon which a few small ornaments resided. A small hob, microwave and kettle completed the facility, making her almost self-sufficient. As they sat on the bed and chairs, Liesel made them coffee, fed them biscuits and told them about the journey she had taken to get there, and Anja told of their adventures, and explained how Nassim's men were watching the port, and that they couldn't trust the authorities.

"I have client," said Liesel "a fisherman, he make extra money doing "fishing trips", moving illegals over the Mediterranean. I see him later. I see if he can take us."

The fisherman arrived in late afternoon, so Anja, Emma and Justin loitered in the alley outside. An hour later, he emerged, pulled his jacket up around his face and slipped out into the early evening. Liesel waved them back into her room.

"He will do it. It will be 4000 Dinar each to go on the boat. It will take us to Valetta, in Malta."

"But we don't have any money," Emma said despairingly.

"I am good girl," said Liesel with a twinkle in her eye, "Very good girl, I do what clients like and they give me extra, I do not tell the 'Patronne'. I save up over 20000 dinar. I will pay. We leave at four in the morning."

Anja hugged Liesel, she was about to risk everything and leave her semi-comfortable life behind.

"He say he sorry to see me go, but he likes me and wants me to be happy. He also give me this."

She reached into her bedside drawer, Emma nearly cried as she saw it was a mobile phone.

"Can I call my Mum?"

"Here, you try," Liesel handed her the phone.

Emma, hands shaking began to dial. It rang about a dozen times before it clicked to answerphone.

"Mum, this is Emma, I'm…"

There was a rustling sound as Emma's Mother, Andrea, picked up.

"Oh my God Emma!" Andrea screamed. "We thought you were dead!"

"Mum" Emma choked with emotion, tears welling in her eyes, "we haven't got much time, we have to catch a boat to-to" in her excitement she had forgotten where the boat was going.

"Malta," whispered Liesel.

"Mum it's Malta, we're leaving here at four, in the morning."

"Where are you?"

"We are in Algeria Mum."

"How's Jade?"

Emma had not prepared herself for the question.

"Jade's…" Emma struggled for the words, "Jade's dead Mum."

Just saying the words to someone from home, someone who knew Jade, made it finally real and hit Emma hard. Her childhood friend was in fact gone. All of the past few months she had focussed on survival and nothing else. She had lost Jade and Sabine, and very nearly lost Anja. Andrea was crying on the phone. Emma regained her composure.

"Can you tell Dad and Uncle Harry?"

Andrea could not bring herself to tell Emma that her father was in a deep coma in hospital and that Harry had been missing for months. That would have to wait.

"I have to go now Mum, we need to save the battery, I'll call you when we get to Malta. I love you Mum."

"I love you Emma."

As Andrea switched off her mobile, she made a note of the number that had just called her; it was her only link back to her daughter. She sat in the kitchen looking out at her pretty garden and broke down in a sea of tears.

Emma, tears streaming down her face, clicked off the mobile and her three companions all gathered round and gave her a hug.

"We must get ready," said Anja.

"What do we need?" Emma replied wiping her cheeks.

"Liesel do you have any plastic bags?" enquired Anja.

"I have a few," she reached into her bedside drawer. "Here."

Anja took the bags, slipped the mobile phone into one and filled the others with biscuits and fruit that Liesel had on top of the cupboard.

"Now we must get some rest, we have a good few hours before we must leave."

Liesel told them that the departure point was from a beach a little way out of town, and it would take about an hour to walk there. They planned to set out at two o'clock, which would get them to the rendezvous point in plenty of time. They dozed fitfully for the next few hours, with only Justin, who had barely said a word since arriving in Oran, falling fast asleep.

45.


At two o'clock, they were ready, and set out on the long walk to the landing point. Emma felt more positive than she had in months, having finally managing to speak to her Mum, safely at home. She pictured her Mum and Dad as she arrived home, their loving arms wrapped round her. After fifty minutes they were at the top of the dunes, they looked out at the dark sea and could hear the sound of small breakers lapping against the shore, and above it a moonless sky. A cool breeze tousled their hair, the sea air in their faces tasted of freedom. A farewell to Africa and the trials they had suffered. A boat ride to Malta, and then a plane ride home.

As they approached the beach, it soon became clear that all was not as they had expected.

There were hundreds waiting. Three lines of people were already wading out into the gloomy wet darkness.

A man in dark clothes greeted them as they arrived, and he directed them to another man, tall, thick set with a full beard. He appeared to be the Captain in charge.

"We are here for the boat." Anja spoke first.

"How many of you are there?"

He counted.

"Four. That is sixteen thousand dinar."

At least the fisherman had given them the correct price. Anja counted out the notes into his hand, which he quickly slid into a pouch around his waist.

"Okay that's for the passage, now do you want to a life jacket and take any food or water for the trip?"

"Yes."

"That will be extra 25 dinar."

Liesel nodded signalling that she definitely wanted a life jacket.

Anja started to count out the 25 dinar.

"Each." The Captain laughed. "Is 25 dinar each."

Anja gave him the extra 100 dinar and collected four rather small life jackets, four small bottles of water and some very small sandwiches in plastic bags. The life jackets, although quite old and battered were a decent fit for Justin and Emma as they were both quite slight, but for Liesel and Anja they were tight, even when fully released.

"Now," said the Captain, "you see the small dinghies out there?"

He pointed across the sea and into the darkness beyond the three lines of people, they could just about make out some movement on the water.

"You will need to join the queue and wade out to them. They will take you to the big boat."

Liesel was scared.

"I can't swim, how deep is it? It seems a long way out."

"That water will only come up to your knees." said the Captain. "All will be fine, is very shallow here." He laughed and greeted the next few people that had arrived behind them.

They all joined the same queue and waded out into the sea. The dinghies seemed so far away. They waded for what seemed like forever as the water went up above their knees. On they waded. The unseen rocks and coral underfoot made it difficult to progress. Emma slipped on a rock and Anja managed to grab her before her head sank under the water. As the water got deeper, Anja lifted Justin up onto her shoulders. Once the water reached their waists, the dinghies seemed a little closer. They were still not close enough.

Worry began to set in as the water reached chest height. Liesel did not like the water, but she knew there was no turning back. Onward they strode, completely soaked, Anja had her head above water and Justin above that. Liesel walked on tiptoe trying to keep upright, with her head just above the lapping brine, Emma was swimming. When they finally reached the dinghy, the seawater was nearly up to their mouths. Anja lifted Justin and the boatman, on the dinghy, grabbed him under the armpits and hoisted him into the small craft. Liesel was next as she was in a state of panic. Anja and the boatman helped Liesel aboard. Then it was Emma's turn. At last, Anja clambered aboard, assisted by Emma and the boatman. The long line of people behind followed suit until the craft was completely full. It puttered into the darkness, as the next dinghy took its' place at the head of the waiting queue.

The small craft rocked as its' bow broke through the small waves in its' path. The larger boat came into view, with a host of people already aboard, and yet another dinghy transferring its' human cargo. They had all imagined that a local fisherman would be out on a fishing trip and just deliver them to the island of Malta, slipping quietly into port and dropping them off, but this seemed like a massive exodus. That amount of people would not be slipping quietly into anywhere.

They were soaked to the skin. The seawater stung their cold faces as it flew towards them from the sides of the dinghy. A minute later, they drew up alongside the larger vessel and a rope ladder was lowered. It was a fishing boat, almost a trawler, thought Emma, but not as big as she remembered from seeing them on the television back home. With their last scraps of energy, they climbed the rope ladder. As soon as they reached the top, they were ushered below deck. The hold stank of rotting fish, with the inside walls stained red. Emma thought she was going to be sick and put her hand over her nose and mouth to try to avoid the stench. They settled down on a rough wooden bench, as near to the open door as they could, as that was the best way to get any kind of fresh air. Even at this time of the morning, it was hot and very humid. They could all feel their clothes sticking to them in the humid atmosphere. It was crammed full of bodies, and when it appeared to be full, a head poked out from the door above.

"Everybody, sit down and don't move. If you need to stand, just stand and then sit down again, none of you must go trying to walk from side to side, if just a few of you try it, we might sink."

There was no room to move and the words "we might sink" filled everyone with terror. It was getting very claustrophobic and hard to breathe and Anja could tell that Liesel was suffering from claustrophobia.

"Don't worry, we'll soon be underway, then we can probably get up on deck once we are out of sight of the port, just breathe slowly". Anja's reassurance seemed to work, as Liesel tried to regulate her breathing.

After what seemed like an eternity, the engines began to turn, and the boat began to move. Anja shared some of the biscuits from the plastic bag with a very young woman who was sitting next to her. She seemed very thin, her dark skin showing the early signs of malnutrition.

They struggled to communicate with the noise of the people around and the engine's rattle. Anja thought her name was Madihah who came from Eritrea. Little more than a child, she was fleeing her home for a better life.

After about half an hour the boat stopped, it seemed that more people were coming aboard. Liesel began to get scared and Anja shouted to the man in charge asking if they could go up on deck. After reaching an agreement with the last of the Dinars, the four of them were allowed on deck, leaving poor little Madihah behind to suffer the sweltering hold. Once loaded with the extra cargo, the fishing boat limped out to sea.

With the trawler completely full, the man in charge closed the hold door and slid a large bolt across, to effectively lock its' inhabitants in the hold. Anja felt a shiver down her back; she had a bad feeling that something might go wrong. The engine clattered and spluttered as they chugged along through the waves.

"I don't like this," said Anja to her friends, "make sure you have your life jackets tied tightly."

They each checked each other's life jackets. They were all tight.

For two hours the boat rolled on the sea, the engine seemed to be struggling and getting louder. A loud clank and the engine fell silent. Emma heard the panicking shouts from below, it sounded like there was water coming up through the hull. The boat listed from side to side, thrown around like a small toy on the sea. The boat was taking on more water as it rolled, dipping one side into the water, before listing back in the opposite direction driven by the power of the sea. Many fell from the deck, tipped into the swirl. Many of those who could not afford a life jacket sank beneath the waves.

Anja knew that their only chance of survival was to jump into the sea and trust that their life jackets would keep them afloat. She signalled to the others to jump, Emma took Justin's hand as they leapt from the boat. Liesel hesitated. She was too scared to jump. Anja picked her up and threw her close to Emma into the raging sea. Before Anja could jump, she heard the noise. Down in the hold below they were beating on the door. Without hesitation, she ran to the door, pulled the bolt back and yanked the door open, before running and diving headlong into the water. The spray hit her face as she flew through the air, landing headfirst into the cold water.

The boat slid over onto its' side and continued to roll, condemning anyone below to a watery grave. As Anja surfaced she spied Liesel a little way to her left, splashing around panicking. Anja swam over to her as quickly as she could, dragging her friend away from the stricken vessel. Bobbing in the water just ahead of them was Emma holding on tightly to Justin. They were all still alive.

46.

The rattle of metal on wood reverberated inside the hold. As if by magic, the hold door opened. A blast of fresh sea air hit them as they piled towards the door, crushing the weaker ones in their path, in a desperate fight for survival. The boat rocked violently. Several of the men that had been beating on the door, fell through the opening and landed face down on the spray washed deck.

From deep inside, little Madihah looked open mouthed at the opening and blinked in disbelief. 'A miracle', she thought to herself, 'we have been granted a miracle'. Light and, more importantly, fresh air streamed through the opening, providing some small relief from the stench that had built up inside. The boat was sinking, but now there was a chance that she might make it after all. Many of her fellow passengers lay dead around her, drowned or suffocated; floating face down amongst the rising seawater, effluent and fish remains.

Madihah began to pull herself along the inside of the boat, hand over hand, towards the light, amidst the floating detritus; clinging on as the boat lurched from one side to the other. All those around were desperate to survive, but as they fought and trampled each other, they unbalanced the sinking vessel. Their chances of survival were quickly beginning to disappear.

Madihah slowly made her way forward and managed to hug the outside of the sloping steel stair rail that ran up the right side of the steps. She was the wrong side of the rail; on the 'wall' side; as opposed to the 'steps' side; and dared not to try and slip underneath, as it would have meant plunging her head under water amongst the grime.

Just as she started to feel completely helpless, Madihah noticed a small bar suspended from the cabin roof just above the opening. No one else seemed to have spotted it.

She stretched up with her left hand, keeping her right hand on the stair rail to steady herself. At full stretch, she could almost touch the bar with her fingertips.

Using both hands to steady herself, Madihah managed to position her left foot up onto the stair rail. She extended her left leg, kicking upwards and simultaneously let go of the stair rail. She nearly toppled backwards. Flailing in the air, her fingertips touched the bar. Her slight frame, floating through the air, had just enough momentum to connect, and she gratefully closed her grip around it. Like a gymnast on parallel bars, Madihah swung herself through the gap feet first and outside onto the slippery deck.

Madihah landed with a thud. As she looked behind her, she immediately saw the problem. Too many people were trying to scramble through the door at the same time. The ones at the front were wedged in awkward positions and were unable to get free. The ones behind pushing, were killing the ones in front, and in turn condemning themselves.

Madihah could not help them; her only option was to try to save herself. A loud crack sounded, and the boat began to roll. With the boat about to sink, she knew she had to jump into the water. Madihah could not swim. She ran to the edge, slid on the slippery deck, and fell head first over the side into the deadly sea swell. As the boat rolled, about a dozen bodies spewed out from the cabin door and slid into the swirling sea.

Madihah came up for air, her arms flapping amidst the waves. Looking around her in desperation, she attempted a doggy paddle, trying not to be sucked down by the stricken boat. The waves tossed her like a rag doll. Under she went. At the complete mercy of the sea.

Her arms splashed, trying to find the surface. Her right hand hit something solid, and for a split second rejoiced that she may have found a piece of wood or floating boat debris that she could hang on to. She was half-right. It was floating, but it was not boat debris. It was a body. Whoever it had once been, she did not know her. As her salty eyes cleared, Madihah could tell it was a woman, with long hair and a pair of cheap chrome rimmed sunglasses, still hanging from a chain around her neck.

As she clutched the dead woman's arm, Madihah looked around her. Bodies everywhere. She was drifting in a sea of the dead. There was no land, just bodies and the horizon, in every direction. There were red patches in the water amongst the corpses. Blood. Blood would attract the creatures of the deep. It could only be a matter of time.

As the water lapped around her, she noticed that a couple of the bodies closest to her were wearing life jackets. The fact that the life jackets had not actually saved their wearers did not inspire the greatest confidence, but there was no time for guessing how these people had died. It could be the fact that these bodies were actually floating, was testament to the fact that the life jackets were not as useless as she first thought. She may yet die out here in the sea, but at least she would die trying to survive.

Using the dead woman as a makeshift float, Madihah kicked her legs in the way she had seen other people try to do it. It was slow progress, and she was so very tired. The biggest problem was the current, and as she moved towards a body, it floated further away from her. It took her at least twenty minutes to get to the first life jacket clad body and she was completely exhausted. The sun was reflecting off the water and making it extremely hard to see what she was doing, so Madihah slipped the sunglasses from around the dead woman's neck and put them on. Transferring her floating corpse preference to a middle-aged white man, she let go of the woman's body and it began to float away. She turned her attention to the white man and more importantly, his life jacket. He was floating face down, as most of the corpses seemed to be. This posed a problem as the life jacket buckles were on his front, and under the water.

It was difficult to keep her head above water, as the tiredness washed over her. Everything was an effort. She had to choose, either feel around under the water for the buckles, or try and turn him over in the water. Neither seemed a great prospect, but she decided to attempt to turn him. Madihah had never learned to tread water, and the best she could do was flap around, and at times her head sank beneath the water and she began to panic. The man's body rolled and she just managed to stop him rolling in a full circle and back to where he had started. The buckles were on top, and she gasped as she saw the massive head wound which had caused this man's death. It looked like he had been struck, with a heavy object, leaving a bloody crater in his skull.

Sickness and revulsion coursed through her body, she had only eaten a small handful of biscuits in the past few days. Her stomach cramped and she wretched violently, but only bile came out of her mouth. She held her breath, and somehow managed to regain her composure.

Running on pure adrenaline, her movements, although painful with tiredness, were deliberate. This was survival, pure and simple. This was no longer a man, but an object that held a vital tool to save her life. She tried to ignore the bloody hole in this man's forehead and set to work freeing the life jacket from the lifeless corpse.

With the buckles finally unclipped, she managed to peel the lifejacket from his body by again rolling him in the water. She had a life jacket. It was quite blood stained, but that was the least of her worries. Madihah struggled to slip on the life jacket, in the end having to let go of its' owner after she had failed to buckle herself in using just one hand.

Madihah looked back at the remains of the boat. It had rolled completely over with just the hull peeping out of the water. In the far distance, a small craft was rowing away in the opposite direction, overflowing with people. It also looked like a few survivors were clinging to the edge of the upturned hull. She tried to doggy paddle towards them but no matter how hard she tried, the strong current took her further and further away from them.

She pushed herself away from the bodies, certain that sharks would soon smell the blood that surrounded her. There was no sign of land in any direction, but any direction would be better than where she was.

Splashing for what seemed like hours, Madihah had exhausted her energy. The adrenaline that had driven her so far subsided and she was starting to feel cold, from having been in the water for so long. After a further twenty minutes, tired and exhausted, she finally leaned back in her life jacket and closed her eyes. A small speck drifting all alone in a huge sea.

47.

The helicopter touched down safely on a parched parcel of wasteland on the western edge of the island of Gozo. Two ambulances were waiting. Harry and Zettler were helped from the chopper, while Francois was carried on a stretcher; her shattered ankle heavily strapped by the local medics.

"Ahm gonna take that whirly bird back home with me when we are done, seein' as how I lost ma plane an' all," Zettler whispered. "You keep them keys safe for me son."

Zettler handed Harry the ignition keys. Harry nodded, slipping them into his pocket.

On the ride to the hospital, Harry sat with Francois, while Zettler rode in the second ambulance. On arrival at the hospital, there was quite a commotion. A clutch of reporters took photographs as the ambulances arrived, but were ushered away by the hospital security staff, as the three friends reached the emergency department.

"We're not used to celebrities turning up here," said a young male doctor as he examined Francois' ankle.

"Celebrities...?" Francois looked surprised.

"You were all over the television and internet, we didn't think you would escape."

All three of them looked confused.

"It was the strangest thing, one minute we were in the waiting room, watching a house makeover programme. The next thing, you were on, in some kind of macabre human auction."

"Auction? Yes, we were part of an auction," Harry nodded, "but we had no idea that the whole world was watching."

"There's a big investigation at the moment, trying to work out how they did it, it was as if someone took over the entire internet and all of the worlds' TV channels."

"Is there a telephone I could borrow?" asked Harry "I really need to call home."

"Here take mine," said the Doctor handing Harry a mobile phone.

Harry dialled and waited for the tone. It rang. It clicked, and a woman's voice answered.

"Andrea, it's Harry."

"Oh my God, Harry, I can't believe it."

"How's Keith?"

"Keith is still in hospital, he's still in a coma. We hope he's going to pull through, Harry…"

Andrea's voice trailed off.

"I have some terrible news, Emma called…"

"Emma?"

"Yes, she called, and I don't know how to say this but, Jade she's…"

Harry did not hear the final word. He knew. He sank down on the floor against the wall. Zettler hobbled over to him, the wound in his leg freshly treated and bandaged. Harry looked up at him.

"Jade's dead."

Harry spoke softly, but he did not cry. He had known all along. The chances of him finding her alive had been too remote. Zettler bowed his head and put a hand on his friend's shoulder. Harry put the phone back to his ear.

"You say you spoke to Emma, where is she, is she home?"

"She's was in Algeria, but now she's on a boat, I think she said it was heading for Malta."

"Is it a ferry?" Harry did not know whether Algeria even had ferries that went to Malta.

"I don't think it is; I think it might be one of those migrant boats, I'm so worried about her."

Harry felt a chill through his whole body. Jade was gone, but Emma was still alive.

"I have a phone number for her, but I keep trying it and it's switched off."

"Give me the number, let me try." Harry was determined he was going to find Emma and bring her home.

He wrote down the number and promised to call Andrea as soon as he had any news. Harry looked up at Zettler, a determined look in his eyes.

"I'm afraid, my friend, we still have work to do."

---

48.

With her arm firmly wrapped around Liesel, Anja swam towards
Emma and Justin. At a safe distance, they watched as the small
lifeboat launched. A mass of people descended trying to climb on
board, but it was already full. Some hung on the sides as it slowly
moved away, oars battling the waves. Some released their hold and
sank. Dead bodies floated all around them. The fishing vessel
pitched to the side for one last time before rolling leaving only its'
hull jutting out of the water.

For a while the four friends floated, watching, waiting for it
to sink. Aside from the floating corpses, all they could see, in every
direction, was the sea. There was no sign of land. Emma spoke first.

"We will never survive if we stay in the water. It's too cold,"

Justin and Liesel had both started to shiver. They decided to
swim back to the upturned boat. With Anja and Emma assisting
Liesel and Justin, they eventually reached the vessel. The next
problem was to clamber aboard the hull. It was curved, wooden and
wet. Their soaking clothes weighed heavy as they tried to drag
themselves aboard. Justin was first, as he was much lighter than the
rest. Emma managed to help him, acting as a surrogate ladder for
him to climb up her body. He hung on as Emma managed to
scramble to safety. Next came Liesel. She was shaking violently
with the cold, and her fear of the water. Anja held her tightly until
Emma was out of the water, then between then they pulled and
pushed Liesel onto the wooden hull. With her strength running low,
Anja finally dragged herself out of the water.

The sun shone overhead as they sat aboard the underside of
the fishing boat. Their clothes gently drying. They still had a few
biscuits and the small packs of sandwiches wrapped in plastic bags,
so they eagerly tucked in, finally realising how hungry they were.

Emma pulled out the mobile phone, took it out of the plastic
bag and switched it on. It still worked. She waited while the display
powered up. She was about to dial her Mother's number when
strangely it rang.

Emma assumed it would be someone wanting to talk to the fisherman who had originally given the phone to Liesel. She clicked the green button to answer.

"Hullo." She said tentatively.

"Emma..."

"Yes?"

"Emma, it's Uncle Harry."

Emma almost burst into tears, she could hear his voice clearly, Uncle Harry, Jade's Dad, a voice from home.

"Uncle Harry, we're on a boat, but we're in trouble, it's sinking, I think we're going to die." As Emma croaked the words, Harry instantly knew she was in big trouble.

"Emma, I'm coming for you, but there's not much time, you need to listen carefully..."

She could hear the urgency in his voice, and a deep whirring sound in the background.

"Emma, I'm going to hang up now, but you need to leave the phone switched on."

Emma glanced at the battery icon; it was showing as half charged.

"I've got a friend who is going to track the coordinates of your phone, but I need to speak to him, so we can find out where you are, so we can come and get you."

Emma could not believe what she was hearing, after surviving for many months, after facing all the dangers they had been through, Uncle Harry was finally coming to save them. She choked as she answered.

"Uncle Harry, I understand."

She wanted to say something about Jade, but it was not the time. There would be plenty of opportunity for that later.

"Bye Emma, see you soon."

The line went dead.

Harry immediately called Hassan back in Marrakech. As soon as Emma's phone had switched on, he had been on the hunt. Using the position of satellites and the nearest land phone masts, he had managed to calculate their position quite accurately. He relayed their position and quickly said to Harry.

"We'll all see you at Father's house soon for the mint tea we promised."

Harry smiled.

"Hassan my friend, it's a date."

Harry handed Zettler a chocolate bar from the sack of food the hospital had provided them. Zettler bit into it, his eyes focussed on the wide expanse of sea in front of the helicopter. The chocolate tasted sweet and creamy.

"That's gotta be the best God-damn candy I've ever tasted."

Out across the waves they flew. The white tops of the swell billowed and swirled below, making visibility difficult. Harry strained his eyes, scanning the water, praying he did not miss them as he blinked. The wind was strong, but Zettler, with his many years' experience, did all he could to follow the course.

Then Harry saw it, peeping out from amongst the spray, a large wooden hulk swaying in the current. Four small, vulnerable souls clinging onto the wreck for dear life. Harry pointed it out to Zettler and he hovered, checking the wind direction. As Harry looked down and could see Emma frantically waving and pointing out to sea. Emma had seen the speedboat fast approaching from the south. She also recognised the hulking figure, standing in the rear of the sleek white craft.

"It's Nassim," she screamed, the combination of the waves, wind and the helicopter hovering overhead made it difficult to talk.

"It can't be. How could they know where we are?" Anja shouted back.

It was true; Nassim and half a dozen other men were speeding rapidly towards them. Zettler hovered as close as he could, and Harry lowered a rope secured to a winch inside the door.

"Emma, you take Justin first." Anja was firm, and there was no time to argue.

Emma wrapped the end of the rope around her right leg and arm, clutching Justin as Harry pulled on the rope. The wind buffeted the chopper and they swung out over the sea. Nassim looked up as one of his men took aim. Nassim forced his man to lower his weapon, shouting as he did so.

Emma could not hear. The sound of the rotors were deafening. Inch by inch, she held on as Harry winched them up. They reached the opening in the side of the helicopter. Harry locked the winch and grabbed Justin from Emma, placed him in a seat, and then swung her aboard. The speedboat was fast approaching the floating hull below. Anja could almost hear Nassim's shouts.

Safely aboard, Emma strapped Justin into a seat while Harry lowered the winch once more. As the rope dangled above Anja and Liesel's heads, a gust of wind forced Zettler to take evasive action and he struggled to keep control. The helicopter shot upwards, circled, then attempted to make its' return. It was the few moments that Nassim needed as the speedboat reached the opposite end of the ships' hull. Pistol drawn he jumped from speedboat to wreck. The rope played in the breeze, as Zettler regained control, dropping it straight in front of Anja. She was ready. Anja grabbed Liesel by the waist and twisted her free arm around the rope. Harry winched the rope and they were suddenly suspended above the water. Liesel was heavier than Anja had anticipated, and she struggled to hold her. Liesel grabbed for the rope. As Liesel moved, she forced Anja to change her grip and she slid from Anja's outstretched arm. Liesel desperately tried to grab a tighter hold of the rope, but as she slid, the rope burned into her palms. The pain shot through her hands, and forced to let go, Liesel plummeting down into the raging sea.

Anja screamed. Liesel could not swim. Nassim was standing on the hull, two of his men close behind, with weapons drawn, watching the drama unfold. Anja had to make a quick decision. She let go of the rope. Falling through the spray, she hit the cold sea with a huge splash, feet first. Under the water, she thrashed about searching for Liesel. Anja's eyes were open. Her vision dulled by the stinging salt. Anja felt something. It was an arm. Liesel's arm. Anja hung on and pulled her face out of the water. Anja sucked in a breath of salty air as she sought Liesel's face. Liesel's eyes were closed. Anja, slid her own body under Liesel's and in a hugged towing position, forced her fist into Liesel's stomach. Liesel coughed and began thrashing around. Anja had to let go for fear of being struck, but swam back to Liesel and with one arm, held her once again. Anja dragged her friend back towards the hull. There was nowhere else to go. Nassim was waiting, a huge grin across his face. His two men helped drag Anja and Liesel from the water and they lay across the hull coughing, trying to breathe.

As the helicopter hovered overhead, Harry, Emma and Zettler had witnessed the whole scene unfold.

Nassim stood over his two captives, then, looked up at the helicopter. He waved to the occupants to listen.

"I only want the boy. Send him down and I will let your friends go free."

Anja wanted to shout to tell them to leave and save themselves, but the heaving of her chest would not let the words come.

Zettler turned to Harry, he looked at Emma and then at Justin.

"You know son, I think I have an idea how we can all get out of this thing alive."

Zettler quickly explained his plan. Harry disappeared to the back of the chopper to get the sack of food that the hospital had given them. Zettler spoke calmly and quietly to Justin relating his plan. Justin nodded.

Harry handed Justin the sack. Justin was calm he knew exactly what he had to do.

Harry carefully tied the rope around the boy, before inching him down on the swaying line. Nassim was pleased with himself. Anja raised herself to her feet and pulled the swinging Justin tightly to her chest. She untied the boy, standing still for a second not knowing what to do.

"Come here boy," shouted Nassim.

Justin, doing as instructed, sauntered towards Nassim.

"What's in the sack boy?"

"Just some food." replied Justin quietly. He reached into the sack, pulled out a green apple and bit into it.

"Want some?"

Justin offered the open sack to Nassim and the big man peered inside. Apples, tomatoes, pre-packed sandwiches, potato crisps and some bottles of water.

"Get in the boat boy," Nassim spoke the words softly and stroked Justins' hair as if he were a kindly uncle.

Justin clambered aboard the speedboat closely followed by Nassim and his men. Anja watched open-mouthed as Justin placed the sack on the pilots' seat and began rummaging around inside. She could not believe they had just surrendered the boy, after everything they had been through to rescue him. Justin, with a determined look on his face carefully placed the sack on the floor of the speedboat. Then Justin ran. Nassim watched the boy's brave attempt to escape, with a broad smile across his dark lined face and laughed heartily.

"He can't get far."

Justin cleared the side of the speedboat with a jump and landed with a thud on the wooden hull. Running straight towards the startled Anja and Liesel, he dived towards them. Arms outstretched, he caught them both off balance and the three of them landed head first into the water. As soon as their bodies struck the water, the helicopter lurched upwards and banked away. Nassim cursed, aimed and fired a shot from his pistol, narrowly missing the spinning tail rotor.

Unfazed Nassim gathered his thoughts. 'Those silly little bitches had tried and failed, victory will soon be mine, the boy is still in the water, and I will take great pleasure in killing those fucking stupid whores'.

It was then Nassim's gaze fell on the sack. It was too late.

Before he could utter another word, the explosion ripped through the speedboat. Large plumes of flame shot into the air and particles of dust and fibreglass, human flesh and bone rained down upon the surrounding water. Burning fuel, mixed with swollen corpses floated out of a massive hole blown into the side of the fishing boat hull, as it gave up its' bloated prisoners along with its' battle to stay afloat. With the hull twisted, its' final supports breached, the trawler finally slid silently beneath the waves.

Anja swam away from the sinking ship, with Liesel and Justin in tow, for fear that it might drag them down with it. The helicopter circled and came in low, with rope dipping into the water to pick them up. Anja, treading water, carefully hung onto Justin as Liesel gratefully scrambled aboard the chopper. Once Anja and Justin were safely aboard, Zettler turned tail and they raced back towards the safety of Gozo.

The helicopter landed just outside Gozo's General Hospital in Victoria. As they arrived at the hospital reception, Harry enquired how Francois was faring. The receptionist informed him that she was still in the operating theatre, and that the operation was taking a little longer than expected, due to the number of bone fragments in her ankle. Anja, Justin and Liesel had their general health checked, and had dressings applied to their cuts and bruises, while Justin was taken straight to the Paediatrics Department for a more thorough examination.

An hour later, a doctor approached Harry with news that Francois was out of theatre, and in recovery. They had saved her foot and it would not be long before he could see her.

Harry breathed a sigh of relief. Emma immediately called home and spoke to her Mother as Harry listened to them chattering in the background.

The police arrived along with an official from the British High Commission. They had come to see Justin, but he refused to see anyone, unless Anja and Emma were with him. Reporters and television crews camped outside the hospital. They wanted to see the boy that had filled their news items for so long.

One of the doctors quietly told Harry that when they had examined Justin, they found a small scar on the back of his neck. On closer inspection they discovered it was where a micro tracking device had been inserted. Harry quickly informed Anja.

"So that's how they were able to track us."

"Yes," replied Harry "it was pretty state of the art by the sound of it, and could pinpoint him within metres, as long as they could triangulate it via satellites and cell towers."

Two hours later, Harry was allowed to see Francois. She looked a poorly soul, pale with scratches around her face and arms and a plaster cast around her lower leg and foot. As Harry entered the room Francois beckoned him to her. As their faces grew closer, Francois reached out her hand and touched his cheek. He kissed her hand, and she drew him closer.

"'Arry, we are safe at last."

She kissed him softly, full on the lips. Francois could tell from the dreamy look in his eyes that Harry had fallen completely in love with her.

49.

Cadenza Leone shuffled in her seat. She felt uncomfortable, squashed into the cockpit of the twin-engine ATR42. Five months pregnant and looking forward to her maternity leave. She had been restricted to light duties, assisting the Italian Coastguard in the search for migrant boats, attempting to cross the Mediterranean. Yawning, she stretched as she peered out of the plexi-glass window and out across the vast expanse of water. Over the radio, there had been reports of an explosion. It was a vast area to cover. If a boat had exploded and sunk, she knew she would never spot it. All that could be left would be bits of driftwood and perhaps some other floating debris.

She unscrewed the top of her thermos flask and poured herself a hot coffee. The pilot beside her stared straight ahead, eyes fixed on the gauges and dials in front of him. 'He's not much of a conversationalist' thought Cadenza, sipping from her plastic cup. Barely three words had they spoken the entire trip. She had not even bothered to find out his name, too much effort.

A glint of light reflected from the swirling sea below. Putting down her cup, she rubbed her tired eyes.

"Can you get us a bit closer to whatever is shining down there?"

Without a word, the pilot, following the direction of her finger, guided the aircraft down towards the water. As they got closer, Cadenza could clearly see the figure of a young black girl in a shabby lifejacket floating on the surface. She was wearing a pair of cheap chrome rimmed sunglasses, the frame of which had bounced a ray of sunlight towards the airplane.

Cadenza grabbed the radio and clicked it into 'send' mode.

"There's a girl, floating just below us."

Cadenza read out the coordinates.

Within minutes, a small Royal Naval launch was despatched and raced towards the location. As the craft slowed to a stop, they pulled the girl out of the water and proceeded to apply CPR.

A young wren blew air into her mouth, while another assisted with chest compressions. The young wren pressed two fingers into the girl's neck. There was a pulse. It was faint, but it was definitely there.

With a nod to the pilot, they sped back to base.

Several hours later, Madihah woke in a soft bed, a female orderly sat next to her. 'This lady has a kind face', thought Madihah.

"What is your name?"

"I am Madihah."

"…and where are you from?"

"I come a long way, many miles, I from Eritrea."

The orderly leaned over stroked Madihah's hair gently.

"Well Madihah, you are in Gibraltar now, and you are safe."

50.

Keith's eyes flickered open. Everything seemed hazy, but all around was bright. 'Am I dead?' he wondered. The sun streamed into the room through gaps in the off-white vertical blinds. Tiny flecks of dust floated through the bright rays and for a moment, he lay there mesmerised. Without moving his head, his eyes focussed on a plain white polystyrene tiles ceiling and a shiny chrome light fitting.

As he became more aware of his surroundings, he felt a soft pillow, and the cool white sheets that covered his body. He was safe. He raised his right hand, in wonder. Holding it up before his eyes, he spent a few moments turning it back and forth, counting his fingers several times. Then he noticed a band around his wrist, it read 'Keith Watson' with his date of birth printed neatly below his name. He was safe, and in hospital.

He could hear a steady rhythmic beeping noise. He rolled his head slightly to his right to see a machine. It had a steady green light, flickering in time with the beeps. Keith lifted his head and glanced around the room.

It was then he saw her, in a soft easy chair just beside his left shoulder. Emma had a deep tan, longer hair than he remembered, lips chapped and sore looking; and she was fast asleep with a green duffle coat carefully draped over her. She lay upright but curled, with her knees brought up to her chest and tucked beneath the coat. She was more beautiful than he ever remembered. His heart skipped, it was at that moment he knew that he loved her more than he could love anyone else.

He lay a while and watched her sleep, her breathing quiet and regular. Emerging from a dream, the memories began to return. The race to get to Morocco. His search of Marrakech; and how he had tried to help the poor young woman in the room to escape. It was the last thing he remembered before waking the few moments earlier.

Emma's breath was calm, punctuated by the odd little whistling sound she always made when she slept. That sound was music to his ears. For a few minutes he lay in peaceful serenity. He had made it home and his daughter was safe.

A door opened, and Andrea appeared carrying two cups of coffee. She looked across at the bed, and with slow realisation, she carefully put down the drinks.

"Keith, you've come back to us!"

Andrea cried, running to his bedside, tears streaming down her pretty face. Emma awoke with a start, taking a moment to register what had happened.

"Dad, Dad!"

Emma jumped up from the chair; her coat fell to the floor, tears rolling down her sunburnt cheeks. Andrea and Emma sat on either side of the bed, each grabbed one of Keith's hand and looked up at him in wonder.

"Andrea, Emma..." kissing his wife and daughter in turn, he tried to say more but the emotion of the reunion was just too much, and he began crying too. They hugged each other tightly, their prayers had finally been answered.

51.

Ikrimah dressed in his best suit, stood proudly in his farmhouse doorway. He watched, as Mustapha's new Landrover approached. It was not brand new, but it was new to him. Hassan ran over to the car as it parked, and eagerly pulled the passenger door open. Leo Zettler climbed out, blinking in the sunshine. Before the big American had chance to shade his eyes, Hassan was at his side, greeting him with a hug.

"Welcome home my friend." Hassan was emotional but managed to stay in control.

"A'hm pretty glad to be home too, son."

The driver's door opened, and Mustapha stepped out, pulling the rear door open as he did so. First Harry, then Francois dipped their heads as they emerged from the air-conditioned vehicle.

"Here is where the adventure really began." Harry noted pointing towards the farmhouse.

Harry scanned the area in front of the door to Hassan's 'den'. Apart from a few scorch marks on the parched earth, no evidence remained of the helicopter wreckage.

Francois leaned on Harry as she retrieved her crutch from the back seat, hobbling as she did so. At the same moment the opposite rear door opened, and Anja popped her head out of the door.

"Come in, we are making tea." Ikrimah smiled as he beckoned them all up the stairs.

The reunited friends talked, as Hassan's mother prepared mint tea. A pile of bread, meat and vegetables covered the table. Harry's eyes lit up at the colourful spread that Hassan's family had provided.

For hours, they talked of their adventures, of those they had met, those they had lost, and in Francois and Harry's case, new love they had found.

They talked of the friends that could not be there with them. Liesel felt she had to return home to see her Mother.

Anja spoke of how lost she felt saying goodbye to Liesel, and the sadness of seeing Emma board the plane for England. Anja knew that Emma needed to be with her Father and were all so relieved when Emma called to say that he had woken from his coma.

Then there was Justin. His parents had flown to Malta, where they were reunited, with the world's press on hand to record every moment. Justin was resilient, still a quiet boy, he had an inner strength unusual in one so young. When a reporter asked what the first thing he would do when he got home was, Justin replied, "I think I'd like to do some colouring."

Zettler explained how the idea about placing the grenades that had been left in the helicopter, into the bottom of the food sack, had come about.

"It was the only way I reckoned we could save all of us. Those guys could have just shot us out the sky, and then we'd have all been 'gonners'. We somehow had to make sure them grenades were carefully placed in their boat, and I figured, Justin was the only one who could do that without raising too much suspicion."

Zettler paused before adding,

"My main worry was what we'd have done if they hadn't gone off."

Mustapha proposed a toast.

"The boy Justin is a hero. We are all safely reunited here today because of him. Let's raise our glasses."

They raised their mint tea filled glasses to toast brave young Justin.

"To Justin."

They talked, laughed and cried deep into the night, until eventually they each sloped off to bed.

Saying goodnight to Francois and Harry, Anja opened the door to her room and stepped inside; the darkness only broken by the brightly coloured table lamp beside her bed. She moved to the bed and sat down. The crisp linen sheets gently rustled, taking her weight, as she leaned back against the host of soft cushions and pillows, that moulded to the contours of her slender form. The silence was amazing.

A wave of emotion washed over her. It was over. The ordeals, the beatings, the near-death escapes. She had survived all of them, and helped to rescue dear sweet Emma, her ever loving Liesel, and Justin, the kidnapped boy that the entire world had been praying and searching for. She had been their saviour. She, Anja, a mere waitress, from a poor village in Hungary.

She took a deep breath and began to tremble. She could no longer contain the tears. Anja sat upright as the drops welled in her eyes and streamed down her face. Quiet for a moment, still shaking, the emotion rose inside her. When she could hold it no longer, she let out the loudest moan, she had ever cried.

There was no one in the room to comfort her, but she did not want comfort. These were tears of relief. Tears of survival. Tears of freedom. All through their entire adventure, she had been strong, resourceful and determined. Now it was over, the emotional tension that had built up inside could be released.

There was a light tap on her door.

"Anja are you okay?" Francois' soft French accent rang clear, despite the thickness of the wooden bedroom door.

Anja wiped her eyes with a napkin she had picked up at dinner.

"I'm, I'm fine…" she sniffed through the tears, dabbing the tiny droplets from her eyes, "…really I'm fine".

As Francois stepped quietly from the door, Anja flopped back onto the comfortable bed, fully clothed. Outside the stars were shining. The distant noises of Marrakech echoed through her mind. It would be another clear sunny day tomorrow. A new day, full of hope for the future. She lay quietly for a few moments before gently sliding into a deep sleep. Yes, she really was going to be fine.

15162074R00150

Printed in Great Britain
by Amazon